Pull the Pin

Pull the Pin

By

Tate Volino

Cover based on United Nations Map No. 3958 Rev. 7, June 2011. Department of Field Support, Cartographic Section.

ISBN 13: 978-0615610146
ISBN 10: 0615610145

ALCHEMY BOOK, LLC

This book is dedicated to the members of the U.S. Armed Forces, past and present, who have sacrificed to ensure that I can say what I want, think what I want, and write what I want. Thank you.

Special thanks to:

Kimberly Parker
Ric Mayfield
Jeremy Ferguson
Ken and Tricia Eales

Also by Tate Volino

Gold Albatross

ONE

Spring had arrived in Uruzgan Province. Mild zephyrs drifted gently through the foothills, replacing the harsh gusts that had prevailed all winter. The change in weather forecasted an inaccurate omen of the violent conflicts that would soon descend upon the region. Here the new season had no characteristic sounds - no birds singing, no insects chirping. Visually, there were subtle changes. There was sporadic movement as mountain goats mapped their terrain and small rodents foraged for food. Occasional, lonely junipers snaked out from between the craggy rocks as they shed the winter snow.

Underneath an outcropping on a steep mountain ridge, a group of men huddled together in the pale, gray light before sunrise. From their position they could see the lower hills to the east and the mouth of the valley that unfolded to the south. The men were speaking in voices so low that they were barely audible even to each other.

Abdul Karim Abdullah sat in the middle of the gathering and surveyed the men on either side of him. Abdul and his men were all similarly attired. They wore long shirts and baggy pants that were common throughout this part of the world. The outfit, known as a shalwar-kameez, was moderately effective for camouflaging them among the terrain, but it was highly effective for blending in with the native populations. Most of the men wore cap-style kufis or turbans, known as lungees, along with some sort of scarf to protect against the cold and dust. However, none of the soldiers were adorned with a karakul hat - the style constantly perched atop the country's current leader. The men's coats provided some differentiation with styles ranging from military hand-me-downs to primitive-looking animal skins.

As he looked from face to face, Abdul's assessments varied widely - from sympathy and pity to respect and deep admiration. Some of the men he had known for decades while others were relatively new followers. Abdul spoke several languages and knew many dialects, but in this setting he addressed everyone in Pashto, the common language of southern Afghanistan.

"Kourash, as always, we must thank you for feeding us so well," Abdul mused, making a gracious bow of his head. Several of the men with full mouths grunted and nodded in agreement. "To enjoy the food of our lands while watching the sun rise over it gives me hope for the future. I look forward to the days when we can once again walk freely among these hills and valleys and know that they are truly our own. Others have made claim to them for far too long. I do not plan to spend the rest of my days hiding on mountain ledges."

His proclamation was followed by another round of guttural affirmations from the men.

"I simply make do with what we are given. We all have different roles and I am just doing what I can to serve our common goal," Kourash replied modestly.

Abdul's praise hit its target right on the mark and Kourash quickly set about the small camp to further prove he was deserving of the accolades. He poured himself a sip of black tea from the weathered tin pot to test the temperature and then topped off the cups of all his compatriots.

Breakfast consisted of the same basic items every day; however, Kourash tried to add variety when possible. There was always plenty of flatbread, which was called naan. The bread was already a staple of their diet, but it also served them well on the excursions through the mountains as its shape and consistency allowed for easy transport. Along with the naan, there was a slab of boiled curd and a jar of apricot mou-rubba, a jelly-like fruit sauce. Finally there was a mix of dried figs and nuts, which also made for convenient sustenance while on the move.

Kourash had connections throughout the region and was able to source adequate rations for the fighters no matter where they traveled. While others in the group carried rifles, grenade launchers, and extra ammunition, Kourash toted a large backpack carefully filled with his cooking utensils and ingredients. He did carry a small, tarnished revolver in his belt, but kept the safety on to avoid accidentally firing it

2

as he went about his duties. Kourash was the only man that had a pistol and he had never fired the weapon. He hadn't even taken a practice shot as the only ammunition he had were the bullets loaded in the cylinder.

After taking a quick inventory of the food remaining on the pewter platter placed on a low rock in the middle of their circle, Kourash divided up the bounty and distributed equal amounts to each of the appreciative men. As he moved about, the men patted him on the shoulder, smiled, and dished out additional enthusiastic thanks.

Abdul sat calmly and allowed the men to enjoy the rest of their meals. When the sun finally broke over the horizon, he decided it was time to start moving. "At this point we must go our separate ways. Wasim will be taking several men and following the high ridge while I will be leading my group around the lower paths. After that we will move south and west, fanning out across the edge of the valleys. We will be assessing the Americans' current positions and where they may be headed in the coming months.

Mirwais will take the rest of you and head east to the lowlands. Cover as many of the villages as you can. Be sure to show them your strength as you arrive, but be humble and compassionate while you are there. Pay top prices for your purchases and give generously at the local mosques. Despite our limited numbers and resources right now, we need to portray a much greater presence. In a few weeks our brothers along the border will begin pushing in this direction and the territory in between will be critical.

Last year we started to turn the tide of this struggle and we need to keep that momentum in our favor. Time is on our side and the longer we can carry on the stronger we become. The Americans thought this would be a quick affair, but they are beginning to confront the same realities faced by many imperialists that preceded them.

We will all regroup at the northern mountain camp in approximately two weeks. Until then, go forth and may Allah be with you."

The men gave a restrained cheer and chanted: "Allahu akbar." - God is great!

3

Abdul was pleased by the fighters' reactions. In a land of rampant pessimism he knew that optimism was a valuable commodity. Nonetheless, he used it in measured doses as the men had collectively experienced so many disappointments and broken promises. He knew that their new campaign needed to get off to a strong start or it could turn into another long and brutal summer of disenchantment.

Abdul was of average height and build. He had naturally brown skin that had been further darkened by his years in the Afghan sun. His face was framed by a long, scraggly beard with patches of gray while deep crow's feet led the way to his dark, sunken eyes. Most of the men in the group shared similar physical traits. Their culture frowned on individuality, so a homogenous appearance was a positive factor for a leader.

Winters in the mountains had always been daunting, but as Abdul aged he suffered even more. Despite years of fighting he showed few visible scars. This led many of his disfigured followers to view him with an aura of invincibility. In reality he bore many wounds. A collection of shrapnel in his legs caused him to feel anguish with every step he took. The steady cold caused stiffness and pain in numerous bones that had been broken and never properly healed. Abdul always made a conscious effort to hide his infirmities in order to retain his image. To ease the pain he chewed opium straw, trying his best to avoid doing it in front of his men.

Abdul stood patiently while the men packed up, said their final farewells, and began to disperse. As the camp finally emptied, Abdul gathered his weapons and made sure nothing was left behind at the site. He guided his group down the slope and then around a ridge that led to more favorable terrain. The team had excellent topographical maps of the area, but for the most part the charts remained stowed away. They periodically used them to make notes of where the enemy was operating; only rarely did they need maps to determine where *they* were going. Despite being desolate and rugged, the mountains had been crisscrossed by travelers for thousands of years. Those intrepid vagabonds had located the best routes and left well-worn foot trails for others to follow. Abdul and his men walked along one of these paths; their backs warmed by the increasingly radiant sun.

The men knew how to navigate the mountains, but they knew very little about the mountains themselves. The Hindu Kush system spreads out like a large hand reaching down from central Asia with its many fingers touching the edge of Pakistan, fanning across Afghanistan, and stretching westward to Iran. The Hindu Kush lacks the height of other ranges in the region, but this makes it no less daunting. The name Kush, meaning killer, was believed to have come about due to the number of Indian slaves that died while being transported across the mountains. The jagged, uneven waves of stone were formed by tectonic uplift that forced the harsh rock to climb from the earth. Over the ages, the terrain grew steadily more difficult as the two dimensional landscape morphed into three dimensions. The geology of the region created a high level of seismic activity and the unstable ground was just another variable in an unstable country.

For inhabitants of the area the challenges were exacerbated by the lack of infrastructure. For centuries attempts to tame the Hindu Kush led to cycles of improvement, but these were invariably followed by periods of decay and destruction. Prominent passes such as the Khyber, located along the border with Pakistan, had an adequate degree of engineering. However, many travelers were weary of these routes as they provided higher profile targets for robbery and ambushes. The Hindu Kush served as a constant witness to the struggles of the people of the region. Unfortunately at the present time it seemed that those conflicts would continue for many years to come.

By late morning Abdul's group arrived at their first stop of the day: a formation known as the Pillars of Ghari. The scale of these towering rock columns was impressive from a distance and truly humbling up close. Abdul, who was leading the line of men, paused at the base and craned his neck back. His eyes looked higher and higher up the sheer face until finally the stone gave way to blue sky. As though he'd been granted some divine permission to enter, Abdul raised his hand and pushed it forward, signaling his men to follow as he made his way through a narrow opening in the wall.

Abdul threaded a path through the natural catacombs until he reached an open, courtyard-like area. The faint sound of the swirling breeze could be heard above, while the men's voices and the metallic noise of their equipment echoed within the chamber.

"Wait here," Abdul said as crawled into a small opening at the base of one of the walls. He re-emerged a moment later, no longer weighed down by his weapons. "Go ahead," he said, motioning to the next fighter. As the men took turn stashing their arms in the hidden alcove, Abdul allowed for a short break in the calm chamber before they headed on through the remainder of the maze.

When they emerged from the other side of the formation it took a moment for their eyes to adjust. Before them the terrain became less severe and paths branched out in numerous directions. They followed a flat ridgeline for a distance until it reached a fork that led to descending paths. Abdul stopped and scanned the mountainside above and across from their position. After a moment he located Wasim's group moving steadily in the same direction. Abdul made a loud, shrill whistle and waved to the other group as a final gesture of encouragement. They acknowledged Abdul before he led his team down one of the paths and out of sight.

***

After signaling back to Abdul, Wasim continued on his way through the higher elevations. His band remained armed as there were limited places to hide a weapons cache along their route and they did not intend to come in close contact with the enemy while doing reconnaissance.

By mid-afternoon Wasim's team had arrived at their destination for the day. When they crested the last barren cliff they were finally afforded a full view of the massive valley below them. At this point Wasim halted progress and reiterated his orders.

"From here on we'll break into groups of two. Move quickly and take up your positions at the normal intervals. Stay ready at all times, but do not take the first shot. We are only up here to look out for Abdul so hold your fire unless you see me start shooting. If he comes under attack we need to provide cover so they can retreat. Take your shot and then move so you're tougher to target and our presence looks greater. If we are attacked keep moving forward. Press on over that next rise and you'll find better shelter. Understood?" Wasim asked.

All of the men nodded in agreement.

"Good, start moving."

Ten minutes later the unit had fully dispersed and Wasim and another member, Atash, began the short descent to their chosen position. They found a sheltered gap behind two large boulders and unloaded their equipment. The space between the rocks gave them a clear view of the hills and valley below. Wasim lifted his binoculars and took a cursory scan of the area. There was no sign of Abdul's men so he settled back and drank from his canteen.

Atash made a deep sigh and eased his aging body down against the back wall of the alcove. The white hair of his beard connected to his white turban and provided a contrasting frame for his dark, leathery face. Now well into his fifties, Atash was easily the oldest member of the group. This was quite an accomplishment in a country where the average life expectancy was just forty-four. Even more so given the fact that most of his years had been spent fighting in some capacity or another.

In light of his seniority, Atash harbored a smoldering resentment toward Abdul. He still respected Abdul as a leader, but believed that he had earned a higher position than he currently held in the pecking order. Atash took the present opportunity to speak candidly with the man he felt closest to in the group. "This is yet another chance to do what we seem to do best: wait."

Wasim chuckled mildly, "Indeed." He knew exactly where Atash was going to head with the conversation and accepted the fact that he was a captive audience.

"What are we really doing up here today? What new information does Abdul hope to acquire? We already know that the enemy is better trained, better equipped, and better protected. Their camp is right where it was last time we were here. I doubt much has changed as they have spent their winter wrapped in comfortable clothes and sleeping in warm quarters. They have the luxury of doing all of their monitoring from the sky above."

"This is true, but complacency is not an acceptable strategy either. They have their strengths and we have ours. Technology is obviously not one of ours so we must rely on our feet, our eyes, and our ears," Wasim replied in a consoling tone.

"If those are my strengths I hate to think what my weaknesses might be," Atash said with an ironic grin as he lifted his right foot and tapped his ear. Atash had lost two toes in a mine explosion. That blast, and countless others, had also diminished his hearing, particularly on the right side. "What I want to contribute now is my continued will to fight."

"And you will no doubt have your chance soon. Be ready to fight hard, but smart," Wasim replied.

Atash continued to talk while Wasim zoned out and just nodded steadily. Wasim was relieved when he finally saw some motion on the hillside below them. He inched forward and braced his arms on one of the boulders. Raising his binoculars, Wasim scanned the terrain below them until he found Abdul's men sneaking along a crease in the rock. He bounced from man to man until he located the leader. A moment later Abdul situated himself and raised his fist as a signal to Wasim. He returned the gesture and then settled back to monitor the situation from above.

***

Abdul unpacked his small shoulder bag laying out his surveillance equipment like a surgeon preparing for an operation. He removed the caps from his binoculars and made an initial survey of the area below. The camp layout had not changed much since their last visit to the valley; however, he noted that its size had continued to expand. This was clearly transforming from a remote outpost to a full scale operating base for the opposing forces.

Abdul opened his notebook and began updating his observations based on what he saw. He had several rough maps where he penciled in new structures and equipment. Although he would never admit it, he was always in awe of his opponent's ability to source materials and equip their troops. After completing his macro analysis, Abdul unlocked a weathered brown case and carefully lifted his long scope. He unfolded the legs of his tripod and threaded the base plate with the set screw. Abdul used his prized possession to get a significantly closer view of the subject below. Now he made mental notes of the faces he could see and the activities of the soldiers.

While Abdul conducted his work the rest of the men in his group did their best to emulate his efforts. For the most part, however, their viewing was more like tourists taking in the sights. They would point out new things, ask each other questions, and occasionally laugh about something they found to be amusing.

Abdul had limited expectations when it came to educating his men - keeping them loyal far outweighed making them smarter. They were in no hurry today so he decided to impart some knowledge to one of the youngest members of his team. He motioned to Kaihan, who happily scurried over and knelt next to Abdul. Abdul tilted his head toward the scope and Kaihan eagerly accepted the opportunity to view the camp through the high powered optics.

"What do you see?" Abdul asked in a thoughtful tone.

Kiahan paused for a moment before answering. He wondered if this was some kind of test and didn't want to disappoint his leader. "I see the enemy."

"Correct," Abdul said patiently. "But what do you see that is important to us?"

"They look very busy."

"That's right. They are preparing for the coming months. There are more men here now and more equipment. From their standpoint they are adding strength, but the way I see it we now have more targets," lectured Abdul.

Kaihan nodded at the wisdom.

"Their expansion requires increased support. The roads feeding this camp will have a steady flow of trucks and they won't be able to protect all of them. The camp is well fortified so they feel safe where they are. That's why they're having fun and enjoying themselves right now. It won't be that way when they come and go. When they venture out they become much more vulnerable," Abdul added.

They had already seen several small groups of vehicles arrive today and Abdul pointed out a cloud of dust in the distance signaling the approach of more trucks.

"Lots of opportunities," Abdul said with an optimistic grin.

Abdul returned to his work and tried to identify individuals on the ground below, particularly those that appeared to be leaders. Off to one side Abdul noticed silver flashes coming from among a group of soldiers. He trained his scope in that direction and saw several senior officers that he recognized. He also noticed a new face.

"It appears that they may have someone new at the top of their ranks," observed Abdul. He called Kaihan over for another look.

Kaihan peered through the scope and saw the officers standing among a number of tiny, white spheres and carrying shiny, metallic sticks. He watched as they contorted their bodies wildly and then looked off toward the horizon.

"Is that some new type of weapon? What are they doing?" Kaihan inquired.

"No, it's actually a game. They are playing golf," Abdul replied.

"Hmm. I've never seen this before. It looks very foolish."
"It is."

2

Major John Lewis glanced up from the reports he had been reading. The steady crackling of gravel pelting the wheel wells of the truck he was riding in had slowed and he realized they were finally approaching their destination. His day had started well before dawn with a turbulent helicopter ride from Kabul to a supply base in Ghazni. There he hitched a ride with a small convoy of vehicles and spent several hours twisting through primitive roads.

He looked around and saw barren flatlands in all directions. The plain covered a vast area; however, Major Lewis still seemed to feel enclosed by the solid line of mountains that fenced in the valley. He wasn't sure if it was a barrier that would keep him in or keep others out. He noted that the landscape assured that no one could sneak up on the installation without being seen.

Their truck stopped and started several times as the vehicles ahead of them checked in at the entry control point. When it was finally their turn the driver opened his door and handed his paperwork to the soldier manning the station.

He saluted the driver and said, "Good morning, sir," before giving the paperwork a cursory look. As he handed the documents back to the driver he looked over at Major Lewis and noticed his uniform. He immediately stood erect and saluted again. "Good morning, sir!" he said again, this time with added enthusiasm.

"Good morning, Private," Major Lewis replied with a nod and a salute. He sat back and looked around with a touch of unease. In an unknown setting he was a bit concerned about being recognized as a senior officer. Although it was unlikely anyone else would see the exchange, Major Lewis knew it was always better to remain inconspicuous until he had a better lay of the land.

The driver pulled forward and drove slowly into the maze of the compound. They wound along the dirt paths past a variety of buildings and equipment toward the middle of the facility. Major Lewis took in the surroundings and was pleased with what he saw.

The base appeared very orderly and the soldiers were moving with a sense of urgency. Everyone was in motion; no one was standing around or loitering.

From an aesthetic standpoint, things were less pleasing. Between the uniforms, the vehicles, and the structures there were many different shades, but only one color: brown. This was obviously in response to the location and in a war zone it was always best that form follow function. The walls and partitions were constructed of HESCO bastions. These earthen barricades were ubiquitous throughout the military installations in Afghanistan. From a distance they looked like thick graham crackers stood on edge.

They peeled off from the other vehicles and pulled into a courtyard fronted by several nondescript buildings. Major Lewis dragged himself slowly out of his seat and exited the vehicle. He yawned and stretched trying to shake off the lengthy road trip.

The truck looked quite different than the one he left in this morning. They had departed in a spotless, brand new vehicle. Now it was covered in dust, caked with mud, and had dozens of nicks and scratches. It was as though the trip had aged it by years. The men gathered their canvas briefcases and walked toward a stone entryway where an officer stood waiting to greet them.

"Good morning, Major Lewis. Welcome to Forward Operating Base MacKenzie. I'm Captain Roth."

"Great to finally meet you, Captain. It's a nice place you've got here."

"Thanks, come on inside."

They headed inside where several soldiers were gathered around a pod of monitors. Everyone stopped and stood up when they saw Major Lewis. He spent several minutes with introductions and a brief tour of the command center. Captain Roth then led everyone to an adjoining conference room where they sat down and unloaded their materials on the table.

Each man unfolded a laptop and laid out his paperwork. The computers had touch screens and the soldiers began to peck away on the screens with styluses. The scene looked like a group of big kids had decided to dress up for game time. At any moment one of them was bound to shout: "You sank my Battleship!"

The first thing on the agenda was a general summary report from Captain Roth, who had been running the base but would now be second in command.

"So tell us, Captain, what is the state of the base?" Major Lewis asked.

"I'd like to give you a simple answer, but this is Afghanistan. Things continue to vary greatly from day-to-day, hour-to-hour. We tend to see extremes in activity. Either we're bored senseless or running flat-out. Feast or famine. Overall, I'd say we are holding up reasonably well, but everyone knows that the quiet season is coming to an end. With the influx of new equipment and new faces, everyone can sense that the fighting is going to dial up again soon."

"Did the troops enjoy having a bit of reprieve at year end?"

"You know how tough the holidays can be. It is such a jumbled mix of joy and sorrow. We do what we can to make it feel like home, but look around, this isn't like home for any of our soldiers. Even those that come from the projects or the boondocks feel like they're in another world. We did video conferences, held special events, and brought in the requisite food and drink. All of those things serve as a nice diversion, but at the same time they drive home the fact that they are spending the holidays on the wrong side of the planet.

They also know that the break in hostilities has nothing to do with the goodwill of fellow man. Mother Nature steps in and forces a truce upon everyone. Moreover, what little economy the Afghans do have here is driven primarily by illegal agriculture. Back home we celebrate the spring with cherry blossoms and fall with pumpkins. Over here it is opium time in April and marijuana harvesting in November. That raises money for the months in between: fighting season."

"It sounds like I arrived at just the right time of year then," joked Major Lewis, trying to lighten the tension.

Captain Roth continued, "Major, I know your track record. You've been to a lot of crazy, dangerous places in your career. I can

13

assure you that you've never been anywhere like this. I'm not trying to scare you; I'm just giving you the facts, sir."

"I understand, Captain," Major Lewis replied with a now solemn face. "I've read the reports, studied the maps and photos. They never tell the whole story. I'm realistic about what we are up against here. Nonetheless, I'm not going to lower my expectations. Part of what I bring to the table is optimism that hasn't been drained out of me the past few years. We finally started having success in Iraq and the morale improved vastly from where it had been. Meanwhile, this place has been going in the other direction and has, therefore, created the opposite effect. My goal is simply to combine your knowledge of the situation with my experience and do the best we can together. So let's start sharing some of that knowledge. Tell me about the territory."

"Alright, we've got some movies for you to take a look at," Captain Roth replied. He powered up a small projector and aimed it at the gray wall. The bland, solid surface made for a perfect screen and Captain Roth began narrating a series of high-resolution aerial videos.

The briefing continued for about an hour with several other officers providing updates. Major Lewis had lots of questions, but he knew there would be plenty of time to dig deeper in the coming weeks.

"Alright, let's head out back and I'll take you to your quarters so you can relax and settle in for a bit before lunch, Major."

"That sounds good. Lead the way," Major Lewis said.

Back outside, Major Lewis noticed that the sun was now brighter and the temperature was mild and comfortable. His mind wandered away from his new assignment and he started thinking about things he'd rather be doing on a day like this.

He followed Captain Roth down a narrow walkway that wound between several buildings. Once inside the barracks the atmosphere felt like a penitentiary. They walked down the stark hallway with the sound of their boots impacting the hard floor.

They passed an uncovered doorway and Captain Roth noted, "Showers and bathrooms in there." Arriving at the end of the corridor, Captain Roth opened the door and welcomed Major Lewis, "And here we have the penthouse suite."

"You're spoiling me already," Major Lewis said as he walked into the room.

"We have lunch scheduled at thirteen hundred hours so I'll swing back by and pick you up then. Need anything else?"

"No, I'm good. Thanks, Captain."

Major Lewis closed the door and evaluated his new abode. The structure had been built last year, but it didn't have the smell of new carpet or fresh paint. Rather it was the musty smell of concrete that welcomed Major Lewis and said home sweet home. The spartan room had a perfectly made bed covered with a dark green blanket. There was a metal chest of drawers on one wall and a small desk in the corner. There was a single fluorescent light fixture hanging from a piece of conduit on the ceiling, but right now the room was lit by the daylight filtering through two narrow, slit windows cut high on the wall opposite the door.

Major Lewis walked across the room and sat down on the edge of the bed. He let out a deep sigh, took off his hat, and rubbed his eyes. Glancing up he noticed that he was looking at his own reflection in a mirror mounted on the back of the door. He got back up and stepped toward it. He stood up straight and pushed back his shoulders. Lewis had spent his entire adult life in the military and he looked every bit the part. He was just over six feet tall with a broad torso and thick legs wrapped in fatigues. The chiseled face was showing fissures as lines and wrinkles grew deeper with years of stress in combat. The square geometry of his head featured a wide, flat chin and ears that appeared pinned to the side of his skull. It was topped off by a fresh flat-top haircut; the short length hid the beginnings of encroaching gray. He mentally reminded himself that with age also came experience. He had faced many challenging situations and succeeded time and time again. Lewis was confident that he was the leader that MacKenzie needed right now.

Off to his right Major Lewis saw that a courteous soldier had performed bellhop duty and neatly stacked his bags. He went over and picked up a small backpack sitting on top of the pile that held some of his personal items. He unzipped the main compartment and took out several framed pictures. He looked at the first few, which were recent photos of his family. He savored the fresh memories of each one before carefully placing them on his desk. Major Lewis had been able to spend several weeks at home in the fall and then again for Christmas and New Year's. Given his current assignment he knew it would be a long time, too long, before he saw them in person again. His method for dealing with the extended separations was detachment. He forced himself to emotionally let go.

The last picture was from the end of his most recent deployment in Iraq. It was a group photo of Major Lewis with several of his officers and soldiers. They were in a semi-circle; each man was standing with a golf club in front of them with their hands placed on top of the grip. It was the kind of photo you would have taken at a scramble tournament or on a buddies' trip. The difference with this picture was that the men were dressed for combat and the sun was setting over the Syrian Desert. The men were smiling with true happiness at a point when they knew they had achieved success. Lewis hoped that in the not too distant future he could take a similar picture with the soldiers here.

Major Lewis sat back down on the bed and decided to relax for a few minutes. There would be plenty of time to unpack the rest of his belongings later. He leaned back, closed his eyes, and let his mind wander. He had just drifted into that comfortable space between being awake and sleeping when a knock at the door sent him quickly back to the former. He sighed and then rolled to the side. "Coming," he said as he slid his hand across the top of his head and grabbed his hat.

***

When Captain Roth entered the dining hall with Major Lewis it was as though the new sheriff had just entered a saloon in the Old West. The boisterous banter quickly fell to a mild murmur as soldiers shot glances amongst themselves and toward the doorway. One soldier was slow to catch on and continued to laugh raucously until a kick under the table brought him up to speed. He quickly stopped and slunk down a bit on the bench.

Captain Roth gave a half wave to let everyone know it was alright to carry on as they had been. The room cautiously came back to life as the two men walked to the small aluminum counter to order.

"How are you doing today, Private Miller?" Captain Roth asked as he perused the fare displayed in metal bins.

"Good, sir, and you?"

"Excellent. Private Miller, this is Major Lewis our new commanding officer."

"Welcome aboard, sir," Miller said with a toothy grin.

"Thanks. I'm looking forward to getting involved."

Private Miller stopped smiling and looked as though he was questioning Major Lewis' statement. "Is this your first time in Afghanistan?"

"Yes, it is. Captain Roth has already been selling me on what a wonderful place it is, though," Lewis replied, picking up on the implied message.

"We all pretty much agree that there's no place else like this. But that's probably a good thing," Private Miller said with a shrug.

"Well at least we have Private Miller to make it feel a bit more like home. He can take the blandest food the military has to offer and give it some life," Captain Roth complimented.

"I just do the best I can," Miller replied humbly.

"Good to meet you, Private. I'll be seeking your counsel on how we can make it even better."

They took their plates and found a seat at a table with several officers Major Lewis had met earlier at the command center. It was a universally understood etiquette that lunchtime conversation would focus on non-military topics unless there was something urgent in nature. Families, sports, gossip, and similar topics were all acceptable conversational fare. Things such as world events were border line as they usually led to something tied to the war.

Basketball was the focus as Captain Roth and Major Lewis entered the discussion.

17

"So, Major, are you a pro or college fan?" asked Lieutenant Simon Warner.

"I'd say indifferent to that aspect, but I much prefer an offensive game to a defensive one. I want to see lots of fast breaks and both teams score in triple digits. Full court presses and teams struggling to reach fifty really don't interest me very much. When the seasons get to the end I'll follow the tournament and the playoffs."

"Do you have any favorite teams?"

"I lived in a number of places while growing up, but most of my formative sports years were spent in the Midwest. As a result, the teams I followed tended to gravitate toward Chicago. It always seemed that even if the teams weren't doing well they at least had a star player that was fun to watch. The Bears have had plenty of solid seasons, the Bulls obviously had their golden years in the nineties, and then you have the Cubs..." Major Lewis said raising his eyebrows.

"They get close every once in a while and then seem to still lose in the end," added Lieutenant Warner.

"Kind of a metaphor for this place. Maybe we should rename this country Wrigley Field," Lieutenant Marcus Davitch interjected.

The others quickly shot glances at him and he held up his hand apologetically as if to say, "my bad."

"So far we haven't had enough staff out here to set up any real teams, but we get in our pick-up games when we can," Captain Roth said, steering away from the serious reality they all knew surrounded them.

"I always try to make sure my men have as many athletic opportunities as possible. A lot of the time we have to improvise the best we can. We can usually get any equipment we need; we just never seem to have any grass. It makes you appreciate those neighborhood vacant lots you always had as a kid and took for granted."

"Yes, unfortunately our golf course may not be up to your standards, Major. I understand you are quite a golfer," Captain Roth said inquisitively.

Major Lewis's expression seemed to brighten immediately as he was offered the opening to talk about his true sporting passion: golf. "I don't get to play as much as I used to when it seemed like every place I was stationed had at least one course, if not two. I do my best to swing the clubs whenever I can."

"So what kind of handicap do you have?" Captain Roth asked.

"Right now I'm probably sliding up to the high single digits. At my peak I could edge toward scratch, but that's been a while. Who's the top player here at MacKenzie?"

"It sounds like he just arrived," Lieutenant Warner offered.

"I always hear that and then I find out that there are plenty of strong players."

"We've got a couple of guys who are decent all around golfers, but our range always seems to turn into a long drive contest," replied Captain Roth.

"Nothing wrong with that," said Major Lewis. "There are plenty of times when I only want to hit one club out there. Good way to release some aggression. Practicing half sand wedges doesn't seem to have the same effect."

"You'll get a chance to see all of our facilities later this afternoon when we take our full tour of the base. I already have a tee time penciled in for us at around fifteen hundred hours."

"Excellent. I can already tell that we are going to be able to work together," Major Lewis complimented.

As lunch continued, Major Lewis spent most of the time listening to the other soldiers to start getting an idea of the people he would be working with here. He had already read over the personnel reviews before arriving, but now he could begin filling in the other traits that you couldn't get from a piece of paper.

Besides scheduling golf, Major Lewis was confident in Captain Kyle Roth's other abilities. Roth had arrived at MacKenzie last summer and had successfully supervised the continued expansion of operations. He had also made progress in improving relations with the local leadership in the surrounding communities.

Roth was in his mid-thirties and closest in age to Major Lewis. He seemed to be middle-of-the-road in just about every way. He was even tempered and non-opinionated. Even his appearance tended toward average: just under six feet tall, with a brown flat top, and no real distinguishing features.

First Lieutenant Simon Warner was more memorable. He stood six foot six with sandy blond hair and wide shoulders. He looked like the corn-fed Iowa boy that he was. His voice still had some of the slow, plains drawl underneath, but most of it had been beaten out by the formal military dialect. Despite his imposing size, the fact that he was ultra-polite made him seem almost timid. Based on his profile, he would do the things necessary to avoid a fight or diffuse a difficult situation. However, once that line was crossed, his fighting instincts kicked in and he became a soldier to be reckoned with.

Major Lewis was comfortable with Roth and Warner. Second Lieutenant Marcus Davitch was the one that concerned him, however. Davitch had come from a violent upbringing with a litany of abusive parents and step-parents. The pattern had followed him into adulthood as he was now on his third marriage. Despite his profession and time away, it seemed as though he was trying unsuccessfully to accomplish what his parents had failed to achieve. This was no doubt in part due to his short temper and combative nature. His heritage included American Indian and Eastern European ancestry. His pitch black hair and pale white skin gave him the appearance of a cinematic vampire.

Davitch had been in Afghanistan the longest; perhaps too long. His strategy and fighting skills were invaluable in the current struggle, however, at some point Major Lewis worried that he may become more of a liability. Despite their differences, Davitch and Warner had forged a strong bond and worked well together. With the two of them on the same team there at least seemed to be a balance, a true yin and yang relationship.

Major Lewis had done his homework on the group, but he knew better than to make pre-judgments. He had been in enough different places to know that the profiles didn't always match the soldiers. Moreover, people who performed a certain way in one environment might behave differently in another.

After finishing lunch Major Lewis spent a few minutes with additional casual introductions. Everyone at MacKenzie already knew of his arrival so there was no need for a ceremonial announcement process. In such an isolated location there was no way to maintain anonymity and Major Lewis would get to know his men quickly.

***

There was no formal agenda for the afternoon, so after a brief update at the command center, Captain Roth, took Major Lewis on a tour of the rest of the base. They looked over equipment and infrastructure and then headed for the area that Major Lewis really wanted to see: the driving range.

Working their way through a fortified maze on the edge of the compound, Major Lewis felt his spirits rise when he heard the sound of golf balls launching off a metal driver mixed with chatter and laughter. When the two men rounded the corner the sounds came to an abrupt end.

"Carry on," Major Lewis said immediately to the young soldier standing frozen with a golf club in his hands. "Let's see what you've got."

"Okay," the golfer stammered, while lining back up on the tee. As he did, the other soldiers standing nearby could sense the pressure and exchanged animated glances and snickers. He settled himself and then let loose with the driver. Despite a decent swing and his best effort, the soldier's shot was a wicked snap hook. The outcome was of course met with taunts and laughs from the other men.

Without cracking a smile, Major Lewis pointed to the next closest soldier, "Alright, your turn."

The soldier's attitude quickly changed as he was handed the club and stepped onto the firing line. He took a few easy practice swings before sending a high, power slice on its way into the warm afternoon air. He looked back meekly for an evaluation from his new commanding officer.

Major Lewis glared at him and then turned to Captain Roth, "I sure as hell hope these guys can shoot their guns straighter than this."

There was dead silence for a moment until Major Lewis finally cracked a big smile and let everyone in on his joke.

"No worries, Major. This unit may not boast the lowest handicaps, but you'd be hard pressed to find a better group of snipers anywhere in Afghanistan. Sergeant Hook over there could hit a flag on a thousand yard hole, likely on the first shot," Captain Roth said.

"Good to know. Give me an inventory of what we've got here, guys," Major Lewis said, pointing to the line of clubs leaning against the wall. He walked over and sorted through the motley assortment of drivers and irons that had been orphaned from their sets many years ago. He picked up a few and sighted them down the shafts the way one would check for a straight pool cue. Finally, he bent down and scooped up a handful of the shabby golf balls lying on the ground. Throughout this exercise he had his lips pursed and he was shaking his head with dissatisfaction.

"Not up to your standards I take it, sir?" Captain Roth queried.

"Definitely not. However, pretty much what I expected. My intentions aren't to come out here to MacKenzie and shake things up, but the driving range is going to need some drastic improvement. These sticks aren't fit for Neanderthals hunting herd animals. Like so many things here in Afghanistan we just need to introduce a little modernization."

"So you don't want to hit any shots then, Major?" goaded Captain Roth.

"I didn't say that, did I?" Major Lewis shot back.

"Then I guess the tee box is yours, sir" Captain Roth said, motioning toward the worn piece of carpet lying on the ground.

Major Lewis grabbed one of the better looking five irons and took a few warm up wrist swings. He stretched with the club over his head and finished with several full swings. He looked like a pharmacist sorting pills as he used the club's blade edge to cull out a few decent golf balls from the pile.

Even though there was nothing riding on these shots, Major Lewis shifted his mindset to golf. He looked at the harsh terrain spread out in front of him and then closed his eyes and took a deep breath. On top of the mental image he had just taken he overlaid a lush green fairway rolling gently into the distance. He could clearly see the color variations created by mower lines and topography changes. He opened his eyes and addressed the ball, but continued to see the image residing in his mind's eye. Major Lewis made a natural, fluid swing and sent his shot on a perfect trajectory off into the desert. He'd fired his first shot in Afghanistan and it was a good one.

The men were duly impressed and watched as he hit several more balls as well or better than the first. After seeing Major Lewis walk up cold and hit such impressive golf shots they knew they would no longer be able to blame all of their shortcomings on the substandard equipment. Apparently there were still some good shots left in these old clubs.

Eventually one of the soldiers handed him the driver. He was glad to see that it at least had a metal head. However, it looked very small, perhaps two hundred and fifty cubic centimeters in size, and it was attached to a steel shaft speckled with rust.

To adjust to the feel of the strange club he took his first swings at about fifty percent of his normal speed. It was a decent drive, but the gallery seemed quite surprise by the lack of distance.

He noticed their reaction and reassured them, "Don't worry, just warming up and getting the feel. This thing is about half the size of my driver."

With the next few balls Major Lewis steadily increased his power and in turn his distance increased significantly. The shots began to have their own soundtrack as the men whistled and emitted various sounds of awe.

Major Lewis was thoroughly enjoying himself, but he didn't want to look like he was showing off so he stepped back from the tee and leaned the driver against the wall. "I better stop now before I run out of good ones."

"That's a pretty impressive swing there, sir. Are you our new commanding officer or the new golf pro at Club MacKenzie?" asked Captain Roth.

"I've got my orders, but I'm sure we'll find some time to work on our games. Since the base continues to grow I think it is reasonable to look at expanding and upgrading our driving range."

"We'd certainly appreciate anything you can do, sir. We need as many diversions as we can get out here," said one of the soldiers.

"So what is your protocol for ball retrieval?" Major Lewis asked, starring out at the white dots littering the landscape.

The men exchanged glances wondering if their answer was going to be a problem.

Noticing their hesitation, Major Lewis added, "Don't worry, unless it is something illegal of course."

Captain Roth went ahead with the explanation. "Well, at the end of the day we'll have some kind of contest and the loser or losers have to go collect. We send out a sweeper for a detection run at dusk and then the gatherers head out with night vision goggles after that. We don't have to do it every day so we try to mix it up so there isn't a discernible pattern. While they are out there we also have the snipers provide cover. The enemy knows that they shouldn't mess with us at night. If any of the local gallery tries to wander on to our range they are going to get mowed down."

"Sounds elaborate. I'm glad you're being smart about it. Nonetheless, I'm not going to teach you too much about the game."

"Why is that, Major?" Captain Roth asked.

"Because I want to be sure to win those contests you mentioned."

Major Lewis spent another half hour chatting with the men, sharing stories, and hitting more balls. It was a pleasant diversion to help him get settled in at his new post. Major Lewis felt that he was off to a good start at MacKenzie, but he knew too well that there would be many far less enjoyable days in the near future.

3

After spending nearly a week at the base getting acclimated it was time for Major Lewis to start venturing out into the surrounding territory. He was glad that most of the internal procedures at MacKenzie seemed to be running smoothly. This would be his first glimpse at the situation outside of the cocoon.

Today's destination was the town of Baza Faqir-e. It was an ancient village located near the Helmand River at the crossroads of several major mountain routes. Captain Roth had arranged for a meeting with a regional leader who used Baza Faqir-e as his center of operations. Additionally, Major Lewis planned to tour the town while the accompanying troops conducted their regular public relations activities.

Baza Faqir-e was approximately thirty miles from the base, but the trip would take well over an hour. After the harsh winter the roads were in even worse condition than normal. There were numerous dangers in traveling these byways, both natural and man-made. Major Lewis was pleased that the trip was without incident and was taking in the barren surroundings as the convoy crested the shoulder of a low hill.

"There it is," yelled Captain Roth over the engine and road noise.

Major Lewis shifted his focus forward and looked through the dusty windshield. In the distance he saw rows of small, white buildings nestled in the middle of a vast plain. A multitude of straight, dirt roads fed out in various directions making the town look like the hub on a spoked wheel.

"Quite a metropolis," Major Lewis said sarcastically, noting only a few structures that appeared to be two stories high.

"Yeah, we're hoping that if they can get a little bigger Wal-Mart might consider building a store here. I'm not holding my breath though," Captain Roth replied.

On the outskirts of town they passed several people who looked on indifferently, but as they moved closer the younger residents seemed much more excited. The drivers slowed down and proceeded cautiously as more children gathered along the way; even an accidental injury could have drastic consequences in situations like this. The soldiers smiled and waved, but shouted for the boys to stay back from the vehicles.

"It's always nice to get a warm welcome," Major Lewis said as he waved.

"We have them well trained, sir. They don't think presents come down the chimney with and old guy in a red suit. Their Santa drives a Humvee and wears cammo. Unfortunately, like most people here they're only your friends as long as you have something for them.

Don't expect any of the adults to join the parade. They'll wait for the kids to come home and then evaluate anything we've given them. We try to keep the handouts pretty basic," Captain Roth replied.

"You can't blame them. We always check our kids' candy on Halloween."

"I guess you're right, but some of the stuff here just seems crazy. I could understand if we were handing out bibles, but even simple things can be misinterpreted. We had some soccer balls that were red and blue with a little bit of white writing and we got complaints that they were too American. There weren't any flags on them, no slogans, just an unsuitable color scheme. And what do you think the writing said?"

"Inflate to ten pounds and made in China," Major answered confidently.

"Yep! Think about that. Some poor worker stitches it together in China, they ship it to the U.S., it comes back around the world to Afghanistan and some kid in Baza Faqir-e isn't allowed to play with it. That's a pretty good example of what we are up against here, Major," Captain Roth said, letting some of his frustration slip.

"I know. We deal with it everywhere. So what did you bring in the sleigh today?"

"We've got plain, white soccer balls now, likely from the same factory in China, to go with the white Frisbees and white kites. We hand out some candy too, but they eat that right away so it never makes it home for inspection."

"And what did we bring for the big kids?" Major Lewis asked jokingly.

"You, sir," Captain Roth replied with a sly grin.

The trucks rolled along the edge of Baza Faqir-e before turning down one of the main thoroughfares. They parked in front of a walled compound and unloaded. The senior officers proceeded inside, leaving the remaining soldiers to handle public relations and stand guard.

After being greeted at the wooden double doors, Major Lewis and his staff were led across a tranquil courtyard to the main building. The property was simple, but well maintained. Major Lewis noted how quiet it was as the only noise was the sound of their boot steps echoing off the walls.

Once inside they were shown to a large, sparsely furnished room. Several men were already there seated on the ornate, but well-worn rug covering the center of the floor. The soldiers acknowledged their hosts and sat down with Major Lewis located in the middle of the group. Captain Roth began the introductions and opening pleasantries.

The Baza Faqir-e contingent were all dressed in the standard Afghan garb and had the uniform appearance of dark skin and black beards. However, the man seated directly across from Major Lewis was the person that mattered at today's gathering. Dehqan was the primary power broker in the region. Although he held no formal title, he was a tribal leader and warlord who had a broad sphere of influence. He was a politician who curried support from the populace, he was the commander-in-chief of the local militia, and he was the arbiter of disputes.

After the introductions were complete Dehqan got right to business. "We welcome you to Baza Faqir-e, Major Lewis. I'm sure you have studied your reports and know all about us. So let us use this time together for you to enlighten us about *your* plans and how it will impact *my* people."

"Thank you for having us. My goals here are to take what we have already been doing and expand and improve upon it," Major Lewis began. He paused to allow his translator to relay the message in Pashto. Although Dehqan spoke English, the translator was there to make sure communication was clear and for the benefit of the others present. Major Lewis had taken part in many meetings such as this during his career and was quite used to taking the regular pauses to allow for the language barrier to be crossed. "First and foremost is obviously the security situation. We'll be bringing in more men, more equipment, and more weapons. The central and southern portions of Afghanistan are garnering more attention and, therefore, will receive more resources. That then allows for the other initiatives to happen such as infrastructure, economic development, and jobs for your people. This won't happen overnight, but that is where we are headed."

"That sounds like a nice plan, but it also sounds very familiar. I seem to hear the same thing from your leaders every time we talk, however, over the past several years we have not seen things improve. In fact, they seem to be getting worse. Perhaps more foreign soldiers and their weapons don't increase our safety; perhaps it has the opposite effect. We have little to offer you other than our support, which has been there since your troops arrived. At this juncture it is important for you to convince me that route is still the appropriate and not an alternative course of action," Dehqan said, staring directly at Major Lewis while the other local representatives nodded in agreement.

Major Lewis knew of their frustration in advance and had expected this tone to the conversation. "I understand your skepticism. We appreciate your support in the past and I hope to earn it going forward. This is just our first meeting and I know it will take time for me to garner the trust of you and your people. This is a very complex fight we are engaged in, but I think we are up to the task. Many of our current efforts appear to be gaining traction and I will use my experience to add new strategies as need be. This summer will be an important test. All I'm asking for is a little more time to achieve our results."

Dehqan looked from side to side to gauge his men's reactions and then shrugged indifferently.

Major Lewis continued, "As for your *alternatives*, now is not the time to join the losing team. You know what kind of place this was when they were in charge and, regardless of what they are telling you, that is what they want to go back to. Despite what they may say, we have no desire to be occupiers. It would be easy to walk away and we would be happy to leave. Nonetheless, we are willing to take the more difficult path rather than leave you in the wrong hands."

"Summer is coming fast so I guess we will see," Dehqan replied unenthusiastically.

"As I said, security and stability are my top priorities. Without that I can't bring in the people and resources to implement the new projects that matter to you. In terms of our current undertaking I am still getting up to speed. So I'm going to let our logistics officer, Sergeant Diaz, lead that discussion.

The group spent the next two hours haggling over the status and details of projects that the unit was supervising and financing in and around Baza Faqir-e. Most of the talking was done by the subordinates of each group and they both blamed the difficulties on the other side. Periodically, Major Lewis and Dehqan would have to step in to reduce the animosity and table discussion items that were log jammed.

Some progress was made before they finally reached a point where everyone knew the meeting was done. Good-byes were exchanged and the U.S. contingent showed themselves out. Although everyone in town knew they were meeting, Captain Roth had already told Major Lewis not to expect a tour of Baza Faqir-e from Dehqan. He would not want to be seen together with the Americans outside of the compound.

Once they were back in their truck Lewis and Roth debriefed on the session.

"I think that went reasonably well," Major Lewis said.

"I agree. I think by the end Dehqan had warmed up to you and will give you a chance. As you can see there is still a lot of doubt and disagreement. However, a lot of what you are seeing is just the nature of how their culture does business," Captain Roth responded.

"And he seems to trust you, which is good."

"We've come a long way since I first started out here. They would either hide and act like nobody was home or shoot at us in most of these villages. We'd just leave them some propaganda and tell them that we'd be back."

"It's obvious that someone is in his other ear so we'll need to keep our projects moving forward and see if we can accelerate a few of those that seem more important to him," said Major Lewis, looking over his notes. "Alright, let's go see what this town has to offer."

***

The soldiers gathered up and drove the short distance to Baza Faqir-e's market area. They dispersed and moved slowly to avoid causing a panic when they arrived. The merchants were like a flock of birds; if something scared one of them they might all suddenly take flight. As expected, the soldiers were greeted with an anxious mix of excitement and fear. Like most residents in the area they were hesitant to be seen working too closely with the Americans. However, they were well aware that these customers carried dollars and were here to spend them.

Major Lewis and Captain Roth walked casually down the main avenue while the soldiers fanned out. The area was timeworn, but well maintained and the white noise of commerce filled the air.

"It looks like most of the vendors are out today, so that's a good sign. If there was an attack planned today someone would have been tipped off and most of the stalls would be closed. Only the really desperate would stay open," Captain Roth noted quietly.

"It seems like a nice size crowd. You don't want too many people around and get stuck in the middle of chaos if a car accidentally backfires. Anything you need while we are out here?" asked Major Lewis, motioning to some of the salesmen holding up their wares.

"No, nothing here. Just grin and wave, Major. Let's head down toward the end, though. I want you to meet that person I mentioned earlier."

When they made it to the end of the aisle, Captain Roth pointed to a stall surrounded by ornate artwork. "This is it, Major."

Major Lewis walked around the large prints up front and found a small boy sitting on a pillow on the floor drawing on scraps of paper. "He's a bit younger than I expected, Captain," Major Lewis said with mock surprise in his voice.

"That's not him," Captain Roth said, turning his attention to the boy. "Where's Zemar?"

Without even looking up from what he was doing, the boy yelled, "Zemar! Amrikhans!"

There was noise from behind a drape and then a thin teenager appeared.

"Zemar, how's it going?" Captain Roth asked while stepping forward and bumping fists with the boy.

"Good, Captain. Who's your new friend?" he responded while looking over Major Lewis.

"This is the new boss that I told you about, Major Lewis."

"Nice to meet you, Zemar." Major Lewis said with a smile. He didn't offer a handshake or fist bump as he didn't want to seem patronizing.

"Good to meet you, Major," Zemar replied.

Major Lewis stared at Zemar for a moment and then tilted his head a bit as he scrutinized the side of the boy's small turban.

"What?" Captain Roth asked, noticing the look.

"Wire."

Captain Roth instinctively put his hand on his M4A1 assault rifle and shifted his position to see what Major Lewis was talking about. He quickly laughed and flicked the dangling wire. "Just an ear bud, sir. We must have interrupted his hip-hop break."

"Sorry," Zemar giggled as he tucked the wire back under his cap.

"No problem," Major Lewis replied as the tension immediately subsided. "So is this all your work?" he asked, looking around the stall, noting the impressive drawings, paintings, and carvings.

"Most of it. I do sell some things for others. There aren't a lot of artists around here anymore."

"You are very talented. Is this just natural or did you have some instruction?"

"It seems to run in my family. My parents helped me when I was little, but most of it I picked up along the way. When I see something I can usually recreate it or use it as inspiration for something else. I do a lot of custom work if you are interested in something different. I've drawn sketches for a number of your soldiers."

"I'll think about that, thanks. I'm new here so my walls are bare and could use a little life. I'll look around a bit," Major Lewis said as he began to peruse the selection.

Captain Roth took the opportunity to see if he could gather any intelligence from Zemar, who, despite his age, was very well connected in the area. "So, have there been any new art buyers in town recently?"

Zemar knew the drill and volunteered only vague references, "Some, but not many. Certainly no heavy hitters. Just trying to run my business and keep all my customers happy."

"Good to know," Captain Roth said, reaching into his pack and pulling out a broad, but thin coffee table book. "Here's a new book I found for you. It has digitized photos of the earth taken by satellites up there," he said, pointing to the sky.

"Wow. These are some amazing pictures," Zemar said while flipping through the pages. "Thanks."

"I thought it was something you would like."

Major Lewis had picked up a landscape pencil drawing and returned to the conversation. "I see a lot of your work features artistic maps of Afghanistan and the region. Where does that come from?" Major Lewis asked, already knowing part of the answer.

"That's another family talent. My father was a geologist and cartographer. I was always playing with his maps when I was a kid and tried to imitate his work."

"Interesting." Major Lewis replied, noting that Zemar referred to being "a kid" like it was some time long ago. He was already aware that both of Zemar's parents were dead so he didn't want to push that discussion. "Well, as I said, you have lots of wonderful pieces here, but this one really caught my eye. How much?"

Zemar thought for a moment on where to set his price. "That's a nice one," he said, marveling at his own work. "For you, ten dollars."

Major Lewis knew that the price was high, way above what any local would pay, and that negotiation was typically part of the deal here. "Hmm..." he mused as he held the picture up to examine it closer.

"You're not going to find anything else like that around here," Zemar added, now worried that he'd priced too high.

Major Lewis reached into one of his pockets and found a stack of bills held by a steel clip. He pulled off two fives and handed them to Zemar. "I really like it. Thank you, Zemar."

"You're welcome, Major. Thank you," Zemar said eagerly. "I always tell Captain Roth to let me know if you need anything else. Always trying to do business."

"Okay, we'll keep that in mind. Well, we have to be going, but it was nice to meet you."

"Same here. By the way, Major. I hear there are some new foreign art buyers headed this way soon. It sounds like they are serious players. So you may be up against some new competition." This was normally something that Zemar would have passed along to Captain Roth, but he wanted to prove his worth to the new man in charge.

Lewis and Roth exchanged glances immediately realizing the meaning of the statement.

"Thanks again, Zemar. Take care."

The two men left to continue the tour of the town. Once they were out of earshot they discussed the interaction they'd had with Zemar.

"It seems like everywhere I go there is a Zemar," Major Lewis said smiling. "An industrious young wheeler-dealer who operates well beyond his years. Clearly a smart, talented kid. I'm really amazed by his English, too. So many young people here have almost no education. I'm glad to know there are some exceptions to the rule."

"He's a good kid. If there were more like him we wouldn't need to be here. He sees us as progress and a bright future so that's why he favors our side. Unfortunately he's stuck in this existence day-to-day so he still has to hedge his bets."

"What do you think about his parting comment?"

"I think it just provides additional support to what we've already been hearing. With our increasing presence the local factions know they have to bring in reinforcements from outside."

"Do you think he knows more details about who and when?"

"Probably not. He'll pick up info on macro changes, but I don't think he has any contacts that are close enough to get actionable data," Captain Roth surmised.

"Based on what you know about the players here, where do you think they will be coming from?" Major Lewis asked.

"Most likely the normal tribal areas across the border in Pakistan. You know we get a steady flow of foot soldiers from there, but my guess is that this would mean a bigger number of better trained soldiers and some higher level commanders to direct them. I think most of the forces in the north are busy enough trying to gain inroads up there. As for imports and mercenaries, they tend to gravitate toward more populated, higher profile areas."

"I agree. That's what I've been debating for the coming months. Whether we should strengthen our hold here and prevent anyone from gaining ground or if we should venture east to try and staunch the flow at its source."

"It's a tough call. If we focus too much in that direction it would leave us vulnerable to a move from the north or from the Kandahar/Helmand area down south."

"I've requested additional intelligence to see if we can get a better grip on some of their numbers and locations. They can't move troops the way we can so wherever they are massing is going to be close to their point of attack," Major Lewis said.

The men stopped as they were overtaken by three small boys who looked eager to see them. The boys held their hands up high and jumped, yelling: "Amrikhans! Amrikhans!" as though the two soldiers might accidentally overlook them.

Captain Roth held up his hand gesturing for them to stop. "Sorry, guys," he said while patting his pockets to show that they were empty.

The boys immediately appeared crestfallen and looked to Major Lewis for hope. He shrugged his shoulders and tried to look apologetic. The boys slunk away sadly having come away empty handed.

"I usually have some in reserve, but the others cleaned me out earlier," Captain Roth said.

"Wait!" Major Lewis called, reaching down to a side pocket near the knee on his fatigues.

The boys rushed back excited by whatever treasure Lewis had located. He pulled out two golf balls and held them in his hand. The boys exchanged glances amongst themselves not sure what they were looking at.

"Balls. For play," Major Lewis said, tossing one in the air and catching it. The boys still appeared confused, but were not about to turn down the dimpled orbs. He handed one to each of the smaller boys and patted them on the head. The third boy gazed with jealously at the strange, white gifts. The boys threw them in the air carefully and said, "Thanks, Amrikhans."

"You're welcome," Major Lewis said feeling good about his deed. He turned and continued to walk with Captain Roth. They had just resumed their conversation when they were interrupted by a loud scream behind them on the street. They swung around and saw one of the boys down on his knees crying loudly with his hands over his face.

"What the..." Major Lewis said, curious as to what had just happened.

The boy got up quickly, yelled some type of insult at the other two, and ran off with tears still streaming down his face. On the ground where he'd been hunched over one of the golf balls sat in the dirt. The third boy quickly snatched it up and tossed it in the air. He waved to the soldiers and the two boys scurried away.

"That went well," scoffed Captain Roth. "What are you going to bring them next time, Major? Maybe some apples with razor blades? Perhaps a live grenade for them to play hacky-sack with?"

"Hey, that's not my fault. The kid didn't use proper etiquette," replied Major Lewis defensively.

"Proper etiquette?" Captain Roth asked.

"Yeah, if his shot was going to hit someone he should have yelled: Fore!" Major Lewis explained, laughing heartily at his own joke.

Captain Roth chuckled and shook his head. "Alright, let me check around on the radio and make sure none of the team is coming under heavy golf ball fire. We'll head to the north side of town and then loop back around to the vehicles."

***

The other soldiers reported no issues on their patrols, but indicated that they sensed an elevated level of paranoia among the citizens of Baza Faqir-e. Even if they hadn't seen the Taliban, the people clearly knew that they had been in town just prior to the Americans' visit.

The convoy made a slow exit from town and headed back on a different route than they had taken this morning. This was a common procedure to make it more difficult for the enemy to plan an ambush. Given the mobility of their vehicles, they also took frequent diversions from the established roads to avoid IEDs.

The afternoon temperature had started to fall as the line of trucks made a steady crawl through a deserted valley on the way back to MacKenzie. Captain Roth was on the radio coordinating their route with the lead vehicle, while Major Lewis tried to match the images on their map to the surroundings outside. The landscape made him think of Zemar's drawing so he retrieved the artwork and looked it over in greater detail. The image was very ornate, but at the same time seemed to have a ghostly emptiness. The scene showed a great amount of natural detail while displaying almost no actual life. He felt their truck leveling off as they clambered out of a dry river wash and back onto the double track road. Captain Roth had just started to pick up speed when a muffled explosion brought them to an instant halt.

Major Lewis immediately looked up and was shocked to see their windshield covered with a bloody, pinkish pulp. In an instinctive reality check he looked at his hands and legs to make sure the substance hadn't come from him. All of his parts seemed to still be attached so he turned to Captain Roth to be sure he was still there. This took less than a second, but seemed to take much longer in Lewis's mind.

"What's your status in the lead?" Captain Roth bellowed in a loud, but steady voice.

"We're cool," the voice on the radio replied.

"Rear?" Roth asked.

"Us too. No damage."

"Everyone else?" Captain Roth continued.

"Nothing...I don't see anything...we're fine."

"Did anyone see where it came from?"

"I didn't see anything airborne. I'm pretty sure it was ground based," said the soldier in the lead vehicle.

Captain Roth looked to Major Lewis who nodded and grabbed his rifle, "Let's check it out."

"Alright, middle vehicles fan out and see what it is. Lead and rear, man the mounted guns and watch the hills," Captain Roth ordered.

They slowly crept out and began to survey the area. Major Lewis swiped a finger across the hood and examined the carnage. It appeared to be clumped with fur. He motioned to Roth who took a closer look.

"Is that an animal?" Lewis asked.

"I think so," Roth replied. He clicked his radio, "Looks like this might have been some kind of critter, boys. Let's be sure though."

"Over here, sir," came a voice from further up the road.

Roth and Lewis joined the soldier who pointed to a fresh crater just off the side of the road. The spot was still smoking and was covered with blast residue and more entrails. It smelled like a ghastly barbeque.

A soldier joined them carrying some kind of leg. "Tastes like chicken!" he said as he feigned gnawing on the limb.

Another soldier was picking through the edge of the crater and using a hand-held laser to take measurements.

"What's your evaluation, Private?" Major Lewis asked him.

"Definitely an older device. My guess is that it was near the road, but over time erosion gradually moved it away without detonating it. It looks like we scared some goats off the road and they triggered it," the soldier reported.

"Any sign that they had a shepherd or do you think they were strays?" Lewis asked.

"I don't see anything that looks human around and there don't appear to be any clothing fragments."

A soldier from the lead vehicle had walked up as well. "We didn't see anyone on the road when we came up. If anyone was tending the goats they probably ran off when they saw us coming down the wash."

"Alright, get a sweeper and make one last check in the immediate area to be sure. I don't want to get blamed for a body that shows up later," Major Lewis instructed.

Captain Roth and Major Lewis stood watch as the men brought their equipment and carefully waded through the scraggly brush.

"We spend millions on bomb detecting equipment, maybe we need to just go low-tech and buy some goats," Major Lewis observed.

"The proverbial canary in a coal mine," replied Captain Roth.

"I wonder what kind of reaction I'd get if I put in a requisition for some sentinel goats? Unfortunately, they'd probably have to be specially trained and bred and still end up costing us millions," Lewis surmised.

"And I think the animal rights crowd would be slightly bent out of shape when they found out," Captain Roth added.

Major Lewis shook his head. "Sure, it's okay for my men to get blown apart, but let's keep a damn goat safe. Still, can you imagine our convoy with a lead of goats on reins strung out in front? It would be just like the pioneers rolling across the plains frontier."

"I don't think many Conestogas were outfitted with GPS though, Major."

The men returned and reported no signs of human remains.

"Alright, let's get out of here and head back to Mac," Major Lewis announced. As he turned to walk back to the Humvee he looked at the oozing windshield and added, "Anybody got a squeegee?"

4

A light fog had infiltrated FOB MacKenzie during the night. The moisture in the air diffused what little light there was in the pre-dawn hour. Major Lewis was now very familiar with the base layout and moved quickly from the command center toward the helicopter pads. He had already completed his morning briefing and delegated duties to be handled during his absence.

Major Lewis entered the small office that faced the landing area and checked in with the soldier that had been on the graveyard shift. He chatted for a moment and received an update on the status of his approaching ride. He made one last check of the paperwork and equipment in his pack before stepping back outside.

His eyes could discern nothing beyond the edge of the base so Major Lewis focused on tuning his hearing toward the dark horizon. A moment later he heard the first faint thumps of rotor blades pounding the mountain air. It was a sound he loved to hear. It was a sound of power, a sound of military superiority. As the helicopter approached the beating grew gradually louder like a percussion section building to a crescendo. Major Lewis finally made visual contact when the pilots turned on their lights and decelerated for landing.

Once they touched down Major Lewis boarded quickly and they immediately rose back into the air. The pilot swung to nose around, cut the lights, and slid off into the darkness.

As they began their journey, the pilot steered a straight line across the valley while the co-pilot began preparing for the mountains in the distance. He paused for a moment and turned toward the second row of seats. "Welcome aboard, Major. How have the boys out here at MacKenzie been treating you?"

"Great group of soldiers. It has been pretty quiet so far, but everyone knows we are gearing up for several initiatives so there is some tension starting to build. I think most of them just want to finish the planning and get to work."

"I know the feeling. You have to do your homework in this place though. The enemy's mindset is so much different here than anywhere else, even Iraq. The players are always changing so it's hard to define a constant foe."

"We recently met with some of the local chiefs and they are clearly riding the fence. Based on what has transpired over the past few years it's hard to know if we should use the stick or the carrot to motivate them. It seems that with the carrot they just want more, but if we get more forceful it will push them away. And right now they see the enemy as a possible option. We need to stamp out the Taliban in this area to make their decision a lot easier."

"And you need to stomp on them hard, sir. They're like roaches: you step on the ones you see and new ones just seem to crawl out of the rocks. You have to go into where they live and eradicate them. And when you do that you make damn sure you get every last one of them," the co-pilot said with clear malice.

"You're absolutely right. The problem is that we have to do that without hitting the wives and children. They know that so they keep them close."

"I hope the tide shifts your way, sir. Should be a pretty quiet trip this morning. It wasn't too turbulent coming across the Kush. Catch a few winks if you can."

"I'll try," Major Lewis said, knowing sleep on the helicopter wasn't very likely. He did lean back and pulled his hat a little lower to relax. He stared ahead at the glowing instrument panel and let his eyes drift nearly shut. The amber light of electronics fused together until it looked like the low embers of a dying fire. There were no stockings hanging over the hearth, but the visual triggered memories of the time he had spent with his family over the holidays. The weather in North Carolina had been colder than normal and the family had spent a good number of evenings gathered around the fire. Major Lewis always missed his family, but over the years and various tours he had learned to manage the separation. His job was a difficult, though important one. His duty to his country and his loyalty to his men were strong counterweights to the sacrifices he had to make. On the other hand, the love for his family was a powerful inducement to do his job right and make it home alive to see them once again.

***

The morning sky was emanating a cool, dawn light as the helicopter made its approach to Raynor Airfield near Kabul. The facility served as the primary cargo hub for the Afghan operations. The massive complex was well fortified and organized with typical military precision. Equipment and supplies were arranged in straight lines and tight patterns.

Major Lewis disembarked and thanked the pilots for an uneventful voyage. He made his way into a nearby hanger that housed the administrative offices. He spent the first hours of his visit handling the authorization of routine requisitions for MacKenzie and meeting with several officers to discuss logistics planning for the upcoming summer offensives.

At this stage most of the supply routes were running efficiently. The military had found some success in countering roadside explosives and were employing other techniques learned in Iraq to avoid insurgent attacks. MacKenzie's remote location created added hurdles for many items so Major Lewis planned to source as much as he could now.

He was a bit dismayed that the items he was most interested in had not arrived yet. The cargo plane had been delayed, but was expected to land shortly after lunch time. He was able to kill some time and grab a bite until the landing was announced.

Major Lewis didn't want to risk the chance that his personal items would be misplaced so he made his way onto the unloading section of the tarmac. The area was a loud frenzy of activity scented with the potent fumes of jet fuel. He waited patiently as forklifts scurried in and out to unload massive pallets of standardized supplies. Finally the bins of smaller items began to make their way down from the plane's massive tailgate. Major Lewis had politely interrupted the receiving clerk and had him search the manifest to locate the appropriate container. When the scanner registered its arrival the clerk directed that it be moved to the side.

The clerk unhinged the rigid, chain link door and motioned for Major Lewis to take what was his. Lewis immediately saw the large case and dragged it out.

"So what's in there, Major?" the clerk asked. "Some kind of special weapon?"

"You could say that I suppose. But more accurately there are fourteen of them and ammunition by the dozen," he said, wheeling the case clear and carefully lowering it to the ground. "It's my golf clubs," he added to help the confused soldier.

"Wow. That's an awfully big case for golf clubs. You could fit a body in that thing."

"I like to keep them well protected. Plus there's room for all of my accessories. I had it custom made when I was in Germany. There was a craftsman who made specialty cases for musical instruments and I convinced him to make a modified version," Major Lewis said as he grabbed the next, smaller piece of luggage. "Do you have some kind of cart I can use to get these over to the helicopter pad I'll be leaving from?"

"Absolutely, sir." He yelled into the radio attached to his shoulder and a moment later an ATV with a flatbed pulled up. Together they loaded Major Lewis's belongings and then headed across the field. After dropping off the clubs the soldier took Lewis to the surplus depot. There didn't seem to be anyone around so Major Lewis thanked the driver and began to wander through the rows and stacks.

The surplus depot was a motley assortment of odds and ends that always seemed to accumulate in a war zone. Items came from closed facilities, damaged lots, confiscations, and often simply over-ordered supplies. Many of these orphans would probably have an interesting tale to tell if they could relay where they originated from and how they ended up on a barren plot in Afghanistan.

Major Lewis took out his pen and pad and started making notes as he paced the aisles. He was making a closer examination of some

Lexan panels, tapping vigorously as though that might somehow be able to simulate a bullet, when he was finally discovered.

"Good morning, sir. Anything I can help you with?" asked a voice from behind him.

Lewis turned and faced the young soldier. "Morning, Corporal. I'm Major Lewis from FOB MacKenzie.

"I'm Corporal Moses, but everyone calls me Moe."

"Nice to meet you, Moe. I found a couple of things I think we'll need and a few others I have questions about. These panels here - full strength Lexan I assume?"

"Yes, sir. Some serious see-through security."

"What are they for?" Major Lewis asked, noting the large, curved shape that made them look like big parentheses.

"They are bus stop shelters. You can hook them together in a row and add benches. I guess they come in handy if a suicide bomber accidentally blows his top *before* he gets on the bus."

"Can you spare a few? Maybe a half dozen?"

"Sure. Nobody has been installing them recently. I can't imagine you have a lot of bus routes out near MacKenzie," Moe asked, probing for the Major's interest.

"No, no. Alternate usage," Major Lewis replied with a smile.

"What else can we get for you?"

"Follow me over this way," Major Lewis said, walking briskly toward his next prize with his new friend in tow. "What are these big saucer-like things over here?"

"Those are some kind of bomb muffler. If you can get it over an explosive device it is supposed to diffuse the strength of the impact. Apparently they work okay on some mines and such, but on larger bombs they fly up in the air and spin like a tossed coin. You don't want to be around when something that big comes back down."

"Again, I'm looking at a different use so no worries there."

"How many do you want?"

"Just one will be fine. They look pretty heavy and I don't want to go overboard. What I'm really looking for is some carpet or mat material. I didn't see anything out here."

"We've got stuff like that inside the warehouse. Follow me," Moe said.

The warehouse facility felt like a cavernous home improvement store with pallets stacked on metal racks in long rows and the beeping sound of a forklift piercing the air.

"We don't have too much carpet here, but there are some small rolls and rugs over in those bins. Help yourself, just remember that we don't offer installation...particularly out at MacKenzie."

"You don't want to come out and see us? Maybe spend a long weekend? That's what I'm doing here - sprucing the place up. It's going to be like a resort when I'm done and you guys will be fighting for a spot at MacKenzie," Major Lewis said, knowing that his base would never be high on anyone's list.

Major Lewis pulled out several of the rolled rugs and unfurled them on the concrete floor. He found a rather ornate one and ran his hand over the surface. Despite the detail, it was relatively smooth and he decided it would make a nice addition to his quarters. The surface and pile height would also make it suitable for putting practice. Although the design looked like something that might be made by a local artisan he could tell it was a manufactured rug.

After a little more searching he found just what he was looking for: several good sized remnants with firm, medium length pile. He gathered up his selections and made sure everything was prepared for transit.

***

Major Lewis made the return trip to FOB MacKenzie on a Chinook transport helicopter. Many of his items made the journey with him, while other requisitions would be arriving via truck in a few days.

When he touched down he was met by a team of soldiers led by his logistics officer, Sergeant Diaz. There was nothing in the payload that required urgent attention, but that didn't stop the men from emptying the hull with wicked precision. Major Lewis loved to see this level of attentiveness and efficiency from his men.

As he stood to the side, Major Lewis barked instructions to Sergeant Diaz. He watched as one of the soldiers with a heavy beard rolled the bomb diffusing disk down the ramp. Major Lewis thought it looked like primitive man showing off his new invention: the wheel. Lewis directed that he roll it all the way to the outside courtyard next to the officers' residence.

Finally, when he saw his clubs he waved them over. "I'll take those," he said happily. With his new rug tucked under his arm and his clubs in tow he headed off to his quarters.

Lewis was exhausted from the trip, but that didn't stop him from immediately playing with his acquisitions. He unrolled the rug in the middle of his room and carefully trampled out the wrinkles. Next, he bent over the travel case, entered his code on the tumblers, and snapped open the locks. Inside everything appeared to be in order. He hoisted his golf bag from the shaped foam insets and gently set it on the floor. He unwound the wrapping that held the clubs in place and removed each one individually, inspecting it and then leaning it against the wall. Major Lewis removed the semi-round head cover from his putter and set it at one end of the rug. He grabbed two golf balls from a side pocket of his bag and dropped them at the other end. After a few practice swings he stepped up and smoothly drilled the balls down the length of the carpet directly into the head cover. He said to himself, "No rust at all, Johnny."

Major Lewis took his time unpacking the rest of his luggage. Different items triggered trips down memory lane for places he'd been and played golf. For all of the violence and death he'd seen along the way, he was glad that there were also lots of positive memories. He was hopeful that he would be able to accumulate more of the good ones even here in Afghanistan. Once he finished, he turned his attention back to his clubs. He quickly determined that he had just enough space in his room to take full swings with his driver. It made a beautiful whooshing noise that echoed around his tiny quarters.

Before he knew it dinner time had arrived and he walked down the hall and grabbed Captain Roth.

"Did you see that we had a UFO crash land while you were gone?" Captain Roth inquired.

"What are you talking about?" Major Lewis asked.

"You didn't see the big flying saucer in the courtyard?"

"Oh that. No, I brought that back with me - surplus," Major Lewis said, trying to infer that he'd gotten a good deal.

"From where? Area 51?"

"If you're afraid of aliens you don't need to be out there with us later tonight. And you'll miss out on the s'mores."

"Oh, I can't miss that."

"I'm planning to fire her up around twenty-one hundred."

"Sounds good."

***

At dinner Major Lewis extended fireside chat invites to several other officers. He had already been working to establish his leadership role with the men and now he needed to work on bonding with them.

The courtyard was a small swath of property wedged between several of the compound buildings. Cloistered off on all four sides it was a calm and quiet spot that offered a view of only the sky above. Over time it had been furnished with a variety of items. The majority of the seating was provided by plastic Adirondack chairs in an assortment of colors. Major Lewis had decided to add his own personal touch by bringing in a fire pit.

At this point in the year most evenings were cool and clear. When the sun dropped below the mountains the mercury fell quickly at MacKenzie. As the first stars peeked out in the darkening sky, Major Lewis tended to the first crackles and pops of the bonfire.

One simple item that Major Lewis had almost overlooked was wood. There weren't any sizeable trees nearby and much of the brush had only small amounts of hardwood. Instead he spoke with the facilities officer who was able to find some timbers from nearby growth that looked combustible and didn't appear to have any chemical treatment. For the first fire Major Lewis had decided to start modest in order to be sure nothing went wrong.

As the men wandered in and pulled up chairs the impact of the fire was immediately evident. They sat down with wide grins and were quickly laughing with nostalgic glee. The flickering light cast shadows that danced on the walls. The fire transported them from a dusty plain in Afghanistan to somewhere else they'd rather be.

The conversation rolled casually around the pit for about half an hour before Major Lewis decided to begin his comments.

"I just wanted to thank everyone for coming out tonight for our inaugural fire - not that you had anywhere else to go of course. I don't have any big announcements or hidden agendas tonight, I just wanted to get everyone together and make fire. I hope everyone enjoys the new addition to the courtyard and that it adds to the atmosphere. Living out here is a strange existence and we don't have a lot of places to gather ourselves. I'm glad we at least have this small area to unwind from the pressure. Alright, who wants to lead the first singing of Kumbaya?"

Everyone groaned.

"I think it's a great addition, sir," Captain Roth said, sincerely appreciating the new center piece in action.

Everyone groaned again, interpreting the comment as brown-nosing.

"I have a few more things on the way as well. As you all likely know I am a golfer so there are some upgrades for our driving range. There will also be some other new sporting equipment arriving soon. You'll find that I expect you to work hard, but at the same time encourage you to play hard. Hopefully you'll discover something you and your men will like and it will help ease the insanity. Does anyone have any questions or anything they'd like to add?"

The group seemed pretty mellow and Major Lewis got no volunteers.

"As for fireside rules, I want you to enjoy yourselves. If you drink, go ahead and drink...a little. If you smoke just stay downwind from those who don't. But make sure you stick to tobacco. The only thing I want to *burn* is the fire - no local vegetation.

I don't plan to talk about our mission here or tell ghost stories, but something I like to do is find out more about the various places I'm stationed. Sometimes when you look into the history of a country or region it can give you added insight into who and what you're dealing with. Lucky for you guys the tales to be told about Afghanistan seem to be shorter than anywhere else I've ever been.

This has always been somewhat of a crossroads so much of what went on here was just part of something bigger nearby. War and conflict certainly play a big role in Afghanistan's past so many events that occurred elsewhere could never develop or play out here. There was no Renaissance, no Industrial Revolution, no period of great English philosophers. Additionally, of the things that did happen, many have been forgotten or destroyed. I would have loved to have seen the Bamiyan Buddhas. To know that they were blown up by illiterate despots is nauseating."

"Can you imagine someone blowing up Mt. Rushmore?" asked one of the soldiers.

"I don't think any of us have to worry about that happening in our lifetime, but if history is a guide it could very well happen at some point in the future. Nature will do its part with ongoing erosion and sooner or later someone will deem it offensive and have it erased. It could be five hundred years from now or five thousand. Eventually it will happen.

The Bamiyan Buddhas survived almost fifteen hundred years. Think about it. That's a period similar to the time of Christ until Columbus sailed to the New World. It's an even more impressive run considering the events that transpired in this region.

Mullah Muhammad Omar had originally decreed that they be preserved, but in 2001 he changed his tune and gave the go ahead to destroy them. Even when the Taliban gave the statues all the firepower they could muster the Buddhas put up a fight. It took several weeks and a couple of different techniques to finally knock them fellas down."

"Do you think they will be rebuilt?" one of the men asked.

"And more importantly, will it be us doing the re-building?" asked another, only half-joking.

"Definitely not any time soon," Major Lewis wagered. "If we fixed them the Taliban would just try to blow them up again. They also wouldn't represent the original intent; rather they would be seen as a symbol of occupiers leaving their mark. Part of the reason they decided to go ahead with the demolition was that outside agencies were offering funding to repair previous damage. The Taliban wanted to take the money for other purposes, which they claimed to be humanitarian. When the agencies said no it inflamed the leaders who gave the order to destroy the statues. I can understand the anger part, but to blow them up in response is like a little kid deciding to take his ball and leave a game when he's not happy. The groups that were interested in preservation wanted to help because the Buddhas were one of the few major items of real significance in this country. Mullah Muhammad Omar wanted to keep them at first because he knew they were a draw for tourists. Why? Because they were unique, not because of any religious significance. Just another chapter in this country's history with a sad ending," Major Lewis lamented.

The men relaxed and chatted around the fire until the outer logs were all black with just a molten orange core. Some of the men were dozing off, roused occasionally by periodic pops from the dwindling fire. It was nearly midnight when Major Lewis snuffed out the final embers with a few handfuls of dirt. He stacked his chair and happily followed the bobbing beam of his head lamp off to his bed.

5

In addition to all of the equipment sourced for MacKenzie, Major Lewis had also obtained key pump components for irrigation projects near Baza Faqir-e. These had been high on Dehqan's priority list as he owned or controlled significant amount of agricultural land in the area. Major Lewis was embarking on a several day road trip to meet with other commanding officers in the region and Baza Faqir-e was going to be his first stop. He intended to deliver the new machinery in person to help build his credibility. Although this could have been handled by the engineering team assigned to the project, Major Lewis wanted Dehqan to see him as being responsible for results.

Major Lewis and his men arrived in Baza Faqir-e early in the morning. Prior to his meeting with Dehqan, Lewis stopped by the market and was glad to find Zemar already there. He wanted to develop as many loyal ties among the populace as possible and he felt that the boy could be very helpful in winning support from younger Afghans.

"Good morning, Zemar."

"Welcome back, Major." Zemar said, extending his fist forward.

Major Lewis did the same, glad to see that there was already a comfort level with his presence. "I've got some business to do here in Baza Faqir-e this morning and then I'm meeting up with another unit to play some golf. Have you ever seen golf before?"

"I've heard of it. Kind of like hockey, but no ice," Zemar replied.

"Sort of. The rules are quite different though. Anyway, when I was young I earned money working as a *caddie*. The caddie carries the golfer's clubs and helps him out with the game. I was wondering if you and some of your friends would be interested in making some extra money working as caddies."

"How much?" Zemar answered immediately, not showing much concern about the job itself.

"Well, the game will last a few hours so maybe a couple of dollars each. And, if you do a good job there is normally a tip, like a bonus." To Lewis the amount seemed very small, but he also knew the scale of the economy here and didn't want to set expectations too high - keep the carrot small to start with.

"Sure. I can have somebody cover for me here and I can bring a few other boys. How many should I get?"

"We should have four golfers so bring three friends that you trust."

"No problem."

"Rather than leave town with us I was thinking we could meet you outside. Just to avoid anyone thinking we are taking you against your will. Do you know where the Khana Pass is?"

"Of course."

"I figured you would. Meet us there in about two hours and then we'll drive to the place we are playing."

"Okay. What should we bring?"

"Open minds," Major Lewis said. "We'll see you there."

Lewis went about the rest of his tasks in Baza Faqir-e pleased that Zemar was open to his idea. He had run it by Captain Roth, who agreed that it was important to improve relations at all levels in the community. The kids loved to get toys and candy, but dishing out sugar highs wasn't a solid long-term plan. For the youth in Zemar's age group it was imperative to see that there were opportunities in the world beyond the narrow range that existed for them right now. Lewis felt that exposing them to a game like golf and seeing how they reacted would be an interesting experiment.

***

Just before noon, Major Lewis crested the low neck of the Khana Pass and saw Zemar sitting at the side of the road with his friends. Several of the supply vehicles had returned to MacKenzie so Lewis was now traveling with a smaller group.

"Hello, Zemar. Glad you could make it," Major Lewis said.

"Hi, Major. Where are we going?" Zemar asked.

"We are heading to a valley not too far away, should be there in about half an hour. We'll have you back here before dark. Are you still up for it?"

"Sure. Business wasn't booming today in Baza Faqir-e," Zemar shrugged.

"Alright, hop in back. We've got some lunches there if you guys are hungry."

The boys climbed into the bench seats in the back of the truck and eagerly dug into the pre-packaged food. As they headed off across the foothills the passengers enjoyed their chance to ride in an Army vehicle. Although the pace was slow, they stuck their arms out the slit windows and tried to grab what little airflow there was. When they hit bumps they would accentuate the impact and fly off the padded seats; certain behaviors were clearly universal.

Major Lewis tried his best to be at ease. Since the incident on their last trip home from Baza Faqir-e he had become wired to watch for goats along the roadside. Driving across a low area that was intersected by a web of small streams, Lewis noted that it would be a great place for a cabin in just about any other country.

"Get down!" yelled the driver as he slammed on the brakes.

"What is it?" Major Lewis asked, looking back to see Zemar ducking while the other boys seemed unfazed.

"Gunfire. Over there," Private Petrofski replied, pointing off to his left side.

"I didn't hear anything," Major Lewis said while looking back and forth over the edge of the dashboard.

"There. Look!" Petrofski exclaimed, directing Major Lewis toward the stream closest to them.

Major Lewis watched and then finally saw it. A straight line of spurts burst along the top of the water. It indeed looked like a line of fire from an automatic weapon, but there was still no sound. He had never heard of insurgents in Afghanistan having silencers and a close pattern of shots would have to be coming from somewhere nearby.

"Hang on, something's not right," Major Lewis said, staying vigilant to the surroundings.

"What's wrong?" Zemar asked from behind.

Again a line shot across the water. "That," Major Lewis said.

One of the other boys saw what they were watching and said, "Maha, maha."

"Do you mean the fish?" Zemar asked.

"Yes, the fish," Lewis said, looking to Petrofski.

"Sorry, sir," he replied.

"No worries, better to be safe. Pull up a bit."

As the vehicle moved ahead and breached the water several lines shot up and moved away from their truck.

"Jesus Christ," Petrofski muttered as the scared fish scurried away.

Major Lewis glared at him, "Watch what you're saying."

"Sorry, sir," he replied, now even more embarrassed. "I didn't mean to take the name in vain."

"I'm not worried about that. I'm worried about them," Lewis explained, motioning over his shoulder. "I don't want anyone accusing us of proselytizing. If they pick it up and say it they could get in more trouble than with most of the four-letter words we could teach them."

Petrofski looked a bit skeptical, but Major Lewis was quite serious. He knew all too well that in different cultures things that would seem innocuous to Americans could be life and death matters. This was particularly true when it came to religion.

They continued on and Major Lewis tried to calm back down. Based on his encounters so far he was starting to question if there were really insurgents in the region or just militant wildlife.

Twenty minutes later they arrived at their destination. As desolate as much of the area seemed, the Ughust Valley was truly in the middle of nowhere. There were no local inhabitants and the small American camp now housed only a skeleton crew of transitory soldiers. At one point the base was slated to be a major southern foothold. However, as troop levels increased and the military's focus shifted south to Helmand and Kandahar the plans were mothballed.

More recently it had been considered for an airfield due to its flat base and long, uninterrupted footprint. Those plans were also on the backburner, but it had been chosen for today's adventure due to the survey and mine clearing activities that had been conducted here. This was a bit of a scouting mission, but in the future he hoped to be able to bring additional soldiers from MacKenzie to play this unique locale.

As they approached the rendezvous point, Major Lewis saw several Army vehicles surrounded by soldiers swinging golf clubs. Their attire was best described as country club cammo: low-cut combat boots, camouflage cargo shorts, khaki tee shirts, and wide brimmed, olive drab boonie hats. Tattered cargo shorts wouldn't be allowed in most respectable clubs. However, the dress code here had some leeway.

Lewis's team pulled up and unloaded.

"Glad you were able to make it for our tee time, Johnny," the senior officer said, embracing Major Lewis.

"Good to see you, Ray," Major Lewis responded, glad to see an old friend in a new place. He had known Major Ramone Cierra for over ten years and this was the third time they would be serving in close proximity to each other. The two men had a common bond in their military backgrounds and also their love of golf. "It's been too long since the last time I took some of your money."

"Ha! You waste no time overstating your skills. I hope you've been practicing up over at MacKenzie. I've been here a while already so I've had a chance to learn the local conditions," retorted Major Cierra. He was a hulking man who looked big even standing next to someone the size of Major Lewis. Several thick rolls of flesh spilled down his neck from the bald head currently covered with a hat. He had a deep, booming voice that further added to his persona as a military leader.

"So playing off the dirt here is a lot different than elsewhere?" Major Lewis said facetiously.

"It's not just our local dirt. It's the altitude, the humidity, the weeds. But rather than talk about it, let's get to it. The valley should have been pretty clean already, nonetheless, I had our grounds crew

55

run the Buffalos and Huskies out this morning for an extra sweep. We've basically got a half dozen holes laid out heading up and then six more heading back. We'll see how twelve holes goes and then we can repeat the first few if we have time. Our typical cross-country rules, Johnny - we'll sight our targets on each hole and then measure for putts once your shot is within twenty feet. Are you ready to roll?"

"Absolutely. Let us get our stuff out and stretch for a minute and then we'll be ready."

Major Lewis introduced the caddies and met the other players that had come with Major Cierra. They spent a few minutes explaining the caddies' job with Zemar and his friends. It was rather comical watching them try to navigate the golf bags at first. One of them insisted that he should wrap the shoulder strap around his head until he wobbled and fell to the ground. Another tried to drag the bag, as though he was walking a dog, to the great dismay of the owner. This was clearly going to be an interesting cultural exchange. Zemar was a great mimic and immediately looked at ease with Major Lewis's clubs strapped across his back.

Major Cierra led the group to the spot marked as the first tee and then used his binoculars with laser distance capabilities to sight and measure a small tree in the distance. Once they were in agreement they teed off. All four men were solid golfers and smashed drives off into the distance to the delight of the onlookers and caddies. The sight and sound of the balls rocketing off their drivers led to a series of ooo's and ahh's as though they were watching a fireworks show.

"I like the gallery that you brought," Major Cierra noted as they walked off down the not-so-fairway.

"We'll see if they know how to boo once they see your short game," chided Major Lewis.

Although certainly non-traditional, Major Lewis enjoyed their version of "cross-country" golf. It felt like the way golf was originally meant to be played. Golfing in the primal fashion seemed even more apropos in such a primitive place. The format also reminded him of his childhood when he and his friends would play park golf. They would make up the course as they went carrying a bucket and a few clubs. Once they arrived at each "green" they would put down the bucket and then have to chip in to hole out. Today's format did have a slightly higher tech element as they were measuring their distances with lasers and using GPS mapping to move along the course.

After hitting their second shots, Majors Lewis and Cierra met back up and walked together.

"So how are things so far over at MacKenzie?" Major Cierra asked.

"Not too bad. How about over at Camp Ross?" Major Lewis replied.

"Good."

Now that they were on the course that was as much work talk as they would have. When they did chat it was catching up on family and reminiscing about prior rounds played. Also, they didn't want to discuss anything sensitive in front of the caddies. More than anything they were trying to detach from the struggle around them and enjoy the beautiful day. Their jobs entailed being on duty twenty-four seven and, therefore, they intended to take full advantage of their R&R when they could.

There was also limited conversation with the caddies. This was in part due to the language barrier, but also due to the fact that they seemed to be taking things in on this strange hike with a group of foreigners. Zemar did ask periodic questions and Major Lewis offered occasional tips about the game and the rules. He tried to keep the rules part to a minimum since even experienced golfers often had trouble figuring them out and interpreting them.

Lewis was very impressed at how quickly Zemar learned and how intuitively he worked. The golfers all had small, synthetic turf mats with them that they could hit off if they chose. The mats were a bit unstable and cost distance so Lewis preferred to hit off the ground if he could. However, if his ball came to rest in a particularly rough or rocky area he didn't want to risk damaging his clubs. Zemar would watch the lie and determine whether or not he should offer the mat to his golfer.

The group was having fun and moving well, reaching the turn in about ninety minutes. They found a cluster of low, flat rocks that looked like benches and parked themselves for a break. One of Major Cierra's men who was walking along, but not playing, handed out drinks and snacks from his backpack. Thus far Major Cierra was in the lead with Major Lewis in a close second. They would be putting for each hole at the end so that could quickly change the outcome.

The men recounted some of their more memorable shots and the caddies were doing the same. Major Lewis took in the scene and noticed how it appeared so normal yet was quite other-worldly based on who they were and where they were.

"Zemar, do you want to take a shot?" Major Lewis asked, tossing Zemar a golf ball.

Zemar looked around at everyone and nervously said, "Okay."

"Here, try my seven iron. Just take your time and swing easy."

Zemar carefully placed the ball on an open spot on the ground and tried to access all that he had learned so far.

"Spread your feet apart and keep your head down," coached Major Lewis.

With everyone now focused on him, Zemar realized he was more nervous than he had been in a long time. He didn't want to look like a fool, but at the same time did not want to damage Major Lewis's club. He started back slowly and then swung down with a fit of speed - a complete whiff. His friends burst into laughter, while the soldiers were more restrained having fully expected such a result.

"Try again," Lewis said patiently. "Just take your time and watch the ball."

Zemar refocused and tried again. Another miss, then another. With his embarrassment quickly evolving into anger with every giggle from behind him, Zemar shortened his swing drastically and chopped a worm-burner thirty or forty yards off to the side.

He looked at the head of the club and turned with consternation to Major Lewis. "How do you do that?" he asked as though Lewis had given him a trick club that could not be hit properly.

"I told you, Zemar. It's a tough game," Major Lewis shrugged.

"Can I try again?" Zemar asked.

"Uh-oh. You're going to get him hooked already," laughed Major Cierra.

Major Lewis reached into his bag and pulled out a few beat up balls that he'd brought just for this reason. He tossed another one to Zemar. "Try again and then we'll see what your friends can do."

The following shot showed minor improvement and actually got off the ground for a brief time. The next boy tried to learn from what he'd seen and employed more of a hockey-style swing. He made contact, but with a check back swing the ball didn't go far. The third caddie decided that he wanted to show the other two up a bit. He made a powerful swing and sent the ball sailing into the air. It was the best shot of the bunch; unfortunately it was followed down range by Major Lewis's club. The boys' eyes all grew wide as they waited in anticipation for impact - as though it might explode. Zemar then turned to Major Lewis to see if he was going to explode.

"Okay. That's enough practice for now. Zemar, have your pal go round that up and we'll get going."

Zemar barked a command at his friend who sprinted off to retrieve the club. Upon return Major Lewis looked it over. It appeared unharmed and still fit for play. The soldiers all loosened up and started the return stretch down the course.

On the way back Zemar began to open up and was more talkative with Major Lewis. He also showed more interest in the golf discussion as though his first attempt at golf had brought him new respect for what the soldiers were doing.

"So is Johnny your first name?" Zemar asked after Major Cierra had congratulated Major Lewis on a good shot.

"My first name is John so Johnny is just a common nickname. I've known Major Cierra a long time so he's the only person around here that uses it."

"I see. It reminded me of a name we have here: Ajani. It sounds about the same."

"I am *a Johnny*. It's a rather common name so there are a lot of Johnnies in the United States."

"I guess we will see if you are Ajani in Afghanistan," Zemar mused.

"What do you mean?" Major Lewis asked.

"The name means: the one who wins the struggle."

"Ahh," Major Lewis nodded. "I'm not sure about golf today, but when it comes to Afghanistan I certainly intend to be an Ajani," he added with confidence before striding off to his ball.

"I can't understand what they are saying, but your friends seem like good guys, Zemar. Have you known them long?" Major Lewis asked after his next shot.

"Longer than anyone else. I've been the most stable thing that they've known since most of their fathers and brothers have left or died. I'm their brother."

"Do they work for you?"

"Sometimes. Mostly I watch out for them and they help me out when I need it, like today. They knew that meeting you outside Baza Faqir-e wasn't some kind of trap. They trusted that I wouldn't be selling them to a bacha baz."

Major Lewis considered what Zemar had told him. *Kind of like an anti-pimp*, he thought to himself. In his background research Major Lewis had come across the term *bacha baz* and Captain Roth had provided additional insight. In parts of Afghanistan it was a common custom for older men to have a physical relationship with young boys. Unfortunately with the high number of bastard children there were numerous targets and few guardians to question the practice. It was something that had long been accepted in the Pashtun culture.

"That's good that you watch their backs. It shows that you have honor, which is a big part of golf. Hitting the ball is important, but only in the context of the rules and how you handle yourself on the course," Major Lewis said.

"I learned honor from my father. Even though he died when I was young I know he was a good man and others always spoke highly of him. It is something that used to exist in Afghanistan, but it has disappeared over the years. Now it can only be seen in relation to Islam and even that is usually manipulated to serve someone's desires."

"You sound like a skeptic."

"I am more educated than most people here so it is easier for me to separate the truth from the lies."

"So why have you stayed here?" Major Lewis asked.

"Do you want to take me to the U.S.? For that chance I'd even consider letting you be my bacha baz," Zemar joked. "Look at a map. There aren't a lot of options for someone like me. We all keep hoping that things will get better and we can make a life here, but it seems to be getting worse."

"Why do you think we are here?"

"Because George Bush wanted to kick some butt after nine eleven. But that was a long time ago. Now I'm not sure," Zemar replied.

After hearing Zemar's response, Major Lewis pondered his own question for a moment. "I think we can provide some stability that will allow for education and the economy to start growing. That's still a very long road from where Afghanistan is now though. It will take years. The concept of education here is so far detached from the rest of the world that it is hard to even know where to begin. In terms of the economy, one of the biggest challenges is the lack of resources. The most commonly grown crops here happen to be illegal in a lot of other countries."

"We have resources besides drugs, just no way to get them," contended Zemar proudly.

"Like what?"

"Lots of things. Remember my father was a geologist. He knew of Afghanistan's resources. Drugs were just an easier way to make money so that's what people did. They didn't care..." Zemar tailed off, clearly getting a little emotional.

Major Lewis decided not to push any further into such big topics. "Just try to remain optimistic and we'll all get things headed in the right direction."

A few minutes later they were distracted by a commotion across the way. Zemar and Major Lewis jogged over to see what was the matter. They arrived at what appeared to be an argument between one of Zemar's friends and one of Major Cierra's men.

"What's the problem?" Major Lewis asked.

"The kid doesn't seem to want me to hit my ball," the soldier said, pointing to his golf ball sitting a short distance away.

The boy looked to Zemar and kept saying, "minoonah, minoonah," and then, "boom," lifting his hands up.

Zemar listened to his friend's explanation and then told the soldiers that there was a mine near the ball. He said that what looked like a small twig on the ground was actually an old wire.

"How can there be a mine?" the soldier asked. "You can tell this place has been totally swept."

Major Cierra had also now come to see what was going on and motioned for his golf bag. From between the clubs he pulled out a telescoping rod with a small box on one end and a foldout antenna on the other end.

"That's the fanciest ball retriever I've ever seen," noted Major Lewis.

"Actually it's to make sure we don't need a leg retriever, Johnny," Major Cierra replied as he carefully fished the tool out to where the ball was sitting and hovered it over the ground. He adjusted the dial on the box and read the display. "There's something there alright. Not sure if it is a mine or not, but let's not find out. Leave the ball there and we'll send the engineers back out here to examine it. Be careful and listen to your caddies," Major Cierra said, giving a wave of approval to Zemar and his friends.

"How many club lengths of relief does he get from a land mine?" Major Lewis asked, feigning a serious rules inquiry.

"As many as he wants," Major Cierra responded, heading back to hit his next shot.

***

By the end of play Major Cierra had separated himself by six shots from Major Lewis. They had returned to the area where they had started and now it was time to putt. Major Cierra had found a rolling patch of hardened earth and had it swept to create a dirt green. To add authenticity he had cut a four and a quarter inch hole and dropped in a flag. They had played twelve holes and, therefore, picked out twelve different locations to hit the putts of various lengths from. The cumulative putting score would then be added to their stroke scores.

The men practiced for a few minutes to get the feel as a number of other soldiers arrived to watch the big finale. Major Lewis didn't expect anything too exciting since Major Cierra was an excellent putter and had no doubt been practicing for their match.

Once they were ready to go Major Cierra began setting up at the first location and took his first stroke. As he did, Zemar decided to be proactive. He walked out and snatched the pin out of the hole.

"Wait, Zemar. You can't do that," Major Lewis said.

"But earlier you told me that you have to pull the pin out when someone putts," Zemar replied.

"Yes, that's correct, but we are playing against Major Cierra, so that's his caddie's job. You only pull it out for me. Or, if you are on their side, you can't pull the pin when it is my shot."

"Wow, you are getting pretty technical on him there, Johnny," Major Cierra interjected. "He was just being helpful."

"Oh, I see, Ray. The rules only apply when you want them to, eh?" scolded Major Lewis. "You should have had the pin out already."

"No, no. We need to be legit. Zemar, let my caddie tend it. I don't want anything getting in the way of my ball going in that hole."

Major Lewis putted well, but still dropped another two strokes to Major Cierra in the putting competition. Everyone shook hands and they settled up their token bets. The soldiers each paid and tipped their caddies and thanked them for a job well done.

"Zemar, we've got to do some quick business here and then we'll get you back. You guys can practice your putting if you want. Just hold onto the clubs!" Major Lewis joked.

***

The trip back to the Khana Pass was quiet. All in all it had been a good day and Major Lewis felt that it was good PR for their cause. They dropped off Zemar and the caddies, said goodbye, and headed south toward Camp Ross.

Major Lewis was now riding with Major Cierra. Just the two of them were in the truck so after reminiscing for a while they took the chance to speak frankly about what they were facing in the region.

"So tell me straight up, Ray. What's your outlook here? Are we just doing time and holding ground or is there a finish line?"

"Honestly, Johnny, I've never been less certain. There is such a gap between this place and the civilized world that it's hard to know what can realistically be done to close it."

"That's what I'm seeing. Even if we do *win* the resulting situation is still pretty bleak. It will be so easy for these people to fall back into the wrong hands, even if that's not the Taliban."

"Well, as always, Johnny, we need to do the best job we can and see what happens. We can't save everyone, especially from themselves. We all want to help these people, but don't forget our most important rules: keep your men alive and keep yourself alive."

"I know, Ray. Maybe I'm just getting softer with age. I see how well my kids are doing and how bright their futures are and I feel a little guilty."

"Don't! Aaron and Jessica are your responsibility. Zemar is not your responsibility. If you can help him - great. If not - tough. We are here for security, not charity duty," Major Cierra stated without wavering.

"Yeah, you're right," Major Lewis conceded. He looked out the window and stared at the iridescent orange sky. The low clouds on the horizon looked like they were on fire, lit from underneath by the sun that had just fallen behind the mountains.

As they drove on, Major Cierra glanced sideways at his old friend. He wondered if Major Lewis was perhaps losing some of the edge that had served him so well in the past.

6

The visit to Camp Ross had been informative and provided Major Lewis with added motivation as he began preparations to go on the offensive. Meanwhile, at FOB MacKenzie a new barracks had been completed and every few weeks new soldiers were arriving. Reports were indicating increased movement of suspected insurgents in the region, but thus far the fighting had been very limited.

It was early Friday morning and Major Lewis was going through a check list with an exploration team. Today they would be heading east to visit several small settlements in a series of valleys across the Hindu Kush. Major Lewis was in no way expected to lead such missions, but he had always felt that it was important to show his men that he truly appreciated the level of danger that they faced.

The first stop was the smallest of the villages. As they approached they saw no movement and made announcements on the PA system to let the inhabitants know that they were coming. Arriving at the edge of town there was still no sign of life. The few small shacks and crumbling structures led Major Lewis to wonder if the settlement had been abandoned. He directed several men to stay put and provide cover while he and several others began carefully examining the buildings. Rather than checking doors, which might be booby-trapped, they shined their lights through windows and holes in the walls. As they moved forward the men began to notice a pungent stench. Major Lewis immediately recognized it as the smell of death; the only question was what and where. They were approaching one of the larger structures from upwind, but as they neared the power of the odor grew drastically. The men sidled up along one wall of the building. Two of the men held their guns at the ready with two others shone their light inside. There were several bodies scattered inside, none of which were moving. Based on their positions they did not look like they were sleeping and several were tied up. They called Major Lewis over to take a look.

"Do you want us to take down the door with the battering ram, sir?" one of the soldiers asked. "The windows are too small to go through."

"No. There are too many of them in there and I doubt any of them are still alive. Somebody killed them and placed them inside. Look in front of the door. There are no marks. There should at least be some foot prints and if those bodies were dragged in there would be tracks. It looks like it has been swept smooth." He looked at the area in front and saw that it was at the base of a small hill. "We've got some new robots arriving soon to do this job, but for now let's bring up one of the Hummers."

The men were surprised that he might consider ramming the hut with one of their vehicles.

When the truck arrived he had them park it about fifty feet away, but facing the opposite direction. He dropped one of the thin ladders in the back so that it made a steep ramp to the ground and instructed two soldiers to remove a spare tire. They made one final attempt to communicate with the bull horn, but again there was no response.

The two soldiers with the tire rolled it over to await further instruction.

"Let's go bowling, guys." He put the tire iron in the center of the rim and directed the other two to help him roll it up the ramp. "Alright, on the count of three let it go and get behind the truck. One...two...three..."

The tire took off, bounced slightly, and then began a smooth roll toward the door. The men peered around the edge of the vehicle in anticipation. It looked good until about ten feet away when it drifted slightly to the side and hit the door jam.

"Damn. Gutter ball!" Major Lewis said with disappointment. "Roll it back up guys. Walk only in the path that the tire just took."

They quickly set it back up on the ramp and Major Lewis made a slight adjustment in its targeting.

"We can still pick up a spare, boys," he said with enthusiasm, despite the grisly goal of their game.

It was another good roll and with a few feet to go they knew the massive tire was on target. It made a low thump at impact and plowed the door down. A split second later there was a pop inside followed by the wooshing sound of flames bursting out from all of the building's openings.

"Nice roll, sir," noted Lieutenant Davitch.

"Thanks. Get some extinguishers and put it out quickly. That's probably it, but be careful."

After the flames were quashed the soldiers looked inside and took pictures. The bodies were all men and they had been shot.

"What's the plan, sir?" Lieutenant Davitch asked.

"Let's leave them for the time being. We'll head to the next valley and tell them what we found. If we need to we'll come back later and bury them. How's our tire?"

"Looks fine. I don't see any damage."

"Load it up and let's go," Lewis ordered.

***

The team followed the same protocol when they made it to the next village, a town called Mahzri. This time, however, there was a flurry of activity. The men heard several gun shots and quickly took up a defensive position with their vehicles. None of the shots appeared to be coming in their direction and the sounds seemed to be getting further away. They scanned the scene and communicated over their radios.

"It looks chaotic down there. The shooting appears to be toward the back of the village and up into the hillside. I see some women and children moving in this direction. Be careful with your fire. We've already got a house full of bodies in the next valley. Let's keep our collateral damage low," Major Lewis said.

They waited for several minutes until they saw a man heading in their direction with his hands up. He was yelling something at the soldiers, but was too far away for the translator to make out what the man was saying.

"He doesn't look armed. Let him get to about fifty yards and then tell him to stop, turn around, and show us some skin," Major Lewis ordered.

As he approached, the tension among the soldiers grew. The translator, Private Webster, began yelling commands through his bull horn and the man complied.

"Alright, have him turn around and tell his story so you can understand it. Remind him to keep his hands up and that any sudden moves will result in his death," Major Lewis added.

The man turned and began babbling again. He was very animated and was talking with his hands. Being that they were still above his head he looked as though he was doing some kind of strange dance.

"He says they came under attack and have fended them off. They got a warning from another village nearby and were able to prepare to fight. They need help to drive them back over the hillside, sir," Private Webster said.

"How many?"

"He says about thirty, sir."

"What's his name?"

"Rashid, sir."

"It looks like that's what's happening. What do you think Lieutenant Davitch?" Major Lewis asked.

"I agree, sir."

Major Lewis took another scan across the landscape. "Alright, we're going to go in from the front and the right. I want to flush them up to that rocky ridge on the left. I'll take the first team and we'll go with Rashid to the edge of town. Lieutenant Davitch, you take the rest to the right. We'll have him drop his men back down and then you sweep across. Don't shoot anyone coming down, I don't want to take out the locals. Rashid can tell us who doesn't belong and we will eliminate them."

"Got it, sir," Lieutenant Davitch replied.

The soldiers prepared their weapons and moved out. Major Lewis had Rashid jump into one of the trucks and they drove into town. Several men stayed to handle the large, vehicle-mounted weapons while others spread out and took their positions along the streets. The buildings were low, hut-style structures and most had thick, protruding walls that offered good cover. Major Lewis monitored the hillside until he received confirmation that Lieutenant Davitch had moved into position. Rashid gathered several of his men and scurried up into the brush where he began ordering the others to drop back.

The militants knew that the Americans had arrived; however, the question for Major Lewis was how they would react. If they followed the villagers back down they might rush into town and attack. It depended on how courageous they were feeling. He kept his soldiers ready and told them to make sure the insurgents didn't get to the edge of the village where they could take shelter.

The village's defenders came down in small groups and Rashid ran back to where Major Lewis and Private Webster were stationed.

A few moments later Rashid began jumping up and down and blurting: "Tor! Tor!"

"The black turbans are the combatants, sir," Private Webster relayed.

"Looks like they made it easy, fellas. The bad guys are wearing black. Take 'em down," Major Lewis directed.

Seconds later the four men who were running at full speed and firing their weapons appeared to slam into an invisible wall. They flew off their feet and flopped to the ground without further movement.

There was a brief pause before another wave descended under a barrage of cover fire from above. The shooting pinned down the individual soldiers so Major Lewis had the truck-mounted Browning M2 take care of this group. The bullets hit the targets so rapidly that the men's' bodies seemed to have brief seizures before dropping next to their compatriots. These salvos were meant to test the Americans' strength and they were clear failures. There was simply too much open space between the town and the brush line.

Everything was suddenly quiet as they waited for the next move. Major Lewis saw the enemy's men sneaking up and to the left among the rocks and foliage. He confirmed with Rashid that their men were out before giving his next orders.

"My team - if you have a clear shot take it. Precision. I don't want chaos. Lieutenant Davitch, let us know when you reach their current position and we'll cease fire."

"Do you want to send a group up to the left to cut them off, sir?" Lieutenant Davitch asked.

"No, just keep sweeping and be careful. I don't think they're going to make any stands now."

"I'm just concerned that if some of them make it over that ridge they might gain an advantage."

"Don't worry, Lieutenant. They won't be leaving the valley today," Major Lewis said confidently.

With the threat of attack gone, the snipers in town set up and took their time waiting for clear shots. They were able to down several more combatants before Lieutenant Davitch swept through.

"Keep the herd moving, Lieutenant Davitch. I'm not worried about any prisoners today. These guys are just foot soldiers. I doubt there's any real leadership that could provide us with intel," Major Lewis said. "Go ahead and get the rocket launcher ready," he added to one of the soldiers on the ground.

They monitored the progress as the team on the hill flushed the enemy fighters up and out of the valley. They headed exactly where Major Lewis thought they would.

"Alright, Lieutenant Davitch. Hold your position."

"Sir, I think we can get the last group that's higher up if we keep moving," Lieutenant Davitch responded.

"No, I don't want them having the high ground on you when you go above the tree line. We've got them covered."

Moments later they saw the remaining insurgents begin scrambling up the rocky switchbacks. Major Lewis waited patiently until it appeared that all of the fighters had emerged. Once they made their way a little higher Major Lewis gave his order.

"Aim at that wall above them and fire the rockets."

"Above them, sir?" the soldier asked.

"Yeah, bury them," Major Lewis clarified.

"Got it, sir."

The soldier sighted a large fissure in the rock wall and sent the first one screaming on its way. He shifted his sight slightly right and fired another one. It took a split second from when they saw the missiles impact until they heard the sound echo down to the valley. Major Lewis watched through his binoculars as large slabs of rock broke loose from the wall. The men on the trail froze in their tracks as the fatal rain began. A massive block fell directly on one of the insurgents and flattened him instantly. Although gruesome, it reminded Major Lewis of Wiley Coyote and he almost laughed. The other men were hammered by the debris and also disappeared.

Major Lewis noticed that many of the town's people had come out onto the streets and were watching the events unfold. As the small avalanche ended they began to cheer loudly. Several of the militia men fired their weapons in celebration.

"Have Rashid tell them to stop. We don't need any accidental deaths," Major Lewis said.

"Sir, do you want me to take another shot for good measure?" the soldier inquired, feeling slightly amped based on the crowd reaction.

"No, we're good. Nobody's coming out of that rubble. That's a few less bodies for these people to bury and less paperwork for us."

"Major Lewis, do you want us to do a final sweep and head back?" Lieutenant Davitch asked over the radio.

"Yes. Document what you can and don't spend too much time. We need to move on." Major Lewis acknowledged. Based on what they'd already encountered today he was very uncertain about what might be awaiting them in the next town.

***

After a brief celebration with the locals the team reestablished itself and headed east. Crossing the first few foothills Major Lewis saw smoke rising into the sky above their approximate destination. He felt that they should hurry, but he had no intention of further endangering the men so they proceeded at the normal pace. With each mile they covered the smoke plume grew more defined.

When they finally emerged from the hills Major Lewis saw a discomforting sight. The town had been ransacked and many of the structures were either burnt out or still smoldering. The fields of crops nearby had also been scorched. Major Lewis had the team move in, but he had low expectations for what they would find.

The men stopped at the edge of town and disembarked. They fanned out and began searching the village for survivors or the attackers. Many of the structures were completely destroyed so they did a cursory look and moved on.

"Over here!" came a call from one of the soldiers.

Major Lewis jogged over to the house and found his men helping a woman inside. There were two other bodies lying prone on the floor.

"They're dead, but she's still alive," said the soldier that was helping her sit up and drink some water.

The woman looked to be in her mid-thirties, although it was tough to tell. She had been badly beaten. Her face was swollen and she gazed vacantly out of the small, barely open eyes. Her clothes were ripped from the assault and she had abrasions on her arms and legs.

"Has she said anything?" Major Lewis asked.

"No, sir."

"Ask her what happened," Major Lewis said to Private Webster.

He quietly asked the woman, but she was unresponsive.

"Get her comfortable and have the medic check her over. Let's keep moving. There are probably more," Major Lewis said.

There were indeed more bodies scattered throughout the village, many of which were burned beyond recognition.

The town was laid out along one of the hillsides and as they moved further in they found homes built into the terrain itself.

"This looks like the Anasazi dwellings in Colorado," Lieutenant Davitch noted.

"Yes, except that people were still living in these," Major Lewis replied.

"It's like traveling back in time."

As they proceeded higher they found several more survivors. They were all women and children that seemed to be in a daze; beaten and stunned by the devastation they'd witnessed. They finally found one older woman who appeared able to talk, but was mostly just babbling. When she saw Major Lewis in front of her she pointed at the American flag on his uniform and said, "No Amrikhans."

"These people have been through a lot already so this must have been bad. They all look like zombies. They also must have been told not to deal with us," Major Lewis observed.

"What do you want to do, sir?" Lieutenant Davitch asked.

"I don't know. This is a mess. We can't take them with us, but we can't leave them here. I think our best bet is to transport them back to Mahzri and find them help there for the time being. We can follow up with additional medical assets. Unfortunately for these people it looks like much of the damage is psychological."

"This is different than most of the attacks I've seen here in Afghanistan. It could be ethnic or tribal fighting. It also looks like someone is trying to send a message," Lieutenant Davitch said, looking in awe at the smoking ruins.

"Absolutely. The question is why. These people haven't been aiding us in any way. Besides, they are out here in the middle of nowhere so what strategic purpose does it serve?" Major Lewis pondered. He rolled out one of his surface maps on the ground and scanned the region. As he looked at the tribal regions in neighboring Pakistan and the developed areas north and south along the Kindu Kush he saw one possible option. "Look, Lieutenant," he said, running his finger back and forth. "I wonder if they are trying to clear an east-west path through here. That would create a bridge for them to cross and put a wedge between MacKenzie and the southern forces and our operations around Kabul. If they are moving twenty or thirty men it doesn't matter. But if you start moving larger numbers and more equipment it would become tougher to conceal."

"Makes sense. If they are moving forces across this area they don't want any locals who could tip us off."

Major Lewis looked at the map once again. There was only one other notable settlement, but it was beyond where they had planned to go today.

"Have you ever been out there?" Major Lewis asked.

"About two months ago. Basically the same situation as here - subsistence farming."

"I don't think we should go there today. We'll send out some air assets and have them take a look. Right now let's start gathering these people and load them for relocation. Don't worry about the fires. They'll burn themselves out and there's nothing here worth saving. I'm going to head toward the fields to see if they found anything."

Major Lewis hiked back down and walked toward the farming area. Looking around he thought about how tranquil the natural surroundings were. He could imagine travelers coming here and finding a secluded oasis amidst the harsh mountains. Today the oasis had been transformed into a Faustian purgatory.

As he approached the blackened meadow of crops, Major Lewis noticed that the scent in the smoke began to change. The somewhat familiar odor gathered in the back of his throat and he could taste it when he swallowed.

"Major Lewis, nothing over here except for more dead bodies," Sergeant Guidry, who had been leading the group, reported with an odd smile on his face.

"Is that smell what I think it is?" Major Lewis asked.

"I believe so, sir. Besides the fruits and veggies they also had some cash crops growing over here."

"I see. At this point we need to focus on the survivors. As long as there aren't any out here gather up your men and head back to town. Tell them to try and follow the lead of our former commander-in-chief," Major Lewis instructed.

"How's that, sir?"

"Tell them not to inhale."

"Oh. Good one. Will do, sir," the Sergeant replied with a laugh.

Major Lewis retraced his steps and radioed to Lieutenant Davitch. "Looks like the enemy at least did us the favor of eradicating the marijuana and poppy stands as well as their processing house."

"That was helpful of them."

"We do have another problem though."

"What's that?" Lieutenant Davitch asked.

"I don't think we have enough Doritos in our rations supply. I have the feeling that Sergeant Guidry and his men are going to have the munchies on the way back to Mac," Major Lewis explained.

***

Major Lewis and his men did their best to help the tormented people from the village. When they arrived back in Mahzri they were glad to see that the locals were willing to take in the refugees. The unit's medic provided instructions for the care of the more seriously injured individuals and left additional medical supplies.

Rashid cornered Major Lewis and attempted to negotiate a supply of weapons as well. Major Lewis was not in a position to fulfill the request, but did his best to reassure Rashid. He indicated that he would request regional Afghan forces to provide security. This clearly provided little comfort to the man. Unfortunately Major Lewis was unable to provide a specific timetable for the Americans' return. Major Lewis knew that the upcoming focus would be to the south so diversions to this area would not be likely for several weeks. The situation highlighted the dichotomy that always existed in modern military theaters - the people didn't want the U.S. forces there until they needed protection. This was the plight of the world's policeman.

The team returned to MacKenzie with no injuries. From that aspect the patrol had been a success. However, the damage and death they had encountered was another story. Unfortunately for Major Lewis and Lieutenant Davitch, they would be the ones that would have to write that story. Major Lewis understood the importance of documenting their interactions with the populace. Nonetheless, the paperwork burden was driven more and more by CYA issues rather than intelligence gathering.

Captain Roth joined them in the command center as they began their debriefing. "I hear you got your first taste of Taliban today. Are you doing alright?" he asked.

"We're fine. Today's numbers are going to pump up the Afghan casualty statistics though. The last town we made it to was a killing field. Those people were just farmers and unable to defend themselves. We got lucky in Mahzri. The locals had been tipped off so they were able to put up a defense. We arrived just in time to clean house. The insurgents weren't expecting us to be there. They took out the westernmost settlement first and then shifted back to the eastern one. They knew that Mahzri would be the toughest to take so they cut off both sides to isolate their target.

"Any prisoners?

"No, this looked like a mercenary force. They were given their orders and told to execute. I have to believe they came from along the Pakistan border. If they returned they could be sent again and if not they were expendable. Besides, you know how much more paperwork prisoners require."

"True. Lieutenant Warner is on his way back from the northern patrol. He reported that all was quiet up that way. Also, I already had surveillance planes directed to fly over the coordinates you provided. We should have details by tomorrow."

"Good. It looks like they are trying to clear a path to be able to infiltrate the central region."

"Our reports continue to indicate that they are sending combatants along the southern border to feed Kandahar and Helmand. I have several strategy reports for you regarding our joint operations with Ross."

"Thanks. I'll start reviewing that after we document today's foray. I hope we are taking the right course of action. I know I'm new in town so it is hard for me to question our orders. Still, I don't want to get blindsided. Anything else I need to know about?"

"We should be getting a major shipment on Monday. The robots will be here," Captain Roth said.

"That should be fun. I can't wait to see what they can do."

7

Adjoining the recently completed barracks was a new recreation area. At this point that basically meant that the rocks had been removed and the surface smoothed over. It had immediately received the nickname "The Yard" as the chain link fence perimeter topped with concertina wire gave it the appearance of a penitentiary playground.

Major Lewis and his men arrived at The Yard on Monday afternoon and found it littered with pallets and equipment. He saw several unfamiliar faces working diligently near crates that had been crow-barred open and headed that way.

"Afternoon, sir," said a studious looking young man who popped up from what he was doing and wiped his hands when he saw Major Lewis approach. "I'm Sergeant Merrick."

"Pleased to meet you, Sergeant," Major Lewis said before making introductions around the group. "What have you got for us today?"

Merrick immediately launched into his presentation with the flair of a snake oil salesman and the enthusiasm of a proud parent. "We have several new units for you, Major. All are state-of-the-art and best in class. The first one is basically your Swiss Army knife," he boasted, handing Major Lewis the remote control and shouldering up next to him. "Go ahead and push the lever under your left thumb."

Major Lewis watched as the shiny, silver creature jumped to life at his command. He moved the robot forward and began driving it around The Yard. He followed its progress with his own eyes and via the full color screen on the remote that displayed the view from an onboard camera.

"You've got standard view, night vision, and thermal. Additionally it links into your facial recognition data base so you can make IDs," Sergeant Merrick said, pointing to the screen. He tapped it and an onscreen menu appeared. "All menu driven. Here are some of your special features. Drive it up against that crate and then hit the ladder icon."

Major Lewis did as he was told and was amazed when it swung out folding arms and pulled itself up on top. "Wow!"

"It can make up to a four foot climb on just about any surface. It's great on stairs and if it does fall it has a self-righting mechanism. However, with the gyroscopes and equilibrium logic it won't fall on its own," he added, inferring that any such problems would be operator error.

"Okay, it can dance. Can it fight?" Captain Roth asked, jealous that he wasn't getting to play yet.

"Two weaponizing options. You've got a one hundred round, semi-automatic forty-five caliber gun or a four round grenade launcher. Both are top mounted and visually targeted so you want to be close to what you are shooting. Of course that's the point of the robot - close quarters interaction.

It's not only nimble, but also tough. The exoskeleton is fabricated primarily with titanium and ceramic composites while the innards are enveloped in Kevlar. In the unlikely scenario that it falls into enemy hands we have remote override and kill switch options," Merrick concluded.

"That's pretty impressive. What else do you have for us?" Major Lewis asked.

"Next up is one of the more specialized units. We call this one Rambot," Merrick said, handing Major Lewis another remote that looked completely different.

"Argg," Major Lewis grumbled. "This is going to be like watching TV at home - different remotes for everything. Can't you guys come up with something standardized?"

"You've got different functions and different subcontractors. Call your congressman. Anyway, let me show you this one because it can take some practice and can be dangerous," Merrick said, taking the remote back. He maneuvered it next to one of the empty crates. "Two primary functions. First, is the piston."

He pressed a button and the Rambot let out a quick hiss before thrusting a bar forward and punching a hole straight through the crate.

"There are several implements that you can add for improved battering. You can also arm it with a charge grenade that will blow through most locks. The other capability is swing and sling," Merrick continued.

He turned a dial and a rotary arm whipped violently against the crate tearing a two foot gash.

"Look at that! That's even going against the grain of the wood," admired Captain Roth.

"Again, several attachments to choose from to meet different conditions. It does not have climbing capability and it is far heavier than the first one. It also can be used for towing up to several hundred pounds depending on the ground surface."

"Can it tow bodies?"

"It can, but it wouldn't be a pleasant ride for the subject."

"Can it hold a golf club?" Major Lewis asked innocently.

"I suppose. Why?"

"Just curious," Major Lewis replied, raising his eyebrows and grinning at Captain Roth.

"It's going to do the most damage with the tools designed for it."

"Sure, but a golf club can take out a Cadillac Escalade," Major Lewis pointed out.

"You can use your titanium driver if you like. I'll stick with the titanium mace," Sergeant Merrick replied.

Noting that Sergeant Merrick seemed to be annoyed by the inquiries Captain Roth piled on, "So if R2-D2 and Rambot were to go head-to-head in a death match who would win?"

"That's a dumb question, sir," Merrick stated with condescension.

"Why is that?" Captain Roth asked.

"Because it's not going to happen. Army policy is explicit that the robots are not to be engaged against one another."

"But smashing stuff like the crates is okay, right?" Major Lewis asked.

"For testing and training purposes the robots can be used *individually*."

"Good to know."

"I see. But just hypothetically, which one is better?" Captain Roth pressed.

"They both have strengths and weaknesses. It would mainly depend on the operator's skill," Sergeant Merrick said, intoning that with him on the controls he would destroy all challengers.

"Now we're going to head into the air, gentlemen. Here we have a short-range surveillance drone," Sergeant Merrick said as a small craft began to hum and rise off the ground. "These are good for up to about a mile in distance and around a thousand feet in altitude. That's reasonable here at MacKenzie, but if you head to higher elevations you'll lose performance in the thinner air."

"It reminds me of a toy we got our son for Christmas. It has a little camera and sends the image back to his smart phone," Major Lewis noted.

"That's actually a fair comparison on this one, sir," Sergeant Merrick admitted. "These are for basic observation and do not have any weapons capability. We call these LCAs - for lights, camera, action. Besides the video feed they have exterior LED lighting that can be used to give signals to other soldiers within the viewing range." He tapped the remote and the outer circle glowed red. He tapped again and it turned to green. "It obviously works better at night. The downside is that once you put them into use your reports of UFO sightings will go up significantly."

"Can I try?" Captain Roth asked eagerly.

"Knock yourself out, sir," Sergeant Merrick said, handing off the remote. He obviously cared less for the flying craft than the robots.

Captain Roth wandered off to play and was entranced like a cat with a ball of yarn.

Major Lewis leaned over toward Segeant Merrick and said, "I think he always secretly wanted to be an Air Force guy."

"I'll be happy to include him in our training the next few days. The rest of the stuff is mainly replacement parts and support equipment."

"All joking aside, we appreciate your help on this, Sergeant Merrick. We could have used Rambot the other day in fact. It's rather bizarre to have all of this technology in a place like Afghanistan. With the way things are headed it won't be long before we are all replaced, of course that might be a good thing."

***

The new toys had been a nice diversion, but the reality of the upcoming offensive quickly took center stage. The soldiers from FOB MacKenzie and Camp Ross would be supporting forces already in place in the northern and eastern regions of the Kandahar Province. Additional full time troops were already slated for deployment to the area; however, the bulk of those units would not be in place for several months. The commanders in Kabul were ordering this operation in an attempt to prevent the Taliban from gaining traction before the arrival of reinforcements.

A portion of the men from MacKenzie were taken south on transport helicopters, while Major Lewis led a convoy that joined up with Major Cierra before proceeding to Kandahar. The first several days had been quiet as they moved through generally unpopulated lands.

It was early morning and Major Lewis stood silently looking out over the horizon and drinking his coffee. He was mentally preparing himself for the long day ahead. The sound of footsteps announced the arrival of Captain Roth.

"Ready to go, sir?"

"Let's do it," Major Lewis replied.

They headed back to their remote command center among the ruins of a crumbling apartment building. At one point this had been someone's living room, now it looked like a child's sandbox. On the floor they had constructed a diorama of the nearby settlements that they would be clearing of insurgents. The structures were represented by bricks and various pieces of debris, while the soldiers were depicted with plastic army men. The enemy was made up of a menagerie of small action figures that Major Lewis had collected and included Zurg, Darth Vader, and Papa Smurf.

Major Lewis was confident in his team, but still went through the motions of reviewing their strategy one last time. When he finished he stood up and looked around at the sullen faces of his men.

"Any questions?" he asked. No responses. "We all know that going in as the first daytime wave is going to be dangerous. You've been trained for this and you know what to do. If everyone fights hard and fights smart we will all be back here at nightfall. It's alright to be scared, just don't be stupid. We are superior to the enemy in every way and today we will have the chance to prove it. May God be with you and let's go kick some ass."

"Yes, sir!" the men barked in unison.

Major Lewis smiled and scanned the faces one more time. There was no sign of fear, only the determined look of men ready to fight.

The men left with a sense of purpose and began the operation. The two pronged attack would encompass several settlements where Taliban were living among the residents and a nearby canyon thought to be used for taking refuge. Major Lewis's team would be replaced by Major Cierra's forces. The second phase and nighttime operations was the more desirable assignment as the enemy would already be tired form the daylight onslaught. The ability to conduct a twenty-four hour assault would also take a psychological toll on the opposition. Moreover, all of the technological advantages that the Americans enjoyed were magnified at night. It was a common understanding among the soldiers that they owned the night in Afghanistan.

Major Lewis would be leading from the sideline today. He established a position on a high ridge north of the towns where he could monitor and direct the action. His plan was to gradually move east as the day progressed. Captain Roth was already ahead of Lewis's location with several snipers to provide cover. He watched as Lieutenant Davitch's team slowly approached from the north while Lieutenant Warner did the same from the south. They intended to make the moves seem like a normal security sweep in hopes of not spooking the residents.

By mid-morning things were still very quiet with little activity in the streets. The teams were going door-to-door performing searches. Thus far they'd found nothing suspicious, however, the attitude here was not friendly.

The first sign of trouble arose when Lieutenant Warner approached a small apartment building. He heard movement inside, but no one responded to their knocking and requests for the residents to come out. Finally, a hunched old woman cracked open the rickety door, looked out, and spoke quietly to the translator.

"She said that the inhabitants are all sleeping and that we should come back later, sir," he relayed to Lieutenant Warner.

Lieutenant Warner smiled at the obvious lie. "Let her know we heard other voices already. Tell her that whoever is awake needs to come out slowly and stand in the street now. We will then perform our inspection quietly and try not to disturb the sleepers when we search under their mattresses."

She peered out from behind her headscarf with conflicted eyes. Clearly she was being placed in the middle of a difficult situation. She asked them to wait for a moment while she woke up her husband and then closed the door.

Lieutenant Warner already had several men surrounding the building and radioed an update to Major Lewis. They heard a conversation inside, but could not make out what was being said. The door re-opened and a slow procession began. Seven men and three women lined up outside and stared down at the ground.

"Thank you," Lieutenant Warner said in Pashtu before entering with part of his team. "We're going to need to be extra thorough here. They were probably trying to buy some time to hide someone or something. Be sure to thermal scan all of the walls, ceilings, and floors to see if they're using humans for insulation."

The men were working their way through the first floor rooms when they heard yelling outside and a scream from one of the women.

"Get down! Get down!" came a command in English.

"Lieutenant Warner, we have a runner," relayed one of the soldiers outside.

"Is he armed?" Lieutenant Warner asked as he rushed toward the front door.

"Doesn't appear to be."

"Track him down. Don't shoot him unless he attacks. We don't have anything inside yet."

Lieutenant Warner reemerged to see the occupants sprawled out on the ground while his soldiers pointed their guns from above. Several troops had left to pursue the man who was fleeing. The soldiers were in top shape, but the runner had gotten a head start and he was not weighed down with equipment. It was a strict rule that the soldiers were to keep their body armor on in all but the most extreme circumstances. The men had no qualms with losing the foot race as the runner could only go so far.

The two men in closest pursuit were two of the newest and youngest men in the unit. They were also obviously the fastest. Private Moreno was from Arizona and Private Burgess was from Florida so they were already acclimated to hot weather. They jogged quickly between houses and spotted their target turning into an alley. Their adrenaline was pumping and they almost seemed to be enjoying the chase. Private Moreno started singing the theme song form COPS.

"Bad boy, bad boy, whatcha gonna do? Whatcha gonna do when they come for you?"

Private Burgess would periodically add a gruff "Haa!" or "Huhh!" to the chorus.

At the end of the alley the young man they were chasing slowed down and looked over his shoulder to see the two soldiers on his tail.

"Looks like he's slowing down, sir," Private Burgess radioed to Lieutenant Warner. "We should have him here in a minute." When he looked back up the man was gone. "Where'd he..."

His sentence was interrupted by a sharp punch to his chest. It knocked him back and then he was turned by a burning lash to his left arm.

"Take cover!" Private Moreno yelled as he pushed Private Burgess toward the side of the alley and jumped into a door well as the bullets began to whiz past them. "Under fire! Need backup! Burgess has been hit!" he screamed into his shoulder mounted radio.

He started firing his rifle blindly around the corner and looked across to check on his friend. Private Burgess was lying near some stairs, but was still partially exposed. His arm was torn open and bleeding at the triceps making it hard from him to crawl. Private Moreno watched helplessly as bullets bounced off Burgess's helmet and body armor. A second shot hit his left arm and he wailed out in pain. Then another hit his leg and Private Moreno saw a dark, red flower of blood burst forth from the camouflage. He wanted to run across, but the spray of bullets was constant.

"We're on our way," Lieutenant Warner called into the radio. "Go! Go!" he ordered to his men.

The local Afghans on the ground were now a liability. Lieutenant Warner pulled out a sleeve of plastic handcuffs, while his men held their rifles even closer to the people's heads. In a flurry of motion, Lieutenant Warner hopped from one person to the next and secured their hands and feet. One of the individuals began to struggle and Lieutenant Warner heard a pop as he forced man's arm backward. The man moaned and thrashed.

"You can blame that on your friend," Lieutenant Warner said insincerely.

The speed of Warner's action impressed one of the soldiers standing guard. "How'd you do that so fast?"

"I grew up on a farm and did rodeos. I roped and tied a lot of animals. I was just reliving the old days," Lieutenant Warner replied with pride. "Guard them. If you come under fire leave 'em there. If they try to get away shoot 'em. We'll be back," he said and then ran off toward the fighting.

Major Lewis was watching the scene unfold below him and directed Lieutenant Davitch to lend support. "They are firing from three buildings at the end of that alley. It looks like they have limited openings on the north side so have some of your men loop around that way. Lieutenant Davitch, just hold them on the south. Draw their attention, but don't get too close unless you've got a clear run at them."

The soldiers were quickly in place and began to return fire as the attack team took their position.

"Major Lewis, they are getting good protection from the concrete awnings over the windows," reported one of the soldiers who had made it to a rooftop. "I can't get clear sights on the shooters."

Major Lewis considered the situation. He was concerned that there were civilians in the houses and destroying them would lead to added casualties.

Just then Captain Roth called in on the radio. "Sir, we have a significant number of individuals moving out from the eastern end of the settlements. They may be taking advantage of the diversion to escape to the canyon."

The situation was deteriorating fast. Part of their strategy was to allow insurgents to exit from town if need be. Major Lewis would rather segregate them from the residents to avoid a hostage or human shield scenario.

"Captain Roth, if you can identify any of them as armed have the snipers take them out. Otherwise let them go. Lieutenant Warner, go ahead and bomb the shooters. We need to get Private Burgess out of there immediately."

Seconds later rockets and grenades hailed down on the houses. The structures exploded and there was a sudden quiet as the debris settled. The facades facing the alley had completely collapsed.

Lieutenant Warner and his men rushed down the alley. Private Moreno was in a state of shock, but uninjured. Private Burgess was writhing in pain. His left arm and leg had been shredded by multiple hits.

"Transport them both back to camp. Stabilize Private Burgess and have them run an evaluation. Get him Medevac'd if necessary.

Secure the area and continue the operation," directed Major Lewis. "What's it look like inside those houses?"

"The insurgents are unreachable now, sir. Looks like there may be some civilians."

"Help any survivors, otherwise move on," Major Lewis added. He was unhappy about civilians dying, but as always his men were priority number one.

Lieutenant Warner circled back to the apartment building and restarted the search. As expected they found several weapons caches. It was primarily small arms, but every bullet taken from the enemy was a victory. They were able to establish that two of the men were related to the woman they'd dealt with. Those individuals were released while the others would be turned over to the regional security force for processing.

The next several hours were without further conflict. It appeared that any other insurgents in the settlements had used the firefight as a distraction to flee.

The mid-day temperatures were rising quickly and the sun beat down on the soldiers in full gear. Several small teams had been left at key points to maintain the area already cleared. The remaining soldiers had regrouped in a small, poplar grove at the east end of the settlement finding what little shade they could. Major Lewis and Captain Roth had descended and rejoined the others.

"We'll take a short break here and then push on," Major Lewis said as he made some drawings in the dirt and set up his toys. "Let's just review our strategy one more time while we've got a minute. The canyon starts with one main gorge and gradually forks into two. The northern spur essentially dead ends. The far walls are too steep and men could only get out of there with climbing gear, which they don't have. However, there are lots of ledges and crevices where they can burrow and hide. There are some caves as well. The other fork can be exited, but it feeds into a flat patch of desert. There is nowhere to hide. We have a group of armed vehicles there. If anyone tries to run it will be target practice.

This is their home field so they are going to know the terrain. For most of the front canyon the wall angles are modest so the lead teams need to stay as high as possible. The trailing teams can slide lower to clamp down on anyone trying to escape. You have the aerial views and topographical maps, but don't only rely on that data. If you come across a spot that looks like an ambush site find a different route. The operation's focus is further south right now so we have limited air assets for backup. If anyone gets stuck *we* have to get them out. Captain Roth and I will be moving along the rim providing as much support as we can.

Our goal is to secure and clear the canyon at least to that split point by late afternoon. At that time we will be moving Major Cierra's men in and pulling most of you back if we are in a strong position. Any questions?" There were none. "Alright, we had a little slip up earlier, but otherwise this is going according to plan. You're doing a great job, keep it up. We'll move out in ten minutes."

***

As bad as the heat was in town, it was even worse in the canyon. The dark reddish rock had absorbed heat all day and was now emitting it upward. Below the rim there was no breeze to speak of. The stifling heat and dead silence pushed the tension higher.

The teams moved cautiously forward through the chasm. There were few signs of human inhabitants other than sandal prints scattered on the established trails.

Lieutenant Davitch was leading his men along the southern face when the spotters up above reported their first signs of movement.

"Davitch, we have three individuals on the move heading east. I estimate that they are just over a thousand yards ahead of you," Captain Roth said.

"I don't have any visual contact," Davitch replied, scanning ahead with his binoculars.

"Move up as fast as you can and get within voice range to tell them to stop," directed Major Lewis.

Lieutenant Davitch and his men accelerated their pace as Captain Roth continued to relay instructions. They were closing the gap quickly when the men must have heard the soldiers coming and fled. Davitch finally saw the subjects and began yelling at them to stop. They ignored his requests and the chase continued.

Major Lewis watched diligently ahead to see where the men were leading his soldiers. He directed Davitch to fire warning shots, but they were to no avail.

"Alright, time to slow them down. Captain Roth, pick one of them and try to have the snipers take out a leg. Stay with low caliber."

"Yes, sir. We'll do our best."

Seconds ticked away as the sniper and his spotter targeted and ran through the variables of the shot. In this situation they could certainly take multiple shots, but pride and professionalism were still paramount. Major Lewis finally heard the shot and then saw a small puff of dust burst from a rock next to one of the men. The near miss appeared to make them even more frantic. He waited patiently for the sniper to make adjustments and take a second shot. He found himself unconsciously slowing his breathing, much the way the sniper would be doing before squeezing the trigger.

The second shot dropped the man in the middle of the line. He fell to the sandy path in pain and began kicking himself around in a circle with his good leg. The man in the lead continued on while the third stopped and began rocking back and forth with his hands on his head.

"Lieutenant Davitch, move in cautiously. Captain Roth, keep tracking the single. Let's see where he goes," Major Lewis said.

Lieutenant Davitch's team descended with weapons drawn upon the two men. Davitch split several men off to continue the hunt for the third. The leg injury was not life threatening so they controlled the bleeding and made him comfortable. The uninjured man was now bound and on his knees. He had a small pistol in his belt, but seemed in no way inclined to use it. They would transport the two men out later in the afternoon when they departed. Prisoners would not be a burden today as there was an Afghan National Police unit stationed nearby that they could be handed off to. Davitch reported the situation to Lewis and moved on.

The chase continued for several more minutes as everyone edged toward the split in the canyon. Lieutenant Davitch had closed to a comfortable range where he could take a shot if need be. The brush was thick so the pace was manageable. Suddenly the air erupted with whizzing bullets and Davitch's men instinctively fell to the ground and crawled to cover.

"Stay down, Davitch," Major Lewis commanded when he saw the shooting begin. "Take out the runner, Captain Roth."

"On it, sir," he replied.

"Warner, have you got the shooters on that ridge?" Major Lewis asked.

"Already targeting, sir," Lieutenant Warner confirmed.

Several seconds later the last insurgent winced and then collapsed onto a boulder near the path. Another brief pause and then a salvo of rockets left faint trails of smoke before slamming into the enemy's perch. They were soon followed by a hail of mortars from Warner's men lower in the valley. The shooting ceased as a dust cloud hovered in place where the men had been hiding.

"Status, Davitch?" Major Lewis requested.

"We're fine, sir. No injuries."

"As long as you're ready, keep moving. I want to secure some additional ground before nightfall," Major Lewis said, consulting his watch and looking to the sun. "Hopefully we can have them completely pinned down past the split with no escape routes."

The teams progressed forward with caution. The quiet quickly returned to the canyon and there were no further engagements. Major Lewis's troops set up positions and were able to take a well-deserved rest while they waited for their replacements.

As the sun slid toward the horizon, Major Cierra's men began flowing through the canyon. With the first stretch already secured they were able to move quickly along the floor of the ravine. Major Lewis had made his way down from the rim to meet up with his friend and hand over control.

"Evening, Ray," Major Lewis said, finding Major Cierra stationed on a pedestal of rocks.

"Evening, Johnny. I was hoping you'd have this whole thing wrapped up by the time we got here. It looks like we're going to have to spend the night now."

"We're right where we're supposed to be."

"I heard you had a skirmish in town."

"It got a little dicey, but not too bad. Same thing in here."

"How's your man?" Major Cierra asked.

"He took a lot of fire, all in the extremities though. He's going to live, but they'll be transporting him," Major Lewis replied.

"What kind of numbers do you think we're dealing with down here?" Cierra asked, looking into the distance.

"We had a few dozen slip out of town, but that's probably for the best. The town should be clean now and we don't have to deal with human shields. There might be an equal number that were already down here. This is a spot they use for hiding, not for training or staying for extended periods. The terrain gets rougher as you head into the canyon so there may be some on the ground. The rest are in the caves. We have most of them identified, but there could be some that we don't have mapped."

"I was reviewing the data and it looks like this set here has the greatest likelihood of being their main hives," Cierra said, pointing to a highlighted area on his map.

"So what's your plan for tonight?"

"We're going to start by sending in the new guy," Major Cierra replied.

"The new guy?"

"Yeah, here he comes now," Major Cierra said, pointing to a group of soldiers pulling a low cart with large knobby tires.

"You're going to lead with the robot? Very bold," Major Lewis said, smiling about the thought of the robot in action.

"Didn't you get some, too?"

"Yes, but I left mine at home. We had fun doing our own testing."

"Did you fight them?" Cierra asked with childish excitement.

"No, but we wanted to. We followed the rules and had a blast smashing stuff. We did, however, take Rambot out to the range and equipped him with a sawed-off driver."

"How'd he do?"

"After a little tweaking he hit a few decent shots, but they had a low trajectory. We made more adjustments, but he just had too much torque and sheared the club head off at impact. It flew about fifty yards downrange. After that we decided to stop before someone got hurt."

"Well, they said these things are battle ready so I'm going to put them to use. And I'd have to say spelunking with some angry Afghans ranks way up on my list of highest and best use for them. Do you want to stick around and see how it goes?"

"Nope. I'm passing the baton to you and we're heading back. I'm sure you and R2-D2 can handle things here, but call us if you do need support. We'll plan to see you the day after next down south," Major Lewis said, shaking hands with Cierra before trudging off into the twilight.

***

The next day Major Lewis and his men headed further south and re-established their base of operations near a quiet town that had been under full coalition control for some time. This was as far south as they would travel and would be their position for the remainder of the operation. At this point they had no other direct assignments, but would serve as back up for other units operating in the area.

The following day they were joined by Major Cierra's team and the two commanding officers held an afternoon meeting to prepare reports on the recent operations.

"Major Lewis, how are you doing this fine day?" Major Cierra asked as he placed his laptop on the rickety table where Major Lewis was already seated and working.

"Excellent. And yourself, Major Cierra?"

93

"Not too bad at all."

"Well, you already know how our excursion went the other day. How did you guys fare after we left?"

"Pretty standard operation; we cleared and secured the area as planned before handing it off to the regional security force. No real problems and no injuries to my men."

"How did your robot do?" Major Lewis inquired.

"As I said, no injuries to my *men*." Major Cierra replied evasively.

"And your machines...any injuries there to report?"

"Kind of a good news, bad news scenario. The good news is that the little fella' performed valiantly in the caves. He located and neutralized the enemy. Unfortunately, he was a little too effective and we lost him."

"You lost your robot already?" Major Lewis asked, trying not to laugh.

"Not so much *lost*. We know where he is. We just can't get to him," Major Cierra admitted.

"Alright, quit messing around. What happened?"

"Everything started out fine. We located the main caves and determined there were men inside. So we got the robot near the entrance and began to explore. As he progressed we used the Hansel and Gretel feature. That's actually pretty cool - dropping signal boosters as he goes so you don't lose contact as you go further in. Eventually we made visual contact and I think we scared the hell out of them. They didn't know what it was and quickly got agitated. It kind of reminded me of the apes jumping around the monolith in 2001: A Space Odyssey. The translator tried to talk with them and get them to settle down and come out, but that made it worse. They didn't appear to have any exit routes so they started yelling at each other about what to do and then opened fire. That little guy didn't even flinch. We warned them that we would return fire if they didn't stop and then on the monitor we see one of their guys getting ready to shoot a rocket. We started backing out, but the idiot fired anyway. It looked like it hit the wall next to the robot and knocked him on his side. We were trying to set him right when we heard a rumble. The rocket had set off a collapse and we could see and hear the ceiling coming down on them. We did our best to get the robot out, but the rock fall kept progressing toward the entrance and buried him. We powered down and thanked him for his valor."

"Wow! That's quite a start for the robots."

"The tunnel was completely sealed so we knew we couldn't get to the robot or the men. We moved to the other major cave nearby and it too was collapsed. After that we did some exploration in the smaller caves and didn't find a thing. The rest of the valley was clear so I think all of the fighters were in those two caves."

"Between the two of us I think we're going to end up just burying all of the problems here," Major Lewis said, thinking back to the ridge in Mahzri.

"Anyway, when we get back north I may be stopping over to borrow your robot."

"I don't think so. Not after hearing about how you treated yours," Major Lewis replied.

"I'm sure I am going to have to account for that thing. I wonder if I can just buy one to replace it and hope they don't notice. What do you think those units cost? A couple grand?" Major Cierra said facetiously.

"I doubt it. I'd guess a hundred grand and up. Besides, it's not like you intended to lose it. You weren't violating any of Sergeant Merrick's rules or having a robot battle."

"I know. But it still feels like my dad lent me the car keys and I went out and wrecked it. I've got that sixteen year-old mentality - do anything other than admit what really happened."

"Ray, I'm sure you'll get over it quickly," Major Lewis said reassuringly. "It looks like we'll be here for a couple of days."

"Yeah, I'm bored already. We should have brought our clubs."

"I was thinking the exact same thing."

"So what is the plan now?" Major Cierra asked.

"Wait," Major Lewis muttered, staring off into the distance.

8

The command center at MacKenzie was coming back to life after being inhabited by a skeleton crew for over two weeks. The soldiers were glad to be "home" and settling back into their routines. Overall, morale seemed to be good as the southern excursion had been hailed a success. Major Lewis kept a positive outward appearance; however, he still felt pessimistic undercurrents. Their operations had been easier than expected and when they were providing support to other units the calls had been few and far between. Reading through debrief reports he saw limited engagement in areas where high numbers of insurgents had been anticipated. Either they were doing a great job of hiding and assimilating or else they just weren't there.

Major Lewis was sitting at the conference table and staring vacantly at a report on the screen when Captain Roth sat down next to him.

"Now that we helped mop up down south we can get back to focusing on our own backyard. Do you want to start preparing for our meeting?" Captain Roth asked.

"Yes. I was just thinking about that. It's nice that my new friend, Dehqan, invited us to his party. Let's review the guest list and then we can start laying out our security strategy," Major Lewis said.

"Besides Dehqan and his underlings, who you've already met, we're expecting Jaweed and his posse. As you know, we don't feel we have a lot to worry about with them. Jaweed is definitely a politician and a manipulator, but there is very little militancy in his background. At a meeting like this he'll be front and center. When things get dicey though, he seems to fly below the radar. I guess that's how he has managed to survive so long.

The next two power players are Farzan and Sumahan. In the past they would have fallen into the warlord category. The combination of our presence and their own aging and maturing has tempered their enthusiasm for battle. They've been patient and our funding for their men has kept the fighters docile. Nevertheless, it's in their blood so any valid reason to fight could quickly bring them off the sidelines. We need to make sure that doesn't happen."

"These two are cousins. Do you know of any family allegiances or rivalries between them?" Major Lewis asked, looking over his intelligence notes.

"Since I've been here it has been pretty much middle-of-the-road. They respect each other's territory and work together when necessary, but they certainly aren't close."

"Alright, what about our free agents?"

"It's a pretty motley crew and we're not sure who is actually going to show up. The two we need to focus on are Hadi and Abdul Karim Abdullah. As best as we can tell they seem to have opposite trajectories right now. Hadi has been a thorn in our side in this region for several years. He has had good success in attacking convoys and hitting strategic targets. Lately is seems like he's gotten a bit sloppy. Too much collateral damage has cost him local support and we think his funding is getting thin. He may be coming to the meeting to figure out how to save himself. That could mean some kind of peace agreement. If this is our opportunity we may want to take it.

On the other hand, Abdul Karim Abdullah, who we call AKA, appears to be gaining momentum. As you know, he has an interesting background. He's been around the world and is far better educated than most of these guys. Unfortunately, that makes him a better local facilitator for out-of-country groups. They see him as someone who can step into a major role in the region in what they see as a future state. That's also feeding his local support. A lot of these people, including Dehqan, are looking down the road to when we might be gone. They are trying to figure out who will be the survivors and align themselves accordingly."

"*When* we're gone?" Major Lewis asked innocently. "I was planning to grow old in this lovely valley."

"You can stay as long as you want. I'll be sure to send you a Christmas card each year from the States."

"In the meantime, let's make the best of this opportunity. I know we've been trying for a while to get everyone together at the same table. I received the layout data on Dehqan's country home and it seems like a good location to have this type of a meeting. There is adequate access from several directions and the surrounding land is relatively flat. What do you think the fields out there will be like?" Major Lewis asked, pointing to an aerial photo on his screen.

"At this point in the season there shouldn't be anything growing too high. The fruit groves are further out and most of those trees will just be starting to bloom. There won't be a solid leaf covering yet."

"And you feel comfortable with both of us going in there?"

"I think so. Dehqan will have his men searching everyone outside. Moreover, this isn't a good forum for taking someone out. Kind of like a meeting of the mafia families - it would just turn ugly for all of the factions involved. As unpopular as we may be in some people's eyes, an assassination at a meeting to discuss peace proposals would not go over well."

"Alright. We'll have Private Webster to translate and Sergeant Diaz in case any logistics items need to be addressed. Davitch can run our support team stationed out here," Major Lewis said, gesturing to the map again. "We'll keep Warner here at MacKenzie to mind the shop. Anything else you think we need to arrange?"

"I think we are good. We'll see what they have to say and then re-evaluate our course."

"Excellent. I really appreciate having your expertise on my team, Captain."

***

Things remained quiet around MacKenzie so Major Lewis was almost looking forward to the meeting. The team loaded up and headed off at their typical meandering pace. For as much preparation as they did it felt anticlimactic to embark at such a glacial speed.

After separating from Lieutenant Davitch's support group, Major Lewis casually took in the surroundings on the final stretch. He knew that they were vulnerable as always, but he remained quite calm. The area, about twenty miles from Baza Faqir-e, was wrapped in green, wavy flatlands. Riding along the dirt road, Major Lewis was surprised by the peacefulness in the middle of a war zone. As they rose to a high point Major Lewis evaluated the landscape and could visualize golf holes laid out among the rolling mounds. This was one of those rare places in Afghanistan where golf could exist naturally without massive earth moving and irrigation. Perhaps at some point in the future, Dehqan could turn his country home into a country club.

In the distance, Major Lewis could see the main house. The building was a broad, two-story structure with a tile roof and large windows. It was unlike any home he had seen in Afghanistan and had clearly been built at a time of greater peace and prosperity. Major Lewis assumed that with some modest modifications it could make do as a clubhouse.

On the edge of the estate the soldiers stopped at a security check point staffed by two grinning guards who were engaged in an animated discussion. It was abundantly clear that this was the American contingent arriving and the translator exchanged a few pleasantries before being waved through.

A strung out chain of men directed them toward the assigned parking. From there they were ushered to a trellised gateway on the edge of a large courtyard. The man sitting at a check-in table looked up at Major Lewis and his men and quickly marked them off the list without saying a word.

"I guess we're pretty well known, eh?" Major Lewis said quietly to Captain Roth.

"I was hoping we'd all get 'Hello, my name is...' name badges to stick on our uniforms," Captain Roth replied.

They entered the airy patio and were greeted indifferently by Dehqan. He was in no position to show favoritism toward any of his guests so Major Lewis did not feel slighted. He offered them a drink and directed them to their seats. There were a number of low benches arranged in a semi-circle and most of them were already filled. Some of the attendees looked up at the Americans and exchanged polite nods, while others completely ignored them and carried on with their conversations.

Major Lewis and his men sat patiently and waited for the remaining invitees to arrive. He was able to identify all of the individuals they had discussed, but avoided any extended eye contact.

Dehqan eventually stepped into the middle of the group and drew everyone's attention. He spoke in Pashto so Private Webster quickly translated in a hushed voice for the members of his group.

"Welcome, my brothers and guests. In recognition of our traditions I have called this council to discuss our current situation and how we can work to make it better for our families and our people. We will give everyone here a chance to tell their position and view. When someone is speaking please show respect and allow them to finish even if you disagree. We will then allow for open discussion and suggestions from the group."

Jaweed started off and spent fifteen minutes saying absolutely nothing. He wanted peace and prosperity without paying any price. He harkened back to better days in the past and was certain that the remembered glory could be reclaimed. The platitudes were so bland that much of his monologue could have been translated to English and used on any campaign trail in the United States.

In the same vein, he of course offered no concrete solutions to the problems faced by the representatives at the meeting. He didn't want to offend anyone and seemed to imply that the tough tasks would magically be accomplished by parties not seated around the courtyard. Major Lewis had to work hard to make sure his boredom didn't display itself as disrespect.

AKA was much slower and more deliberate in his approach. He talked in a low voice and considered each word as he spoke. "We must have *local* security and *local* leadership. Only men from this area can bring peace and establish control over the region. Furthermore, only we can determine who truly belongs here and who doesn't. All countries experience conflicts, but throughout its history Afghanistan has consistently drawn foreign powers into its disputes. These interventions never solve the problems; rather they extend and exacerbate the conflicts. The time has come to show that Afghans can lead their countrymen without foreign interference," AKA proclaimed, directing pointed glances at Major Lewis and his men to reiterate to everyone present just who he was talking about.

He covered several other topics and when he was done he sat back down on the bench. Surprisingly, one of his subordinates, a man Major Lewis recognized as Atash, stood up and began a vocal rant. AKA had apparently not been forceful enough in his comments so Atash brought some stronger rhetoric to bear. He was clearly not as well educated as AKA and Private Webster had difficulty making a smooth translation. When Private Webster passed along a statement regarding the village of Mahzri and the atrocities the infidels had committed there Major Lewis quickly stopped him.

"What? Is he trying to pin that on us? Are you sure he said that?"

"Yes, sir. That was quite clear."

"Unbelievable," Major Lewis said, rolling his eyes as he realized the level of spin that would be working against him.

Atash was clearly speaking out of turn and AKA grabbed his forearm to rein him back in. Atash grudgingly sat back while still muttering.

Major Lewis wondered if Atash had been freelancing or if the outburst had been staged to say things AKA didn't want to say. No matter the intention, the show had clearly increased the tension at the meeting.

The next speakers tended toward the middle ground and were hesitant to be as controversial, even if that was their true opinion.

When it was finally the Americans' turn Major Lewis stood up and presented the comments that he had outlined. He thanked everyone for coming and indicated that more dialogue such as this could improve relations and dispel misconceptions among the participants and the people they represented. He tried to focus on the positive and highlight things that were working in the region. As he spoke the level of interest shown by the others was somewhere between tedium and apathy. He wanted to ad lib about the situation in Mahzri, but decided to take the high road and wait for the open discussion. When he was done he politely thanked everyone again before returning to his seat.

Dehqan once again took over the meeting and began the open discussion. He reminded everyone to keep an open mind and an even tone to prevent tempers from flaring.

Atash wasted no time jumping back into the fray and ignoring the guidelines that Dehqan had just presented. "If we are to have a true council and make real decisions it needs to be made up only of Afghans. The assembly of elders is *our* tradition. The Americans have their way of doing things and they want to impose their so-called freedom upon us with the usual violence."

He went on for several minutes before AKA reeled in his leash. Major Lewis was pleased when the men that followed struck a more moderate tone. They all had gripes, but most of them centered on more practical issues. Sergeant Diaz was able to provide updates and solid timeframes on a number of the reconstruction items that came up, which quickly undermined Athash's tirade.

When it seemed like everyone else had had a chance to speak Major Lewis stood up and took the floor. He thanked everyone for their input and expressed his optimism going forward. He wanted to be polite, but could not let the comments made by Atash go unanswered.

"As we saw today, there are a number of different opinions on what is occurring in this region. That is to be expected and it is no different in our country. What we can't have, however, are varying sets of *facts*. Today I heard certain statements that were not misled opinions, there were simply lies. I can say that with confidence because I was in Mahzri on that day and saw with my own eyes what happened. I took part in the operation that saved the lives of many Afghans and eliminated a group of terrorists. Those fighters, most of which came from across your border, were the ones responsible for the slaughter of your countrymen.

I worked with Rashid to save his town and I witnessed the relief our role brought to his people. The damage inflicted upon the neighboring communities was done *before* we arrived. I'm not sure where some of the people here are getting their information, but it is flat out wrong. I know the truth because I was there helping and protecting Afghan citizens," Major Lewis said, his voice rising steadily as he spoke. When he finished he was staring directly at Atash. Major Lewis was daring him to rebut, but instead he sat silently under the Major's gaze.

Major Lewis was pleased that no one else seemed to want to take up Atash's position. He hoped most of the others were reasonable enough to know the truth about Mahzri. Nonetheless, Major Lewis knew how quickly misinformation could spread in a land with such an uneducated populace. Framing the Americans as the aggressors would of course be an easy sell.

In preparation for his tour in Afghanistan Major Lewis had read a report about a unit operating at the western end of the Hindu Kush. A patrol came across a set of dinosaur bones and excavated several of the larger, exposed ones to hand off to scientists. A group of local residents saw the bones and did not believe the soldiers' stories about dinosaurs. One of the men started yelling that the Americans had killed a giant Afghan and were trying to cover it up. It would have almost been comical - believing there were modern-day giants hiding in the mountains, but not believing dinosaurs existed in the area millions of years ago - had a riot not broken out. Luckily there were no deaths, but a number of civilians were injured in the melee.

Dehqan sensed the tension and began to wrap up the meeting. He tried to bring everyone back to the concept of finding compromise and encouraged everyone to stay for lunch and continue the discussion. Major Lewis knew Dehqan was a man stuck in the middle who was trying his best to keep all sides in check.

No one wanted to leave and reject Dehqan's hospitality, however, all of the different factions kept themselves segregated during the meal. After eating quickly, Major Lewis excused himself and went outside to make a call to Lieutenant Davitch. Their greatest concern for violence today was after the meeting. However, Lieutenant Davitch reported no suspicious activity from their lookout positions.

Major Lewis took his time returning to the house and walked through a beautifully manicured garden that was thick with the scent of blooming flowers. From a sensory standpoint it was like nothing he'd experienced since arriving in Afghanistan. Casually walking through a hedged maze, Major Lewis stopped in his tracks as he turned a corner and came face-to-face with AKA. There was an uncomfortable moment while they stared at each other silently, wondering what to do.

"Hello, Abdul," Major Lewis finally offered.

"Hello, Major Lewis," AKA replied in English.

They looked at one another for a few seconds longer, sizing up their opponent.

"This is an amazing garden that Dehqan has grown," Major Lewis said.

"This property has been in his family for several generations and each one has successfully maintained what they inherited. There used to be many places like this in Afghanistan, now they are far rarer."

"I have found that to be the case in many places I have served. We see ruins and remnants of what were once marvels. Time takes its toll."

"So does war," AKA replied.

"True. But it is also how you respond. Wars come and go, but what the survivors do in the aftermath is a measure of the society."

"Your country has been able to rebound, but the United States is still very young. Besides, the United States has never enjoyed the presence of a foreign army on its soil. It is a much different experience when you are invaded."

"We haven't been invaded, but we've been attacked. I think our responses speak for themselves. Beyond that we've had a pretty solid record in reconstruction for our enemies as well."

"Including Afghanistan?" AKA asked mockingly.

"Unfortunately the conflict here is still ongoing. We'll need to assess that once it's over, which will hopefully be soon. And again, it depends on the people who live here and what they are willing to accomplish," Major Lewis countered.

"This conflict could be over today and we could begin rebuilding tomorrow."

"Really? I must have lost that in the translation at the meeting just now," Major Lewis replied, knowing exactly what solution AKA had in mind. "How would we accomplish that?"

"If the foreigners leave we can move forward with restoring Afghanistan."

"Yes, but in what form?"

"The form that *we* choose."

"Who is we? All Afghans or just the select group of self-chosen. Do women get a say? Do Hazaras have a voice?"

"You see that is a big part of the problem. There is a great divide between what you *think* this country could be and what we *know* it can be. Not every land can be reshaped in the model of the U.S."

"I agree," Major Lewis admitted, questioning his choice of words as soon as he'd said them. "But there are many forms of government that can insure basic human rights. Strong leadership and repression don't have to be synonymous. Besides, do you really think that the fighting would end with our departure?"

"I'm not that naive. In fact it would probably get worse before it got better. But I think it would be a quicker path to peace. This has always been a warrior culture. That is how we solve things. That is how we restore balance."

"I guess we are left with a bit of a chicken-or-the-egg problem. Do we leave to end the battle, or do you end the battle in order to have us leave? I haven't been here long, but I don't see any chance of balance with our exodus. I see chaos."

AKA simply shrugged in response, content with the argument he'd made.

Major Lewis pressed on, "So how do you decide who is in charge? I can see you are the leader of your group, but your friend Atash doesn't seem to understand the chain of command."

AKA laughed off the suggestion, "Atash is passionate about the struggle, but he knows his place. We are not trying to take control, just offer an alternative. It's no different than your political parties."

Major Lewis knew he wasn't going to change AKA's opinion about anything while standing in Dehqan's garden so he decided to try to find out more about his foe. "Abdul, I know you have been elsewhere in the world, including the U.S. Tell me, why are you here?"

AKA paused to think about the question, "This is my home. This is what I know. I have seen many places, but this is where I belong. So tell me, Major Lewis, why are you here?"

"This is my job. I go where the boss tells me to go."

"So I get to choose where to be and you are told where to be. We obviously do have different definitions of freedom, Major."

Major Lewis allowed a slight smile at AKA's twist of words, "I had complete freedom in choosing my career. Part of that choice was accepting the hierarchy of the military. I also knew full well that I would be sent to dangerous places. So what is your vision for this place? Where do you see it in ten years? Twenty years?"

"Again, you see some kind of glorious future. I'm realistic and look to the past. This has been a good country in the periods between the wars. If you and the Europeans are no longer here in ten years, Afghanistan will be as it should be. My vision is simple."

"And what will the people here do? What kind of economy will there be?"

"We have agriculture, we have textiles, we have trade. We have survived without technology and without your forms of entertainment. We do not have all the *needs* that Americans have. Our needs are far more basic and our wants are not excessive."

"Agriculture? Does that include the drug trade?" Major Lewis asked.

"We grow many different crops here. The fact that some of those things do not meet your standards is your issue, not ours. People here have always used these plants for various medicinal purposes and they always will. You haven't stopped drug usage in your country and you won't stop it here. You tried prohibition of alcohol and it was a total failure. Instead they legalized it and made it acceptable in society."

"Yes, but alcohol is your issue. How can you be so opposed to booze, but condone marijuana and opium?"

"We don't condone it, but we are able to accept the fact that it is part of the culture."

"The Taliban policy seems to be whatever is convenient. First they allowed it and then they crushed it violently. It served the cultural need of cash generation and repressing the portion of the population that became addicts," Major Lewis pointed out.

"All countries have some people who lack self-control. You can try to help them, but at some point they have to help themselves. Is rehabilitating drug addicts part of you mission, Major? It seems like you are already busy with so many other things."

"It's not our primary focus, but when it impacts stability we will address it. Besides a one-legged economy, what about leisure activities? Without a war you should have a lot more free time. I know of many things that the Taliban didn't allow. I'm not sure what they actually did approve of."

"I'm sorry to disappoint you, Major, but we aren't going to run out and buy golf clubs. We consider things like that a waste of time. We enjoy spending our time with family and friends and honoring our religious beliefs. Again, simple things."

"Wow, you make it sound like a Norman Rockwell painting. Have you ever even tried golf?" Major Lewis asked, defending his passion.

"No, but I have seen it. I have no interest in chasing a little, white ball around."

"How do you know? It seems like a very close minded perspective to dismiss something without every trying it. Part of the reason we play in sports in the West is that we can indulge our competitive urges without killing each other."

"We have games and contests, but they are not the focus of our lives. Survival takes precedence."

"Why just survive when you can thrive? That is part of the mentality that we *do* want to bring from the U.S. to other lands."

"Your people have already been here for many years and I do not see anyone thriving."

"We have a process and it is working. The situation here is not great, but we have it under control. I fully intend to continue the progress and improve things further. What we don't need is interference," Major Lewis said, intoning that he was losing patience with AKA.

"Of course, Major. And you really shouldn't have any concerns here. It is the southern lands that need your attention."

Major Lewis scrutinized AKA's face as he made the comment, looking at him the way he would if he thought someone was bluffing at the poker table. "We're taking care of that as well." Major Lewis checked his watch, debating if there was anything further to gain from this conversation.

AKA grinned at the gesture. "There is another difference between us, Major. You have the watches, we have the time."

The comment confirmed for Major Lewis that he was done. In his mind *this* was a waste of time. By comparison, chasing a little white ball around seemed downright productive. "Enjoy the rest of your day, Abdul," Major Lewis said with a nod.

"And the same to you, Major," AKA replied.

Major Lewis walked around AKA briskly and returned to the dining hall without looking back. He gathered up his team and once again thanked Dehqan for being a gracious host. He waited until they were walking out before telling Captain Roth about his conversation with AKA.

"I just had a chat with AKA in the garden," Major Lewis said.

"Really?"

"Yes, he was out for a stroll so we talked about the lovely weather we've been having."

"Really?"

"No. We just carried on with the same line of thinking they brought to the meeting earlier. I didn't find out anything enlightening.

He clearly isn't someone looking for the middle ground. And he won't be golfing with Major Cierra and me any time soon."

"What?"

"He mentioned golf so he must know that we've been playing here."

"Oh, I see."

"Anyway, these guys are going to be pains in our asses. We'll need to keep tabs on them and have a strategy for dealing with them. Did we get good video?"

"Yes, sir," Captain Roth responded. "I made sure to get up close and personal with everyone to obtain good facial footage."

Captain Roth was wearing a tiny camera hidden on his collar hooked to a recording device. The images would be fed into their database to be able to identify all of the local players with facial recognition software. A common complaint among the soldiers in Afghanistan was the inability to differentiate the good guys from the bad guys. This was another problem they were combating with technology.

"Excellent. Overall, I think things went pretty well. Other than Atash and AKA I believe a lot of the men are reasonable and willing to work with us. We just need to keep delivering on our promises. Let's pick up Davitch and get back to MacKenzie. I feel like hitting some golf balls out at the range just to spite AKA."

9

Following the meeting AKA and his men loaded into a small pickup and began the trip back to Baza Faqir-e. The truck was a loaner from Dehqan and they had to return it to town. Compared to the Americans' vehicles it was a sad sight. It had body damage on all sides, a white hood that didn't match the dark blue color of the rest of the truck, and only one headlight. The interior was tattered and options like a radio and air conditioning had never been on the original equipment list.

AKA and Atash were squeezed into the bench seat in the cab while one of his other men drove and fought with the manual transmission. It was an unpleasant ride made worse by the overpowering stench of body odor emanating from the three men.

AKA was not pleased by Atash's outbursts at the meeting, but he wasn't going to berate his subordinate in front of the others. "Atash, I understand your anger, but you need to be aware of the forum where you show it. We made our position clear to our brothers, however, a meeting like this is not going to change the Americans' strategy," AKA said.

"I guess I am just not as blessed with patience as you are."

"Patience is exactly what we all need to have right now. We are so close to having the support we need to battle the Americans on our terms. To move now would be counterproductive. What are we to do? Attack their compound in this meager truck?" AKA asked, motioning toward the cracked dashboard. "And we don't need to incite them to come after us before we are ready. Soon we will have additional vehicles, explosives, and weapons."

"I will find the patience," an exasperated Atash assured his leader. "How were your discussions with the American?"

"As expected, he tried to convince me that they had the situation under control. He then warned me not to interfere."

"What did you think of him as an opponent?"

"Like most of the Americans he is a professional soldier. They are always going to be more competent and better equipped than the other foreigners that send token regiments. Nonetheless, he is still vulnerable while on our land," AKA said with confidence. He wanted to portray strength in his opinion even though he did have some doubts after meeting his foe. "He is new to the fight here, but his men have been here longer and are already weary. Our upcoming offensive and the Afghan summer will take a far greater toll on them. The tide will turn sooner than you know, Atash. Remain strong."

"I shall," Atash replied, once again confident in AKA's plans. "What is our next move?"

"When we return to Baza Faqir-e we will continue trying to undermine any progress that the Americans have been making. We may switch to a more forceful approach if they gain favor. Also, we need to pay someone a visit," AKA responded.

***

When they arrived in Baza Faqir-e, AKA dropped off most of his men at a home where they were staying. He and the driver then continued on to the market where AKA found his way to Zemar's stall.

"Hello, Zemar," he said when the boy noticed his arrival.

"Abdul," Zemar replied when he recognized the man. He looked around to see if any other men were with him. Zemar was relieved to see that he was alone.

"What have you been doing lately?" AKA asked as he looked casually at the items for sale.

"Running my business," Zemar said indifferently.

"I see that. I understand that you've gone international with your operations. Doing some work with the Americans now, Zemar, eh?"

Zemar did his best not to show any reaction, but inside he felt his stomach tighten. "I try to do business with everyone. That's good business. You never know how things will turn out so it is wise to have many different customers."

"Indeed. You are a smart young man. In fact I'm glad you know one of my new friends, Major Lewis. We just met this morning and had nice conversation. You know him better than I do, though. What can you tell me about him?"

Zemar shrugged, "He's just another soldier passing through. He controls some of the money coming here so I offered to sell him whatever I can. He bought one of my pictures. That's all."

"And took you golfing?" AKA persisted.

Zemar again felt a twinge inside. "Just a job. We went there to work for him and his men, not to play."

"That's good. Trying to learn a game like golf won't benefit you much here, particularly in the future. The Americans can waste their time doing that when they retreat back to their homeland."

"While they're here I'll do business with them just like everyone else. The more customers the better."

"I'm not saying you shouldn't do your business, Zemar. Just be careful not to get too close to certain customers. Make sure you are selling your *artwork*," AKA said gesturing dismissively to the displayed items, "and not information. That can be a dangerous business and one you should avoid."

Zemar did not like being threatened and wanted to blurt out something like, "Or what?", but when it came to AKA and those like him he already knew what "Or what?" meant. In his mind he was contrasting the meeting he'd had here with Major Lewis and the one he was now having with AKA. Both men wanted to know about the other, but their approaches were diametrically opposed. Finally Zemar replied, "Don't worry. I'll watch my step."

"See, I knew you were a smart boy. You need to think not only about your future, but that of your friends and *family*. Take care, Zemar," AKA said, before turning to leave.

As Zemar watched AKA walk back down the street he ran the last part of the conversation over and over in his head. He had always worried that his friends could be used as pawns, but the fact that AKA had emphasized the word "family" was more troubling. He made one additional comparison between AKA and Major Lewis. Major Lewis at least had the ability and the willingness to buy some of his work.

It was a slow day so Zemar went in back and listened to music to calm down. A short while later his closest friend Yasir arrived in a chipper mood. He immediately noted Zemar's somber appearance.

"Zemar, it's a beautiful day in Baza Faqir-e, what is troubling you?" Yasir asked.

"I had a visitor earlier," Zemar replied.

"Who was that?"

"Abdul Karim Abdullah."

"Oh, what did he want?"

"Just to warn me about doing business with the Americans."

"Did he threaten you?"

"Not just me, but those who are close to me," Zemar said, looking directly at his friend.

"I see. What should we do?"

"Nothing for now. However, I sense that it will become much more dangerous in the coming months. You are the only one that knows about my secrets right now. Depending on how things go we may need to change our plans and do so quickly. It is difficult to know who to trust, but I have full faith in you, Yasir."

"And I have the same trust in you, Zemar. You have always been a good and true friend. Whatever you decide is best, I will be there to help you."

***

After attending Dehqan's local meeting, Major Lewis soon departed for a regional meeting further north. The first portion included only U.S. and coalition military leaders and went very much the way all such meetings had gone recently. They were focused on threats in the south and along the northeastern border with Pakistan. Major Lewis continued to lobby for more support in the central region, but only received modest commitments for equipment and soldiers. He planned to continue his requests, but for the time being he knew that he would have to make do with what he had in place.

The second day proved to be far more interesting. Meetings with a number of Afghan leaders were scheduled in the morning, while the afternoon was reserved for "entertainment".

The conference was being held at what was once an opulent hotel. There were still hints of elegance in the towering lobby and the spacious meeting rooms, but over time most had been pillaged or destroyed. The lobby was now staffed by heavily armed soldiers rather than bellhops or concierges. The hotel still operated in some capacity, however, as far as Major Lewis could tell none of the attendees, including himself, were actually staying at the hotel. Most were set up in secured campgrounds nearby.

Similar to Dehqan's meeting, the Afghan contingent was made up of men with varying backgrounds. What was quite different here was their attitude toward the Americans. Although they were justifiably not happy with the overall state of their country, they did not blame their problems on the U.S. and NATO forces. Rather they were openly appreciative of what the foreign soldiers had done. Their perspective was different, as these leaders had allegiances to the Northern Alliance that was instrumental in helping to overthrow the Taliban. The discussions made Major Lewis feel much more optimistic about his role here. However, he also realized that the opinions here still clashed with those held in the south, which would likely lead to further conflict well into the future. Beyond their military support, none of these men would ever win humanitarian awards. They still believed in a male dominated culture and also had ethnic and racial views that were far from those in the U.S. These were traits shared in some ways with the Taliban, just without the deeply religious underpinnings.

During lunch Major Lewis was seated next to a man known as Sindo. He appeared to be in his mid-forties and looked similar to many of the other Afghans that Major Lewis had met. What differentiated him was a constant smile that conveyed a positive personality. He spoke in broken, but reasonable English and the two men were able to carry on a steady conversation.

"How have you found our southern lands to be?" Sindo asked.

"Hot," Major Lewis replied.

Sindo laughed, "This is warm, but soon you'll see hot."

"I know it's going to get worse. I spent two summers in Iraq."

"If it gets too bad just go climb the mountains. Cooler up high."

"That's something Iraq didn't have. We have them back home, though. I live in a state called North Carolina and our Smoky Mountains have similar heights to the Hindu Kush. However, in Uruzgan the Kush are a lot more barren."

"That's good for you. Less places for the bad guys to hide."

"Yes, but they still have the caves. We had some issues with that down in Kandahar recently. I'm hoping to focus on our territory in the coming months, but as you know our superiors have other targets right now."

"You are wise to pay attention to your neighborhood. The threats here are always changing. When you are looking forward they come up from behind."

"What's your secret for survival?" Major Lewis asked.

"You must watch like the owl," Sindo said, swiveling his head back and forth. "Always looking in every direction."

"Have you ever spent time down south?"

"Not for many years. We have lots of things to keep us busy in our own provinces."

"I was just curious if you knew any of the players that we might be dealing with down there."

"Like who?"

"I actually just met one of the men we're worried about. His name is Abdul Karim Abdullah. Have you ever heard of him?"

"I do know of him, although I haven't heard his name come up in a while. Several years ago he tried to move up in regional power, but was marginalized. Last I knew he was trying to build up his own force."

"That's correct. We think he has only had limited success and now, in order to get bigger, he is aligning himself with fighters from the Pakistan tribal regions."

"He is likely out of options so that does not surprise me. His strategy has probably been to wait you out and then assert control and gain power when you leave. Now that he sees you still here and growing your presence he needs to take action. Sooner, rather than later, would be my guess."

"What about tactics?"

"As I recall, Abdul is a very smart man. You need to be very careful with him. He will seek strategies to inflict the most damage possible. As you know, there are no rules here. He will negotiate a cease fire with you while his men are loading their weapons. And if he is getting desperate he will also use whatever means are available. The foreign fighters will bring with them explosive experts and even suicide bombers. An already dangerous place will become even more so."

"We were already considering those scenarios, but thank you for your input," Major Lewis said, thinking about his plans for AKA once again. His first thought was AKA's suggestion that if the Americans left it would minimize the fighting. Perhaps he was right. Unfortunately withdrawal was not an option. He started to seriously consider the option of proactive removal. They had discussed arresting him, but that might only embolden his followers and would be a temporary solution to a long-term problem. Drone strikes were having solid success along the border, but to remove an Afghan like AKA was a bit trickier to justify. First, they didn't have any concrete evidence on him yet. Second, he wasn't a high enough profile candidate to justify the time and high cost of establishing drone surveillance.

Sindo could see Major Lewis pondering the situation. "Don't worry yourself any further about Abdul right now. He'll be there when you return. Enjoy the rest of your lunch and soon we will go to the match." Sindo's smile was reassuring and Major Lewis followed the advice.

There was no formal announcement, but as lunch concluded the attendees began to stream steadily out of the hotel. Sindo gathered several of his friends and Major Lewis joined them in a procession heading toward a field located about a mile away. As the column of men neared the field the level of laughter and merriment grew rapidly. In the distance they could hear the baying of horses and the white noise of a growing crowd. For the Americans, like Major Lewis, there was a sense of strange anticipation. Today's entertainment was a Buzkashi tournament.

In anticipation of the event, Major Lewis had researched this ancient Afghan sport that dated back to the time of Genghis Khan. Along with seemingly all forms of entertainment, these violent contests were banned under the rule of the Taliban. However, it quickly reappeared after their fall and reestablished itself in the following years. At this point it was once again considered the national sport of Afghanistan.

The game was believed to have originated hundreds of years ago when invading armies would steal livestock while on horseback. In turn, Afghans developed similar skills to retrieve their stolen property. Buzkashi, which meant "goat dragging", was played with many animals and the carcasses typically weighed over seventy-five pounds. This of course excluded the weight of the head, which was removed.

In the game two teams of riders on horseback, known as chapandaz, face off in a circle with the carcass placed in the middle. The teams then battle each other for several hours to carry the carcass and drop it in a goal zone. Similar to professional sports in other countries, the best Buzkashi players were supported by sponsors and were some of the best paid people in the country. Based on what he'd read, Major Lewis was eager to see the medieval melee in person.

They entered through a check point that had limited security as the guards warmly welcomed everyone that entered. Although far more primitive, the scene reminded Major Lewis of going through the turnstiles at Soldier Field in Chicago for a Bears game. There was no massive stadium or JumboTron television, but there was the same carnival like atmosphere with patrons and vendors mulling about busily before the game began. The pungent smell of burning hashish was a notable difference.

The field was situated at the bottom of a natural bowl and the gradual hillside surrounding it served as the stands for the crowd. Sindo exchanged greetings with many of the other attendees as he led their group to a prime viewing location. From their vantage point he identified to Major Lewis a number of regional dignitaries that had already arrived. Beyond the viewers from the conference, there was a wide variety of politicians and businessmen interspersed with local commoners. The event clearly drew Afghans out and brought them together, something Major Lewis had not yet seen in Afghanistan.

The festivities moved into full swing when the last of the riders arrived and the pre-game show began. The riders displayed varying feats of skill: full speed sprints, prancing in tight circles, and rearing the horses up on their hind legs. The horses were bred and trained for the sport. They were magnificent animals that were better fed and cared for than many of the people in Afghanistan.

The riders themselves looked very much like Major Lewis would have expected to see in a documentary about Genghis Khan. They were burly men with leathery faces. Their size was a combination of genetics and a hearty diet. They could afford opulent clothing and they were adorned in pants and jackets with rich colors and extraordinary patterns.

One thing that struck Major Lewis as he scanned the field was the complete lack of any safety equipment. No helmets, no knee pads, not even a pair of gloves. This was truly a raw sporting event. From a legal perspective there were no concerns about injuries or liability. If a player broke his neck you simply got a new player. There were also no groups protesting cruelty to animals or the fact that a dead bovine was the "ball". At a time when even Spain was banning a national tradition like bullfighting there was no such sentiment here.

Most Western observers would see Buzkashi as barbaric, but such a term would probably be taken as a compliment by these men. From Major Lewis's perspective it was better that they were dragging animals instead of humans. He was also glad to learn that the carcass was typically cooked and served to the poor afterwards. He assumed that the meat would be a tad dirty, but very well tenderized.

With the match ready to begin the electricity in the crowd was almost overwhelming. There was a flurry of activity as patrons sent runners scurrying to place final bets. Gambling was also haraam, or prohibited, in Islam. However, most of the people in the crowd didn't look like they were going to take a break for prayers either. Sindo made several different bets and offered to place one on behalf of his new friend. Major Lewis declined politely based upon the honest fact that he had no idea what he was doing.

The local governor fired a rifle, which had live rounds rather than blanks, and the two teams charged. There was a thundering of hooves as two clouds of dust converged. It looked like two waves of water colliding and then rising upward as they met in the middle. For several minutes it was more like a sumo match with horses hitting and bouncing back. Major Lewis could not see anyone take hold of the animal and assumed that it was simply being trampled at this point.

Finally, there was a break away and the entire crowd's vision shifted at once. The horseman emerged and tried to find an exit path, but was quickly sandwiched between two opposing riders and lost his prize.

The match continued at a wild pace and nearly half an hour passed before Major Lewis noticed any kind of slowdown. The moves became more measured and strategy started to be more of a factor. The crowd went crazy when the first points were counted as a young rider flung the dead calf into the scoring circle. That was his only victory of the day as the older, more experienced players asserted themselves as the afternoon wore on. Major Lewis was glad that Sindo had chosen a location higher up on the hillside. He had a better view and did not have to flee in panic when the horses occasionally flowed into the surrounding spectators.

Major Lewis was so engrossed by the spectacle that he barely noticed the fact that he'd been on his feet for three hours. This was the end of Buzkashi season and they were playing an extended length match. The volume of the cheers gradually started to waiver and the horses were finally tired. Even though one team had taken control, both sides continued to put in their best effort down the stretch. The referees finally declared time and announced the winner.

The field cleared as horses were taken away to be rested and the players mixed with the crowd. The winners were surrounded by cheering fans and gamblers who had made the right wagers. The losers did not receive a boisterous welcome, but were shown polite respect for having participated in the dangerous game.

Despite having lost more than he won on his various bets, Sindo remained in high spirits. He put his arm around Major Lewis and asked, "So, Major, what did you think about our Buzkashi game?"

"I'd have to say that I really enjoyed it. There are some similarities to other sports like polo, but I've never seen anything quite like it. Our sport of football is very rough and the professional games are played in stadiums that hold tens of thousands of people. The ball they use is nicknamed the 'pigskin', however, there is a big difference compared to Buzkashi - in our case the pig is not still in it!

This was raw and wild yet still possessed strategy and skill. I can tell you had fun, Sindo. I guess you didn't lose too badly."

"Oh, I lost a lot. But it is part of the game. Having a wager takes the excitement even higher. Just think of it as paying extra admission to see a better game. Do you bet on your professional sports, Major?"

"Some people do, but not me. We have pools where you get to bet on tournaments and playoffs. That's for lightweights like me. Serious gamblers can bet on specific games and even individual plays. We have a place called Las Vegas where gambling is legal and you can bet on anything. They call it Sin City."

"I have heard of Las Vegas. Sin City sounds like a place I'd like to visit," Sindo laughed.

"Many countries have a place like that where vice is concentrated in one location and, therefore, tolerated. I don't think Afghanistan has ever had such a place, though."

"No, unfortunately not," Sindo lamented. "Too often people here have confused sin and fun. I don't think any less of anyone who wants to pray five times a day, but they should not have a problem if my friends and I want to enjoy ourselves from time to time."

"That sounds very reasonable. Tolerance and everything in moderation."

Sindo's expression changed slightly as he pondered issues bigger than the Buzkashi match. "Our country is not in a good place now, but it is still far better than ten years ago. There was more safety for a time under the Taliban, but what good is that when you can't enjoy yourself? You aren't afraid of your neighbor robbing you, but you are petrified that they might report you to the government for something you did. I hope in the future our country can find a middle ground. And I hope you can help get us there."

"I think we all want to get there, Sindo," Major Lewis agreed. "Even in the U.S. we swing from one direction to the other. Luckily we always seem to find our way back to the center."

"We aren't going to solve any more problems today so it is best to worry about them tomorrow. In a few hours we will be having a big dinner at my friend's home. You would of course be welcome. Can you join us?"

"Sindo, I would love to. Unfortunately I have a dinner with our leadership scheduled tonight. In fact, I'm already late for a meeting so I need to get back to the hotel. Thank you again for your hospitality this afternoon and if you do make it down into Uruzgan I hope you will visit us at FOB MacKenzie."

"I will. Be safe and I look forward to seeing you again my friend."

They shook hands and Sindo gave Major Lewis a hearty pat on the shoulder. Major Lewis said goodbye to the others and began walking back to the hotel. He stopped and looked back at the crowd still mulling happily around the field. The afternoon had provided an enlightening view on Afghan culture that he'd not previously witnessed - the laughing, the smoking, the singing, the gambling. It was as if the true nature of Afghanistan was shining brightly through the dark veil of the Islamic Republic.

10

As hot as it had been already, Major Lewis knew that summer had officially arrived in the days following his trip to the north. It was the type of heat he knew all too well from Iraq. In the morning it felt even hotter than when he'd gone to bed. Major Lewis had always been able to get his sleep, even in war zones, but these temperatures made it difficult for him to wake up feeling rested. He grabbed a quick breakfast and tried to get energized for another day of patrols.

The troops were ready and the line of vehicles headed out just before sunrise. They were heading north today and the passing mountains provided periodic shade, albeit with little relief from the brutal air temperature. Eventually the convoy separated into two groups and fanned out across a rugged and sparsely populated area.

At mid-morning Major Lewis's team was stopped on a hillside and surveying the area around them when the radio came to life. Lieutenant Warner had been making periodic calls, but now he just had the line open and Major Lewis could hear the frantic activity taking place. He could hear Lieutenant Warner barking orders over a steady stream of gunfire. He instinctively looked in the direction where he thought they would be, but there was too much distance between them to see or hear anything directly.

"What's going on Warner?" Major Lewis called urgently.

The seconds ticked away and there was no direct response, just more sounds of chaos.

"Warner!" Major Lewis yelled. "Where are you? Do you need back-up?"

Still no reply. He heard several of Warner's men shouting profanity-laced war cries followed by the unleashing of firepower close to the radio. Despite the sounds of the situation unfolding, Major Lewis was comforted by the distinct, pulsating resonance of the M240B machine gun returning fire.

Finally, Warner returned to the radio. "Sir, a rocket hit one of our vehicles and when we dismounted to help they opened fire. We've got several wounded and possible casualties. We're in a bad spot here. They caught us by surprise, but we're taking control. We're going to push them back and then pull out as fast as we can. Don't come in here yet. I'll let you know when we're on the move and we'll meet you back at the rendezvous location."

"Alright, keep me posted, Warner," Major Lewis directed. He turned to his men who were standing by attentively. "Load up and move out. We're going to head back and need to be ready to support Lieutenant Warner's team. Let's go."

The route back to meet Warner had already been traversed so the unit was more confident retracing their steps. With the engines revving and road debris flying, Major Lewis realized this was the fastest he'd driven since being in Afghanistan. En route the sounds of the fire fight kept repeating in his head and his protective instincts were telling him to head out to Lieutenant Warner's location to help his men. He was in charge and could do what he thought best, but he trusted Warner's judgment. He was relieved when word finally came over the radio that Warner's team was in transit.

Major Lewis was standing outside his Humvee when he saw a snake of tan dust start to rise along the horizon. It weaved its way back and forth for several minutes until the vehicles began to crest a nearby rise and pull up alongside their fellow soldiers.

"What have you got?" Major Lewis asked after locating Lieutenant Warner.

"Two dead: Specialist Kramer and Private Carmichael. They were in the front seat of the truck that took the rocket. It was a powerful ordnance. The armor was trashed. The other two that were in the back are alive, but in bad shape. Finally, two more that took gunfire. Their wounds seem pretty modest."

Major Lewis threw a map up against the side of Warner's vehicle, "Alright, let's make a direct run to this town here and we'll call in the Medevac to meet us there. We'll take the lead. Come on."

As soon as they were back on the road Major Lewis made the necessary calls and received an estimated arrival time. Once the medical aspects were in place he switched gears and tried to call in air strikes on the ambush site. He provided coordinates and estimated the enemy's location based on the information Warner had provided. The initial response sounded positive, but after a check of available resource the request was denied. Major Lewis quickly appealed; however, the officer in charge did not want to take the action because of the fact that the troops had already evacuated the area. They were no longer in immediate danger and they also could not direct the aircraft to the proper target. With the fighting now over there was no way to be certain the available targets in the area were all hostile. Major Lewis was not in the mood to argue so he simply shook his head and hung up the satellite phone. He hated the idea of leaving armed and militant insurgents with a chance to escape, but he hoped that Warner's men had at least inflicted a fair amount of damage before departing.

After that the men rode in silence the rest of the way to the extraction point. Major Lewis alternated between staring out the window and rechecking their position on the map in an attempt to keep his mind from the dead and wounded soldiers traveling in the caravan.

The team slowed their pace when the small town came into view. The helicopters had not yet arrived at the flatland area located just north of the settlement. The vehicles parked in a circle and Major Lewis quickly got out to check on his men's conditions. A few minutes later while he was speaking with one of the injured soldiers Private Webster politely interrupted him.

"Sir, several men came out from town and want to speak with you."

"What do they want?" Major Lewis asked impatiently. "We're here to get our soldiers flown out, not deal with their problems right now."

"They said that they were expecting you, sir," Private Webster said meekly, sensing his superior officer's aggravation at being disturbed.

"Expecting me? I don't remember having any appointments on my calendar today. Tell them to wait at a distance. I don't want anyone interfering with us right now."

"Okay, sir. They want to speak with the person in charge and said they thought you were here for the Americans."

"Americans?" Major Lewis asked as he looked toward the ramshackle village. He wondered why anyone would be there, let alone any Americans. "Warner! Where's the helicopter?"

"Less than ten minutes, sir."

"Alright, Private Webster, tell them we'll meet with them shortly. I don't know of any missing soldiers around here."

"Yes, sir."

Major Lewis went back to attending to his troops until he heard the thundering helicopter approach. He directed the loading and stabilizing of the men and ignored the raging dust cloud as they lifted back off into the sky. Once they were under way he stalked off to find Private Webster and deal with next situation.

"Alright, what's their story?"

"They say they are holding two young Americans. A few days ago they stopped a van traveling nearby and when they searched it they found two men wearing shalwar-kameez who were clearly not Afghans. Several of the townspeople accosted them and accused them of being spies. They let the others go. The two men initially claimed they were doing humanitarian work and then said they were tourists. They are being held in town."

Major Lewis again looked toward the dwellings. It seemed unlikely that the locals would be making up a story like this or that this was some kind of trap.

"Okay, let's get a few men and go see what we've got. I can't believe there'd be some stray do-gooders way out here, but who knows. Private Webster, tell them that we'll go with them. Let them know that if anything strange happens we'll flatten what's left of their town. I'm not putting anyone else on a helicopter today. Once we get there they need to bring them out into an open area."

"Will do, sir," Private Webster replied.

The locals led Major Lewis and his soldiers to a group of interconnected shanties. One of the Afghans directed the others to retrieve the prisoners. They returned leading two young men with their hands bound behind their backs and loose shackles jingling around their ankles. It took a moment for their eyes to adjust to the bright sunlight.

Seeing Major Lewis standing in front of them one of the two men finally spoke, "Jeez, what took you guys so long? We've been stuck in this dump for like days now, man."

"Who are you?" Major Lewis asked, not appreciating the tone the prisoner used to address him.

"I'm Luke Winslow and this is Garrett Davenport. We're both American citizens. Can you tell them to let us go now?" he said, lifting an ankle to highlight the bindings.

"Where are you from and what in the hell are you doing here?" Major Lewis responded, ignoring the request.

"I'm from Connecticut and he's from Pennsylvania. We came over here to help out and were taking a tour of the country when we got hi-jacked, man."

"Help out?"

"We were looking to do some, like, volunteer work or something, but when we got here there wasn't much available. We met a guy in Kabul that was running tours across the country so we decided to see the sights until something else panned out. The first couple of days were pretty cool and then these guys Shanghai'd us, but let Fritz go - with all of our money and stuff of course. Very *un*cool."

"Fritz was your tour guide I take it?"

"Yeah. He seemed like a good dude. Said he had relatives all over the country that we could stay with. Somehow we kept sleeping in the van though."

"You should really check references next time," Major Lewis said facetiously.

"Definitely, man. He did get us these sweet man jammies to wear though."

Major Lewis shook his head in disbelief. "You do know that you are in Afghanistan, right?"

"Sure."

"And that it's dangerous and unstable?"

"That's part of the reason we came - to see it first person. But the U.S. is running this show so we figured we'd be okay."

"What we're running are combat operations. I just had two of my men blown up this morning."

"Sorry to hear that, man."

"So what's his story? Does he talk?" Major Lewis said, motioning to the other prisoner. After listening to Winslow he wondered if he even wanted to hear anything from the friend.

"I can talk," Davenport muttered.

"He's been a bit under the weather. Caught a little stomach bug when we first got here and hasn't been able to fully recharge since."

"Sounds like you guys have really been having a nice little vacation. Now that the cavalry has arrived, what's your plan?"

"I think we've seen enough of this place so we were hoping to hitch a ride back to Kabul and then head back to the States."

"How are you planning to pay for that?" Major Lewis asked.

"We pay taxes, man," Winslow joked. "But once we get to Kabul we can get some money wired and I'll hook you up."

Major Lewis appreciated the fact that Winslow would actually consider paying for his transport. "We don't run a taxi service, but we'll see about getting you home. And we might be able to scrounge up an IV for Mr. Davenport here. Do you guys still have passports?"

"They do," Winslow said, motioning to the locals who were watching the conversation. "Fritz was nice enough not to take those."

Major Lewis turned to Private Webster. "Alight, let's see what we can negotiate here. We need to get moving."

They summoned the highest ranking local official and walked out of earshot of the two prisoners.

"Ask them if we can see the passports to confirm who these guys are," Major Lewis instructed.

Private Webster passed along the message and one of the men quickly produced the documents from a pocket inside his shirt. Major Lewis verified the names and handed them to Private Webster.

"Tell them that we will take these men into custody and determine whether or not they should be released or detained. Let them know that we are not carrying much to compensate them for their efforts, but we will bring them additional supplies in a few weeks when we return to this area."

The men discussed the offer among themselves for a moment and then replied via the translator.

"Sir, they appreciate the offer, but would prefer if we could do them a favor now instead."

"What's that?"

"They want our medical officer to examine two children that were recently injured while playing on the mountainside."

"Not that I really want to take these two stooges back with us, but I can't turn down kids." He looked at his watch again. "Alright, I guess we have some time. Call in Lieutenant Gillum and have them lead us to the patients." He turned and hollered toward the prisoners, "Hold tight, fellas, we need to take care of something first."

They radioed for the medic and followed the local men through town. Inside one of the huts made out of corrugated metal and deteriorating plywood they found a woman tending to two small children who were lying on the floor. She was ecstatic when she saw the Americans enter. She jumped up and began talking quickly.

"Yes, we're here to help," Private Webster assured her. "Please calm down and tell us what happened."

She continued to talk quickly and speak with her hands.

"She said that the kids were playing and some large rocks came down on them. The boy was pinned down by his leg and the girl was hit in the head and arm."

Major Lewis surveyed the limp children and could see a significant amount of swelling as well as bruising on their already dark skin.

"Tell her that we will do what we can and that the medic will be here in a minute," Major Lewis said, hoping that Lieutenant Gillum would be able to provide good news in a quick fashion.

Lieutenant Gillum soon appeared and began examining the little boy first. "His leg is definitely broken, but most of the other injuries are superficial. I should be able to set the leg in a decent cast and treat the other wounds."

He then checked the girl. One eye was swollen shut, but when he pried it open she still had adequate vision. He then unwrapped the bloody makeshift bandage on her hand and saw the gruesome damage. Her hand was a swollen, oozing mess with the remnants of fingers splayed out in unnatural directions. The soldiers all cringed, but tried not to display their concern for the sake of the mother.

"What do you think, Lieutenant Gillum?" Major Lewis asked.

"We're going to have to take it off, sir."

"Where?"

Lieutenant Gillum looked it over again. "I could probably do forearm, but elbow would be the best."

"Alright, tell her, Private," Major Lewis said, gesturing toward the woman.

He began to explain what they needed to do and the woman immediately began to cry and get hysterical. The children both lay motionless despite their mother's reaction. Luckily, several neighbors intervened and tried to calm her down. Still sobbing, she went over to each of the children and embraced them. She told them to be strong and that these men would help them. The senior local official confirmed that they agreed to treatment and Lieutenant Gillum quickly began setting up his equipment.

One thing that Major Lewis had observed during his time in different countries was that there was a universal awe of the Americans' medical abilities. Despite a lack of education and in the face of varying religious beliefs they understood that the Americans always took care of their own and even extended their expertise to their injured enemies.

Lieutenant Gillum cleaned and set the boy's leg first. The child let out a cry of pain when the bone was being positioned, but otherwise was incredibly quiet during the ordeal. Gillum then turned the boy over to his assistant to finish cleaning the other wounds.

Major Lewis carried the little girl to a cot they had set up near the door in order to provide adequate lighting for the procedure. He then instructed Private Webster to have most of the onlookers that had gathered to move away.

Although the girl was young and severely injured, Lieutenant Gillum had unfortunately seen worse.

"Are you going to be able to put her under?" Major Lewis asked.

"It's going to be tricky. I'm going to jack her with some local anesthesia in the arm and then dose her with some via IV. The removal will be pretty quick, but I need to spend some time closing everything up."

"Take your time and do it right," Major Lewis said, ignoring the urge to look at his watch. "We've got plenty of time."

Lieutenant Gillum methodically conducted his work while the others waited. Major Lewis put in a call to MacKenzie to provide a status update. Another hour passed before Lieutenant Gillum finished. He gave a thorough list of post-op instructions to the mother via the translator and left a full supply of antibiotics and extra bandages.

During that time Winslow and Davenport were held back in their quarters. Initially they protested, but Major Lewis told them that he didn't want to be presumptive about their release. If something went wrong with the girl's operation he knew that they would need to renegotiate their agreement.

When the mother determined that both children were going to be fine she heaped praise on Lieutenant Gillum in front of the others. Immediately, they summoned the prisoners and let Major Lewis know that they were free to go. From the looks on the locals' faces it appeared that they were very glad to be handing the two men off. Based on his initial conversation with them, Major Lewis could probably tell why.

They unlocked the ankle bindings and untied the prisoners' hands. Both men showed relief and wiggled their limbs freely.

"Alright, Private. Cuff them in front," Major Lewis directed.

"Dude!" Winslow exclaimed as Private Webster approached.

"You're *our* prisoners now. The base said you aren't on any terrorist lists, but until I get some better information you will remain restrained. Furthermore, if you make any wrong moves around my men or put them in danger in any way we will punish you accordingly. That includes leaving you two *dudes* on the side of the road. Are we clear, Mr. Winslow?"

"Yes, sir," Winslow said politely.

Davenport just nodded.

Major Lewis noted the "sir" in Winslow's response and felt certain the message had been received.

The locals seemed to delight in the little show and were snickering amongst themselves as Private Webster re-cuffed the men. The mood in the town had shifted drastically in the preceding hours and the locals invited the American troops to stay for dinner.

Major Lewis did not want to be rude, but he knew they had to return to MacKenzie. "Private Webster. Tell them thanks for the offer. Unfortunately we have to leave. Hopefully in the future we will be able to return and take them up on it. Let them know that we will be sure to check on the children. Also, tell them that in two to three months we will be bringing her a prosthetic arm. Make sure they understand that the arm will be paid for by Mr. Winslow and Mr. Davenport."

As Private Webster finished the locals clapped and surrounded the prisoners, patting them on the chest and back.

Winslow gave Major Lewis a confused look.

"You said you came here to help, right?" Major Lewis asked. "I just gave you the opportunity to put your money where your mouth is. The U.S. taxpayer is going to have to pay for your ride back to Kabul. When you get there I am going to put you in touch with some people who will help you acquire a new arm for that little girl that Lieutenant Gillum saved today."

"Will do, sir," Winslow nodded in agreement.

They said their final goodbyes and joined the rest of the soldiers to depart. It had already been a long day and they still had a few hours of driving ahead of them. Major Lewis had no interest in spending that time with his two new acquisitions so he had them placed in another vehicle. He enjoyed the ride back to MacKenzie in silence.

***

The next morning Major Lewis met Captain Roth in the command center. They had returned late and Major Lewis had sent Winslow and Davenport to a containment quarters until he could figure out what to do with them.

They first reviewed the attack and went over intelligence reports that Captain Roth had gathered. There had been no recent reports of insurgents operating in that area and nothing that would predict an assault of that scale. Major Lewis wasn't sure if they were dealing with a random attack or the start of a summer offensive. Either way he wasn't going to have his patrols become target practice for the enemy.

Captain Roth reminded him that even in "peaceful" times U.S. forces often came under attack here. He also pointed out the fact that Major Lewis's team could have been the one that took the hit. "I understand that you like being out on the lines with the men, sir. But MacKenzie keeps growing and at some point you are going to have to focus on being an operational leader more than a field leader," Captain Roth lectured.

"I know, Captain Roth," Major Lewis replied, in no way offended by his subordinate's comment. "It's hard for me though. That was a brutal day out there yesterday. Still, I felt like that was exactly where I needed to be. It's hard enough to deal with losing our men, but to do it from back here is even tougher."

"My concern is for you as well as your career. Regional command is going to want you delegating more of the offsite duties.

When I called in yesterday they appeared to be questioning what you were doing out there."

Captain Roth knew from a selfish prospective that Major Lewis's actions served to keep him safe from the front line. However, he also accepted the chain of command and was more than willing to do his job when and where necessary.

"So what else did you find out about Tweedledum and Tweedledee?" Major Lewis asked, changing the topic.

"Garrett Davenport appears to be a run-of-the-mill slacker. However, Luke Winslow is a different story. Look at this," Captain Roth said, handing Major Lewis several pages.

Major Lewis flipped through them and scanned quickly. "You've got to be kidding me," he said in astonishment. "Are you sure this is the right guy?"

"It has to be. The dates, addresses, photos - they all match up."

"Wow. This is quite a résumé. I guess I know what we need to do now."

"What's that, sir?"

"See the boy in action," Major Lewis answered.

"I can't wait."

They continued on with their work and dealt with the serious tasks at hand regarding the casualties and wounded soldiers. At least Major Lewis was now looking forward to his next meeting with Winslow much more than he had been.

***

After lunch, Major Lewis headed out to the driving range and started hitting golf balls. He was pleased with the improvements that had been made since his arrival. The area had been expanded and the new mats bristled with a brilliant green. Besides the balls that he had imported initially, they had also received several boxes of donations so the quality of their ammunition was greatly improved. What really took their facility to the next level, however, was the installation of the Lexan bus shelters. These panels bracketed the hitting areas, which allowed the bays to be segregated. This protected the players from the threat of sniper fire as well as the golfers next to them.

Major Lewis continued to hit even as he heard Winslow and Davenport approach. "Good afternoon, Mr. Winslow," he said before sending another shot down range.

"Nice facility you got here, man," Winslow said with honest admiration.

"I'm glad you like it," Major Lewis said, leaning on his club and turning toward the men. "Probably doesn't measure up to the high end country clubs up there in Connecticut, though."

"So you did your homework I take it?"

"It's pretty hard to hide these days, even in Afghanistan. Of all the things I imagined I'd come across in this country the number one ranked amateur golfer in the state of Connecticut would not have been high on the list."

"It's a small state," Winslow replied in his first show of modesty.

"You're also ranked in the top twenty-five in the entire United States."

"Yeah, but I haven't really been posting many scores lately."

"I guess it's a bit difficult to get your rounds in when you're shackled in a third world hut," Major Lewis said, turning to the silent partner. "You're looking better already, Mr. Davenport. It's amazing what a bag of electrolytes can do for a fella."

"I appreciate what your men did for me, sir," Davenport replied in a reserved, but healthy voice.

"Nonetheless, I don't imagine you want to stay around here. You want to go home don't you?"

"Yes, sir. Very much."

"Well, you're in luck. We've lined up a couple of options in fact. We have a luxurious helicopter ride or a scenic transport convoy set up for next week. The first option will be a lot quicker and is probably safer, too. But rather than letting you choose I thought we'd make it a tad more interesting. I'm sure Mr. Winslow can beat any one of us straight up in golf, but we do have some big hitters out here at

MacKenzie. This gentleman over here is Private Charles Maynard, the base's reigning long drive champion. If you can out hit him you two will be flying to Kabul in style. What do you think, boys?"

Winslow sized up Private Maynard briefly. "What are the rules?"

"Simple. I'll let you warm up and when you're ready it's one drive. We've got a couple of good drivers. I'll let you choose, including mine. I have two brand new Titleists so you hit the same ball, no tricks."

"Let me see your driver," Winslow said to Major Lewis, who happily passed it over. He studied it for a moment and looked at the adjustable hosel. "Do you have the wrench?"

"Sure do," Major Lewis replied, producing a small pouch from his golf bag.

Winslow quickly cranked the torque wrench and made a modification to the club's set up. He took a stance, looked at it, and made a few waggles.

"Alright, let's do it," he said confidently.

"Is this a joke?" Davenport interjected, suddenly looking sick again at the thought of possibly spending more time on the winding back roads of Afghanistan.

"Quite serious. Do you think we're all business? We have to have some fun out here," Major Lewis explained. "Now, I hadn't thought about proper golf attire. I see you are still wearing your Halloween costumes. Would you prefer some shorts and a T-shirt?"

"No need. These things are seriously comf', man. Free swinging," he said, taking practice swings back and forth.

"Seriously *comf*, eh? You sound a lot more like a surfer than a golfer," Major Lewis noted.

"I surf, too. That's the main reason I went to school in California. That, and the fact that it's a long way from Connecticut."

"Well, we don't have any waves out here to compete on. Besides, Charlie doesn't surf, do you?"

"No, sir," Private Maynard answered.

"So golf it is!" Major Lewis proclaimed.

Winslow began a gradual warm up with Major Lewis's 5-iron while Private Maynard continued to pound balls unmercifully. Winslow looked like a golf Messiah hitting one perfect shot after another with his long, flowing frock blowing in the desert breeze. Winslow was just over six feet tall and looked long and lean. He was very much the prototype of many current top golfers: good height with adequate muscle tone, but not overbuilt. His shaggy brown hair would have looked at home under a logo visor. The unshaven face was patchy and scraggly and could possibly be converted to an acceptable goatee at best.

When he started to hit the driver he began with perfectly straight, line-drives and worked his way to a high draw that rode the wind for maximum distance. They were not going as far as Private Maynard's shots; however, Major Lewis sensed that Winslow was working at perhaps seventy-five to eighty percent.

Major Lewis was enjoying the show, but decided it was time for the main event. "Ready?"

"Let's do it," Winslow said excitedly. He seemed to have changed personas and was now in his competitive game mode.

Major Lewis flipped a coin and Winslow won. "We'll let Private Maynard have the honors."

The tension started to build as Private Maynard took the tee and Major Lewis tossed him a brand new ball. "Alright, these things are expensive, make it count."

Private Maynard had plenty of confidence and he knew there was really nothing riding on this, but he could still feel his nerves reacting. He lined up from behind and visualized his shot before taking a final practice swing. He hammered the ball and it took off on a great trajectory before drifting slightly to the right. Everyone there knew the fade would cost him distance. Next to the teeing area one of the sniper spotters targeted and located the ball. They sighted it with a laser and checked the distance relative to the yardages marked on the range.

"Three hundred twenty-six yards," the soldier declared.

"Not my best," Private Maynard said with disappointment.

"Nice shot," Winslow commented as he took the tee. He went through his routine, ratcheting up the power with each practice swing. After addressing the ball, he showed no hesitation and then hit a shot that seemed to carry forever. The ball hit and lurched forward with top spin. Without waiting for the measurement call he walked back and returned the driver to Major Lewis. "I've never flown on a helicopter before. I'm looking forward to it."

Major Lewis looked to the spotter. "Well?"

"Three seventy-two."

Major Lewis shook his head with a mix of admiration and disgust.

11

As soon as Major Lewis learned about Winslow's background the wheels in his head had begun spinning. The timing of their encounter had been fortuitous. Major Lewis and Major Cierra had scheduled a team golf match between MacKenzie and Ross for the coming Saturday and now Major Lewis had a secret weapon. The real question was whether or not he could just use Winslow for some teaching and coaching or if he could legitimately include him on the MacKenzie team.

The matches were going to be Afghan modified versions of the Ryder Cup event. They were going to be playing again in Ughust, but had selected the name Khana Cup for alliterative purposes. Major Cierra had already boldly predicted that the name would soon be changing to the Ross Cup. The two majors had determined the golf format and rules, but there had not been much discussion about the team composition as the pool was assumed to be pretty limited.

Following the Long-Drive-to-Kabul contest Major Lewis secured Winslow's commitment to play for MacKenzie. He was more than willing and knew there wasn't much else to do before he departed. Major Lewis had some reservations about taking a civilian back outside of the base, but those were being outweighed by his desire to beat Camp Ross. If Michael Jordan agreed to be on your pick-up basketball team you certainly couldn't leave him at home.

The next hurdle was making sure that Major Cierra wouldn't cry foul when they showed up with a ringer. He didn't want to speak with his rival via phone as that would give Cierra too much time to prod for details. Instead he decided to sneak it into a confirmation e-mail that he was already planning to send. He simply noted, "I have a new guy at Mackenzie who seems pretty good. Are you okay if we bring him to play?"

Major Cierra replied and confirmed the event information. He added, "I'm fine with the new guy as long as he's not a *professional*."

Seizing upon the clear demarcation between amateur and professional status in golf, Major Lewis quickly replied. "Nope. He's good, but definitely not a *professional*." He was now confident that Major Cierra would gripe, but not be able to disallow Winslow's spot on the team.

In the two days leading up to the matches Winslow spent much of his time at the range. He hit almost no shots himself, however. Instead, he was coaching Major Lewis's other players to prepare them for the event and even giving instruction to other soldiers who were just beginners. When word spread that a highly talented visitor was giving free lessons interest in golf at the base spiked. Major Lewis didn't want to work his horse too hard and let Winslow know that he wasn't obligated to keep teaching. Winslow said it was his pleasure and was happy to spend all the time he could with the men.

Davenport was still in recovery mode and happily spent much of his time resting in his room trying to stay cool.

* * *

On match day the group left early as there would be both a morning and an afternoon session. Despite the departure time, a number of soldiers were up to send them off. Major Lewis was extremely pleased at how much importance the Khana Cup had taken on and he owed much of it to Winslow.

Major Lewis had once again enlisted Zemar and his friends as caddies. He thought it would be another good cultural exchange to see the spirit of the matches between the two camps. In the vein of "economic stimulus" he had also commissioned Zemar to acquire or produce a trophy for the event. For inspiration he provided Zemar with printouts that showed the actual Ryder Cup as well as several other major trophies.

When they stopped to pick up Zemar he was holding a small canvas bag and a roll of paper tied with a string.

"Good morning, Zemar. What's in the bag?" Major Lewis asked with curiosity.

139

"The Khana Cup, Ajani," he replied, using the nickname he had given Major Lewis. Zemar walked over to Major Lewis's truck and proudly removed the prize from the bag. It was a shiny, bronze-toned chalice with a wide mouth and a thin stem. The cup was mounted on a small, round slab of marble.

"That's awesome, Zemar," Major Lewis said as he hefted the trophy and turned it in his hands. "Did you make this?"

"I got the cup from a family that owed me some money and bought the marble from another guy. I just put the two together. No big deal."

"It's exactly what I was looking for. Did I give you enough money to cover the cost?"

"Yeah, I owe you some change," Zemar said, reaching into his pocket.

"Keep it, Zemar. You definitely earned it," Major Lewis said, still marveling at the trophy and feeling even more inspired to win it today. "What's that?" he added, motioning to the roll under Zemar's arm.

"That something for you, Ajani," he said, handing it over. "You can open it later. It's just another drawing I did. My friends and I appreciate your business and I thought you might like it."

"Thanks, Zemar. I'll check it out later. Why don't you guys get in and we'll get moving."

***

When they arrived at Ughust and began unloading, Zemar noticed Winslow, who was back in his shalwar kameez, and nudged Major Lewis. "Who's he, Ajani?"

"That's our ringer, Zemar."

"Ringer?"

"He's an extremely good player, one of the best in the United States in fact, and he's going to play for us. Since he's almost certain to win his matches that makes him our 'ringer'. What's even better is what a surprise it will be for Major Cierra."

Zemar nodded and could appreciate the role of the ringer from the excitement shown on Major Lewis's face.

Winslow had finally changed clothes while at MacKenzie, but had willingly changed back into local garb for the match. Major Lewis thought it would add even more to the memories of the first Khana Cup.

Major Cierra and his men had arrived early and already had the course checked and set up. An additional putting green had been established after the sixth hole so they would do half of the putting before turning back. Cierra had brought additional soldiers to serve as their caddies and contribute support to his team. They had an air of superiority about them as Major Lewis marched his own motley mix of men and boys toward the staging area.

"Good morning, Ray," Major Lewis said, shaking hands and ceremoniously placing the Khana Cup on the hood of Cierra's truck. "Looks like the greens keeper was out early this morning. Everything look alright?"

"Morning, Johnny. I think we're in good shape. We did some sweeps and didn't see anything. It doesn't look like anyone's been out here."

Most of the men knew each other so there were brief hellos and Major Lewis quickly introduced Winslow. "Gentleman, this is Luke Winslow, the new guy. Why don't you all go get warmed up and I'll finish going over the lineups with Major Cierra," he said shooing the players off. He spent a moment savoring the look on Major Cierra's face.

"Who the hell is that?" Major Cierra said, clearly looking for a punch line to the joke.

"I told you. He's the new guy," Major Lewis replied innocently.

"Why is one of your soldiers dressed like a local? Is he CIA or something?"

"He's not one of my soldiers. We picked him and another guy up a few days ago. Turns out he's a pretty good golfer. He's an American and you said he could play."

"Alright, Johnny. I'll play along. Let's get going. I want to win this nice trophy you brought me," he said, admiring the cup and rolling it in his hands.

"Nice, eh? Zemar did us right." He restrained his trash talk, letting his friend utter as many words as he wanted. He was plenty confident that Cierra would be eating them before sundown.

The morning matches were going to be team format. Each camp would have three, two-man teams. The first round would be twelve holes of foursomes. Next would be twelve holes of alternate shot. Following a lunch break there would be afternoon singles matches.

Major Lewis had strategically placed Winslow with his weakest player in the foursomes as he knew Winslow could carry anyone. They were the first group to go out and everyone gathered to watch them tee off. Winslow's partner led off and hit a less than stellar shot.

"No worries. I've got you partner," Winslow said confidently as he took the tee box and smashed a perfect ball down into the desert.

"Come on!" growled Major Cierra in disbelief.

As surprised as he had been before, his expression now was truly priceless.

"Good luck, boys," Major Lewis said as they strode away. "I'm feeling pretty good about that pairing," he continued, turning to savor Major Cierra's disgust.

"I'll ask you again, Johnny. Who the hell is that?"

"I already told you. One of the best young golfers in America who just happened to wander into Uruzgan Province in time to compete for the Khana Cup. And yes, I can prove he's an amateur. I brought some newspaper stories about him - should make for good reading on your way home."

Major Cierra was clearly fuming. He knew what would have been a good battle, but decidedly in his favor, had just been tilted decisively the other way. Major Lewis had fully expected his friend to be surprised, but he was beyond pleased to see that Cierra was visibly rattled.

In terms of lineup, the two commanding officers had agreed to be in the clean-up group in the team events and would also play the final singles match. As they played their foursomes round together, Cierra was notably quiet. Major Lewis knew his opponent was trying to focus, but also knew that Cierra played better when he was in a jovial, social golf mode. Cierra managed to play well enough to hold on for their team and after putting did win the point. The congratulations from Major Lewis were not well received as Winslow had destroyed the other team and MacKenzie's final team had unexpectedly taken the third match for a point.

In the alternate shot format Major Lewis decided to adjust his teams. He paired himself with Winslow for two reasons. First, he felt that together they could beat Cierra's best pairing. Second, he unabashedly wanted the chance to play together with a golfer of Winslow's caliber. He would have preferred the opportunity to do it on a real course over eighteen holes, but he certainly wasn't going to pass on this option.

The first matches had gone around at a good pace and it was mid-morning when they began the second loop. The sun was gaining strength and the temperature was rising quickly. Before heading out the men replenished their water supplies and slathered on extra sunscreen. Winslow took his already outlandish outfit to a new level by adding a wide-brimmed, camouflage boonie hat and a pair of aviator sunglasses. He was now the golf sheik of the Ughust Valley.

From the first shot Major Lewis felt confidence like he hadn't in a long time in his matches against Major Cierra. Winslow was able to put them in perfect position and if Major Lewis hit a stray shot his partner had no problem righting the ship. Major Lewis didn't want to bother Winslow, who seemed quite focused. He didn't mind quietly watching golf being played at a different level, but did strike up conversations when it felt natural.

"This is obviously a lot different than your normal playing conditions, however, it doesn't appear that you are having any problem adjusting," Major Lewis commented after Winslow hit another amazing shot off the hard pan surface.

"You just have to modify a few elements of the swing and change your expectation level. You play the ball back in the stance a bit so you can hit it clean and keep the lower body quiet. Then try and hit *good* shots, not necessarily *great* shots."

"If these are just good I can't image what your great shots look like on an actual course. You're striking the ball so well."

"The real difference is that I don't have a lot of versatility out here. I'm trying to hit every one straight with a middle trajectory. If I try to hit high fades or low draws then you'd see some squirrely shots. You're hitting the ball pretty well yourself, Major."

One thing Major Lewis had noticed was that Winslow lost a lot of his surfer-speak and attitude when he was playing. It was tough to tell which version was the true persona.

"Thanks. I'm just trying to hold my own against the competition," Major Lewis said, motioning toward Major Cierra.

"Competition? You mean those guys? We've got them covered, no worries, Major," he said confidently with a nod to Major Lewis.

Major Lewis hated to admit it, but Winslow had really grown on him the last few days. Major Lewis had had a similar experience with an embedded photographer in Iraq. Initially Major Lewis saw him only as a burden, but that changed as he got to know the man and saw his work. Despite having very different opinions about politics and the war, the two men eventually found common ground and developed a mutual respect. "I want to thank you again for working with my men the last few days and coming out here today."

"It's been my pleasure. Of all the things I thought I'd be doing over here, this is one of the last things I would have imagined. The truth is I'm enjoying the game more than I have in a very long time."

"Spending any time in this country puts everything else in perspective."

"That's part of it. I also think I just needed to get out of my element. I've never been around soldiers before. Your men are a lot different than I expected. I sort of thought the foot soldiers would be kids from the 'hood here because they have no place else to go. But everyone I've met is smart and professional. I've taught kids before, but they're all like me - privileged. They felt like they deserved everything they got. Your guys show real appreciation."

"We do have some 'hood boys. However, you can't judge them just by their address. Most of them are good men that unfortunately grew up in difficult circumstances. They see the military as an opportunity to escape, not just something to do for a few years. Regardless, the true demographics of the armed forces would surprise you. The 'poor get sent to war' perception is a vestige of times past. We no longer have a draft and the modern battlefield is a vastly different place."

"You guys do have some wicked equipment."

"I'm a definite believer in fighting smarter rather than harder."

"Well, I have a lot of respect for what you're doing out here. People have told me that I have a killer instinct on the golf course. That may be true, but I don't think I could ever kill someone. Maybe, like in self-defense, if someone attacked me. That's it."

"I'm not going to ask you to shoot anyone, but I do expect you to help me kill Major Cierra today."

"Yes, sir!" Winslow barked in response.

Major Cierra and his partner were playing well given the circumstances. However, they were clearly outgunned in the match up. Major Cierra was walking alone toward one of the target greens when Major Lewis decided to peel off and join him.

"Anything new down at Camp Ross?" Major Lewis asked.

"You already know what is going on at Ross. Don't come over here to gloat."

"I wasn't going to gloat. You guys are playing great."

"Yeah, and still losing," Major Cierra pointed out.

"Come on, Ray. Don't be bitter. If you'd found him first you know he'd be on your team today."

Major Cierra shrugged, not wanting to answer. "Yeah, you're right. That doesn't make me feel any better though."

"Just take it in and enjoy the show. Think of him as a goodwill golf ambassador. He's not like most of the kids we know in that age group. It is interesting to juxtapose him against our guys. I thought he was a complete punk until I saw him spending time giving my soldiers lessons. Now I realize he's a decent guy, despite the abrasive first impression."

"How long do you have him?"

"We're flying him and his pal out in two days. If I had him a little longer I'd gladly lend him to you."

"Thanks, Johnny. We'll see what he's really done for you in the singles where you won't have him to bail you out."

"It kind of a sounds like you are conceding this match already," Major Lewis teased.

"I'm not conceding anything," Major Cierra said, stomping away toward his ball.

Two holes later the match was over...

By lunchtime MacKenzie had a solid four to two lead. With six singles matches in the afternoon session there were still a lot of points available. Major Lewis was happy with his line-up and he would be playing the anchor match against Major Cierra.

Following the short break the singles matches headed out one by one. Despite the heat, Major Lewis could see the energy flowing in his players. The men from Ross looked flat. Besides the play of Winslow, the Mackenzie team was also getting a surprising boost from their caddies. The young Afghanis were starting to learn the game and were showing support for their players. The caddies' respectful cheering could be heard across the matches and proved unsettling for Ross's golfers. It was like a professional golf tournament where a distant burst of applause would cause a player to back off from their shot.

Zemar had come into his own as a caddie. He quickly picked up terminology and was always trying to learn the rules and nuances of the game. A baseball cap and towel over his shoulder helped him look the part.

"Ajani, it looks like your plan was successful. Is Major Cierra mad at you though?"

"He's a little cranky. He came here expecting to win and it's not going to happen so he needs to adjust. He'll get over it."

"I think you deserve to win. You came up with a better strategy."

"That and the fact that I have a better caddie," Major Lewis said, patting Zemar on the shoulder. Zemar turned and smiled at the compliment and fatherly gesture. The interchange also made Major Lewis suddenly realize just how much he missed his own son. His dealings with Winslow recently had already led him to consider his role as a father.

With each tour, being away from his family became more and more difficult for Major Lewis. He knew it was wrong to supplant those emotional shortcomings via Zemar. He also knew better than to get too close with anyone in a war zone. Emotional ties could cloud judgment, which was unacceptable when decisions were often truly life or death.

"Ajani, tell me about Mr. Winslow. Why is he here?"

"That's a good question, Zemar. From what I can tell he was running away and this is where it led him."

"Running away from what? Was someone chasing him?"

"Maybe not so much running away as looking for something."

"The United States has everything. What couldn't he find there?"

"I know it's hard to believe, but even people who have every material thing they could want can still feel like something is missing. He has some family issues as well. He wanted to put some space between him and his father. I guess Afghanistan was about as far away as he could get."

"Did his father beat him?" Zemar asked matter-of-factly.

"I doubt it. My guess is that his dad pushed him a lot in ways that he thought were important, but Mr. Winslow did not necessarily agree. Golf was likely one of those things."

"He should be glad he has a dad," Zemar said jealously.

"I agree. Hopefully he'll come to that conclusion as well before too long. So tell me about your new picture," Major Lewis added.

"It's something I've been working on and thought you might like it. It is a gift, no charge."

"Thank you, Zemar. I'm sure I'll love it. You are very talented and create some amazing artwork. In the U.S. we have a number of art schools where you can develop your skills and learn new ones. I did some checking and unfortunately there don't seem to be many facilities like that in Afghanistan."

"Of course not. Even now art is seen as a threat. Anything that allows and promotes self expression must be discouraged. Sometimes people look at my work and tell me how much they like it. Then they won't buy any because they're afraid if they display it someone might interpret some improper message. It becomes very frustrating."

"Don't let it stop you, Zemar. You have a gift and you shouldn't have to hide it."

"I'll try, Ajani."

***

When the two senior officers finally had the tee, Major Cierra's mood had improved. He seemed to have already acknowledged the eventual outcome of the competition and now just wanted to enjoy the round with his friend. Reverting to his more jovial playing style, Major Cierra felt better and golfed better.

The sun started to slide away as the afternoon wore on. The final pairing worked their way back toward the starting area where the rest of the players had gathered. Word had already come back to them that their match was now moot. MacKenzie's players had continued their dominance and already cleared the six and half point threshold needed to win the Khana Cup.

As the two leaders walked up the final hole one of the soldiers picked up a bull horn and formally announced their arrival. Both of the Majors tipped their hats and acknowledged the small crowd. They finished up and tallied the points before Major Cierra hosted the award ceremony.

"I of course wanted to thank everyone for being out here today. Hopefully everyone had a good time on another balmy Afghan day. Special thanks also go to our local friend, Zemar, for sourcing the perfect prize.

Before we have the official presentation let me first recognize my former good friend, Major Lewis. He is obviously the recipient of our stealth captain award for sneaking in Mr. Winslow over there. As we all now know it was a strategic master stroke. That being said, which had to be said, I do also want to congratulate the rest of the Mackenzie men for playing great matches. Nice job fellas."

He paused for a moment of polite applause.

"Now for the hardware," Major Cierra said, holding up the trophy. "In recognition of a fine victory, I'm pleased to present the Khana Cup to the captain of team Mackenzie, Major John Lewis."

There was more applause along with a mix of victory barks from team Mackenzie as the two majors exchanged a sincere handshake.

"Thanks, Ray. I too want to congratulate our players and thank our caddies. It's a great honor to win today and be taking the Khana Cup back to Mackenzie. In some ways I hope this will be the only time we are all here to play for it. If and when we do have a chance to compete again I look forward to the opportunity to defend it."

***

It was well into the evening when the MacKenzie team arrived back at base. They received a warm welcome from the soldiers that were still up and about. The enthusiasm grew when they found out that the team had achieved victory and brought home the Cup.

Major Lewis was tired and he dragged himself and his clubs back to his quarters. He set everything down and then sat on his bed and cut the binding on Zemar's drawing. He unraveled the scroll and examined the drawing inside. True to Zemar's style, the picture consisted of a map of Afghanistan superimposed onto an Afghan man. It was incredibly ornate and Major Lewis marveled at how Zemar had woven the two images together. Rivers were wrapped down arms into blue veins and folds in the subject's clothing made up the gray, wavy peaks of the Hindu Kush Mountains. The man had one hand over his chest and was clutching his crimson heart that had morphed from the outline of the Day Kundi Province, just north of Uruzgan. There were small notations in the worm-like symbols of the Pashto alphabet that Major Lewis assumed represented locations on the map.

Major Lewis sat there for several moments noting the details and considering the image. One overriding thought kept coming through: what a tremendous talent was being wasted in the heart of Afghanistan.

***

Two days later Major Lewis was up early to see his visitors off on their trip to Kabul. He walked down to the helicopter pad where Winslow and Davenport were already waiting near their ride. Both men were now wearing military issue olive drab T-shirts and cargo shorts. They had no luggage, just small plastic bags sitting on the ground next to them.

"Good morning, fellas," Major Lewis said, shaking hands with each of them. "Taking some souvenirs home with you?" he asked, motioning toward the bags.

"This has been a remarkable trip, sir. That outfit is the only tangible thing I have to take back. I plan to wash them thoroughly and keep them around for special occasions - you know - like Halloween and observing Afghan holidays. I'll have to add a collared shirt if I want to wear them to the club though," Winslow said.

"So where are you going to go when you get back stateside?"

"I was living with some buddies in California so I'll stop there first. Then I'll probably head east to visit the family. I haven't seen them in a while."

"What about you, Mr. Davenport?" Major Lewis asked.

"I'm heading home. I'm going to have my mommy cook me food and I'm going to sleep in my own bed. I have a teaching job lined up in the fall, so I'm just going to relax until then."

"Sounds like a good plan."

"I may try the teaching route myself," Winslow said.

"Really?"

"I'm going to look into teaching golf. There's really a lot more in it when you have people that want to learn. Maybe I can find a program for adults or kids who actually appreciate it."

"Are you going to play at all?"

"I think I will. I'll need to get the game back in shape - you know - hit off of grass, putt on grass. There are a couple of amateur events in the late summer and fall that I'll shoot for."

"What about going pro?"

"Probably not. I've played in several regional professional events as an amateur and that lifestyle just isn't calling me right now."

"It's good that you can admit it."

The pilot returned and let them know that they were cleared for departure. He climbed in and fired up the engines.

"Gentleman, it has been an interesting week to say the least. I want to wish you the best and safe travels home."

"Thank you for everything, Major Lewis. You do a great and worthy job out here," Davenport said quietly.

"Thanks again for bailing us out and putting us up here at MacKenzie, Major. Keep yourself alive and get home to your family in one piece. I hope we get the chance to play again someday," Winslow said, looking Major Lewis directly in the eye.

"I'd like that very much," Major Lewis said as the chopper blades began to spin and the engine noise increased. "Time to go, boys. See ya'."

They ascended the stairs and strapped into their seats before giving a final wave goodbye.

Major Lewis watched as they rose into the air and then banked off into the distance.

12

Luke Winslow was apparently not just good, he was also lucky. Beginning the day after he flew out of Kabul a wave of violent attacks hit the capital. There were car bombings, suicide attacks, and direct assaults on government buildings and hotels. Most of them were targeting foreign individuals and interests. The U.S. forces in Kabul were strengthening their already tight security. These measures put everyone on edge and made interactions with the Afghans even tenser.

The high profile attacks garnered most of the attention, but as Major Lewis sat in the command center reading his briefing reports it appeared that the entire country was coming apart at the seams. Violence was increasing in the already volatile areas and new incidents were occurring in areas that had been relatively calm.

Major Lewis was preparing for two big events in the upcoming weeks. The first was providing logistical support and security for a public works project in the eastern part of their region. It was primarily road work and related infrastructure. These projects were particularly dangerous in Afghanistan and would normally be handled by Afghan security forces. Workers not only faced the threat of new attacks and mines, they also had to negotiate ordnances that had been accumulated during the decades of conflict along Afghanistan's major thoroughfares.

The second was the arrival of a group of soldiers who were being transferred to Uruzgan. The unit had been operating in north eastern Afghanistan along the Pakistan border. It was a region of secluded valleys that had been pacified, but was now experiencing renewed fighting. The Army decided that there were not adequate forces to send reinforcements to the area so the decision had been made to vacate instead. There was a buffer region outside of the area so the hope was that the problems would not spread significantly. Furthermore, a number of local militias had formed and senior military leaders assumed that the different factions would preoccupy each other until the U.S. could redeploy. The unit had suffered a number of casualties, including its commanding officer.

He looked up for a moment at the Khana Cup, now proudly displayed on a small shelf. The matches had been a victory for FOB Mackenzie, but in light of the country's deteriorating state the Cup had quickly lost some of its luster. He was glad that they had been able to play the event when they did. Major Lewis knew it was going to get very hectic and would be a while before he played again.

***

Major Lewis tried not to question his orders; however, it was difficult for him to understand who had approved road improvements during the summer. The area where they were working was a baked, flat plain of nothingness. The good news was that there was no place for the enemy to hide. The bad news was that there was no place for the soldiers to hide either. The men set up canopies and large umbrellas that offered only modest relief.

Based on the location and time frame, Major Lewis had established rolling shifts of soldiers to monitor the project. He was pleased that the road was close enough and a temporary camp location wasn't required for the soldiers. The engineering personnel who were staying at MacKenzie were also being ferried back and forth from the site. Each day a team would roll out early and return in the evening. Only the Afghan workers who had been hired as laborers camped in the area. Several men were being paid extra to provide night time security, however, Major Lewis questioned if any services were actually being provided.

Preliminary site work and bomb sweeps had already been conducted and the first several days had gone smoothly. Major Lewis visited the site and found what he expected: a handful of men doing a modest amount of work and a much larger group doing nothing. Other than the way they were dressed, it was highly reminiscent of every other road crew that Major Lewis had witnessed in action.

With work now underway, Major Lewis was hopeful that it was simply going to be a time consuming babysitting exercise. The hope proved short lived when two days later they received a frantic radio call from one of the soldiers at the site. He reported that there had been a massive explosion and that there were numerous dead and injured, including many of the MacKenzie troops.

Major Lewis quickly organized his team and set out for the location. As they cleared the mountains and reached the edge of the plain, Major Lewis saw a large, dark smoldering mess where the crew had been working. It looked like a giant fist had punched the earth and left a massive black eye.

The men quickly crossed the terrain, watching carefully for a potential attack. As they closed in Major Lewis saw several clusters of ragged looking men gathered near the burnt out debris and newly formed crater. What little movement there was seemed to be in slow motion.

Upon seeing the rescue team arrive, one of the surviving soldiers wandered toward the vehicles. He was stained with a combination of burns and soot and bleeding from several wounds. Major Lewis knew who he was, but had trouble recognizing him. Major Lewis helped the soldier sit down against the Humvee's tire while his troops rapidly fanned out to help the others.

"Corporal Rosen. What happened? Were you attacked?"

"No. They just blew it up, sir," Corporal Rosen said in a daze.

"Who are *they*?"

"Don't know. Must have been some of the workers," he continued as one of the medics hung an IV bag from the truck and fed a needle into his arm.

"Were they armed?"

"Not sure. A new fuel truck had just arrived. One of the graders was stuck on the side of the road so we had all gathered to help out. We heard engines rev and then the fuel truck slammed into one of the supply trucks that was coming from the other direction. There was a small explosion, but before I could get far there was a massive one. Everything from the supply truck went flying like shrapnel and then a giant fireball erupted. It was huge, sir. I've never seen anything like it. Luckily, I was somewhat shielded on the back side."

"Alright, just stay here and rest."

Major Lewis moved on and began to survey the twisted remains of the equipment. The scene brought on quick flashbacks from Iraq where he'd seen many similar scenes along the roads. Many times on patrol they would pass a bombed area that had been repaired, however, the black shadows were ghostly reminders of what had happened there. Those scars were already healing while this wound had just been inflicted.

The area was surprisingly quiet. Most of the noise was coming from his men who were treating the wounded. There were only a handful of survivors from the large group that had been working there and they were shell-shocked. The noxious fumes of scorched fuel and petroleum products were overwhelming. It masked, but could not conceal, the appalling scent of burnt flesh. There were bodies and limbs strewn in a pattern away from the spot where the blast had occurred. Some of the remains looked like incinerated scraps of what had earlier today been men. Major Lewis also saw corpses that had been hit by the shrapnel shower from the supply truck. Those bodies were mainly intact, but had holes punched directly through them or random chunks missing. They had the appearance of incomplete jigsaw puzzles.

His men already knew what to do for the survivors, so Major Lewis had time to examine the scene and contemplate his next step. In the mix of emotions now filling him, anger was certainly foremost. Anger toward the attackers, toward the people who scheduled the roadwork, toward the person who got the grader stuck. More senseless killing. Major Lewis wondered: *Who did this hurt?* The road would still be repaired, just by another crew that would pave through this mess. Major Lewis also pondered his next issue: *Who do you blame? Who do you punish?* It sounded like the perpetrators had driven the trucks and there was now nothing left of them. Some group might claim responsibility for the attacks; however, without any hard proof it would be difficult to know if they were behind it or just trying to garner attention. Major Lewis and his men would photograph the scene and write up their reports. Unfortunately they weren't able to do any forensic investigative work. Major Lewis also knew that resources from Kabul would not be sent to this remote location.

A few minutes later Major Lewis cleared all of the initial thoughts from his mind and focused on his job. He helped out with the few survivors and coordinated their action plans depending on the level of injury. Over the next few days a cleanup crew would be organized to clear the debris and patch the road. It would be at least several more weeks before new equipment could be sourced and a new road crew hired. Major Lewis was already dreading the order that he would receive to restart MacKenzie's involvement in the project.

On the way back to MacKenzie, Major Lewis was on the radio and following up on his injured and killed men. Such discussions were obviously never pleasant. This evening, though, he found himself particularly aggravated. The anger that he felt at the blast site had returned and grown. He had no proof of AKA's involvement in the attack. Nonetheless, the image of his adversary kept coming to the forefront of his mind.

***

Following the disastrous attack, MacKenzie was left mourning another loss and preparing to receive the group of transferred soldiers. The base was losing a number of men whose tours were coming to an end. These troops would normally be replaced by new soldiers, but this shuffle would keep net numbers about flat so there would be no outside additions at this time.

Major Lewis met the troop helicopter when it landed and welcomed the arriving soldiers.

"Good morning, Sergeant, I'm Major Lewis, the commanding officer here at FOB MacKenzie."

"Major, glad to meet you. I'm Sergeant Terrance. I've heard good things about you and we're looking forward to joining your team."

"Welcome. Follow me and I'll show you around." The two men headed off, while Captain Roth led the others to their quarters and orientation.

"Tell me about things up north," Major Lewis said.

"Lately it was pretty tough, sir. We had a clear mandate when we arrived and it felt like we were gaining traction. Almost overnight the pendulum swung and we were on the defensive. We could hold our ground, but not take any new territory. Attacks seemed to come from everywhere. When that happens paranoia starts to set in. We either needed to go full force or get out."

Major Lewis appreciated the candid appraisal. He didn't think Uruzgan was in that state yet, but remained concerned about the direction of the conflict. "I think we are in a solid position currently and I hope you and your team can make us stronger. Summer is here and things are heating up. I want us to keep the momentum and stay on the offensive. How are your men holding up?"

"Losing Captain Lozano was a major blow. He was an excellent leader and a great soldier. He was supposed to be attending a negotiation meeting when the team was ambushed. He'd clearly been set up. It made us just want to start killing anyone that might be responsible."

"I understand," Major Lewis said, reflecting on his recent emotions after the incident at the road project. "The attack east of here last week was carried out by two of the men killed in the explosion. I want justice for my fallen soldiers and terminating the parties who ordered the attack will make me feel vindicated. The question is whether or not it will solve the problem or make it worse."

"I feel the same, sir. So many of the people we helped showed no appreciation. I guess we shouldn't expect anything, it just becomes disheartening."

"My hope is that we can turn the corner. Iraq still has problems, but when I left it felt like a different place than when I arrived. In our operations one of the main goals is to clear area so that the inhabitants can live safely. The goal becomes unachievable when those inhabitants still want to kill each other and also kill you," Major

Lewis stopped and looked out toward the horizon. He realized that he was probably doing too much thinking out loud with a soldier he had just met. "There are some unfriendlies in Uruzgan, but we still have more support than opposition. If we can weed out the bad apples and prevent other combatants from entering and getting established we should be fine. We'll get you and your men back on a positive path."

***

Major Lewis let the new men settle in and gave them limited assignments to ease their transition. He could do it for a short time and then they would need to get up to speed as he did not want the existing forces to resent the recent arrivals for not carrying their weight.

During the second week Major Lewis had a visit to Baza Faqir-e planned. He took most of the new unit with him to start familiarizing them with the area and because he knew it would be a low stress task.

When they arrived in Baza Faqir-e they made their normal rounds and then split up. Dehqan was not in town so Major Lewis headed right for the market to see Zemar. He wanted to say hello and also gather information.

Zemar was tending to his shop and was glad to see Major Lewis. "Good morning, Ajani."

"Hello, Zemar. We were in the neighborhood so I just wanted to see how things were going."

"Are you planning to play any golf soon?" Zemar asked.

"Unfortunately no. We have been very busy and will stay that way for a while. Some new men arrived at MacKenzie recently and I brought them to Baza Faqir-e today."

"Why didn't you bring any of them to my store? I could use some new customers."

"Sorry. I should have done that. People aren't shopping?"

"It's been slow. It seems like everyone is on edge. There have been attacks all around, but none in Baza Faqir-e. People start to assume that you are due to be hit."

"Did you hear about the explosion where we were doing road construction?"

"Yes. A few local families had relatives working out there."

"It was a pretty simple attack. Still I don't believe it was just a worker going haywire. Did you hear anything about it?"

Zemar moved closer to Major Lewis and instinctively looked around. "Ajani, you know I want to help you, but I have to be careful. Along with the violence comes a lot of suspicion. People aren't sure who to trust and there is a mixture of fear and anger. They want the killing to stop, but they are afraid of the consequences of taking action."

"Zemar, that's why we are here. Did AKA have anything to do with the highway attack?"

Zemar looked around nervously again and lowered his voice further. "I don't know of anything specific. However, his name has come up. Rumor has it that several of the workers had crossed paths with some of AKA's men and they asked a lot of questions about what was going on out there."

Major Lewis could sense Zemar's agitated state. He pressed on anyway. "Do you know of anyone who can confirm that for me?"

"Not directly. Besides, they would be afraid to talk to you."

"Are you afraid to talk to me?"

"Yes, Ajani. We know your men and weapons can win any fight. However, you can't be everywhere at once. It seems like whenever you are here they are not and vice versa."

"We have rules that need to be followed when it comes to engaging Afghans like AKA. Within that framework if I can get evidence that he is even tangentially involved in the killing of our men we can crack down on him."

"I don't have any evidence yet. What I do know is that AKA is becoming more active. He now has vehicles and new weapons. Someone is giving him support and money."

"You don't think it is Dehqan, do you?"

"Doubtful. Dehqan serves as a balance. I don't think he's worried enough about AKA that he'd throw all of his support that way right now."

"I don't want you to endanger yourself in any way, but if you do get information let us know. We will take the appropriate action," Major Lewis said, starting to worry that he had put Zemar in a difficult position.

"I will, Ajani."

***

The next day Major Lewis arrived for lunch at the cafeteria with Captain Roth just after mid-day. There were no patrols or projects scheduled for today so most of the soldiers were on base. The room was completely full and the men appeared to be in good spirits as there was a steady roar of voices and laughter.

The two officers grabbed their meals and squeezed in at a table with Sergeant Terrance.

"So what did the men think of Baza Faqir-e yesterday?" Major Lewis asked.

"That it's like most Afghan towns - rather unremarkable. It's still more than we had up north though. Those valleys had nothing but po-dunk little settlements."

"Unfortunately, that's about the best we've got out here."

"At least it's a little taste of civilization. If you spend too much time out in the sticks you start to lose touch."

A few minutes later their conversation was interrupted by an impromptu singing session that was loud enough to trump all of the other noise in the room.

"As I was saying earlier," Sergeant Terrance said, pointing to the soloist. "That's Private Kubiak. I'm worried that he's gone BRAWOL."

"BRAWOL?" Captain Roth asked.

"He's still here, but his brain is AWOL. He was always a bit of a clown; it just seems to have kicked up a notch since the ambush. He was really tight with Private Santori, who was also killed. Rather than mourning he has been crazier than ever. We assume it is his coping mechanism."

Private Kubiak continued to belt out the lyrics to AC/DC's Thunderstruck with tiny ear buds feeding only him the actual music. Private Kubiak was in his early twenties and had a full array of tattoos on his thick, muscled arms. He wore his hair in a dark Mohawk and heavy stubble covered his pock-marked face. He looked like he would be right at home in a mosh pit.

The laughter of the other soldiers appeared to fuel his flames. He was now up and dancing near his table adding air guitar and drum movements to his show.

Major Lewis was inclined to let the act continue, however, he grew concerned when Private Kubiak began bumping into men and drumming on their heads. When things became physical other soldiers would normally respond in-kind. In close quarters many of the men didn't want their small comfort zones invaded. Major Lewis had just elbowed Sergeant Terrance to go reign in his man when Private Kubiak snatched a banana off the tray of Specialist Lott. Private Kubiak tried to use it as a microphone, but as he turned he realized that Specialist Lott had grabbed his other wrist.

"Alright, funny guy. Show's over. Please put my banana back where it was," Specialist Lott said calmly.

The room immediately went quiet.

"Chill out, he's just messin'," one of Private Kubiak's friends pleaded.

Private Kubiak's face had changed. He suddenly looked dead serious. "Okay, here's your banana!" he blurted before smashing the piece of fruit on Specialst Lott's forehead.

The officers all yelled commands, but they were a second too late. Their authority had been superseded by emotion. Specialist Lott tried to subdue Private Kubiak. In turn, several of Sergeant Terrance's men jumped up to aid their friend. There was too much nervous gun powder and too many short fuses in the room. The lines had already been drawn and the battle was on.

In an instant the room was divided into three groups: the fighters, the onlookers, and the men rushing to break it up. The fighters were yelling and making noise by knocking over tables trying to get to each other. Fists and feet were flying, but unlike barroom fights in the movies there were no loud cracks and smacks. It was just the dull thuds of appendages impacting heads and bodies.

The onlookers quickly backed off to the sides. Most of the men probably wanted to help stop the fight, but didn't want to get drawn into the fray by accident. They would either let the fight end on its own or wait for those who could mete out punishment, like Major Lewis, to step in and give direct orders. Others among them simply wanted to observe with the fascination of kids watching a school yard brawl.

Lieutenant Warner, who happened to look like a bouncer, led the officers and other soldiers that moved across the room toward the swarming mass of angry men. Warner quickly assessed the situation and picked the best place to start. He began forcefully grabbing one man at a time and swinging them behind him to be passed down the line. The plucked soldiers continued to yell, but stopped struggling as soon as they were parted from the others. As order began to be restored the remaining fighters got in their last tired shots. Despite its short duration, the fight left several of the men bloodied and exhausted.

Lieutenant Warner propped Private Kubiak against a table so that Major Lewis could address him.

"Son, we're all under a lot of pressure out here. But that's no excuse for this," Major Lewis said, motioning to the disarray surrounding them.

"Sorry, sir...I was just screwin' with your boys...we're cool," Private Kubiak said between panting breaths while dark blood curled from his split lip.

"No, you're not cool," Major Lewis said, turning to Lieutenant Warner. "Get his face fixed up and isolate him."

Major Lewis began walking back toward his table and then realized that everyone was silent and staring at him.

"Finish your lunches, clean up this mess, and get back to work. The fight's over. If I see or hear anything else there will be serious consequences."

The men immediately did as they were told and Major Lewis calmly sat back down to eat.

"Captain Roth, go ahead and order up a psych evaluation on Private Kubiak so we can determine whether or not he'll be staying with us."

"I'm sorry about that, sir," Sergeant Terrance said sheepishly.

"There's nothing to be sorry about. It wasn't your fault. We just need to make sure that they were just blowing off steam and not seeding a feud. To some extent a fight can be beneficial. Taking the mental baggage and exorcising it physically. It also confirms that the soldiers you are here with are fighters. I fought with my brother all the time and if we ever had a common enemy I knew that I'd want him by my side."

"So when you guys fought who won?"

"He was younger so I usually kicked his ass. However, he learned to compensate by fighting dirty. I'm quite sure he'd be able to hold his own here in Afghanistan."

13

Zemar lived in a small house on the edge of Baza Faqir-e that had once belonged to one of his uncles. Zemar was living there when his uncle died two years ago and with no one else to claim the property he just stayed. He shared the home with several of his friends who had no place else to go and lived there rent free.

Zemar had just returned and was talking with Yasir when he heard a truck pull up. Through the small, rectangular window he saw several men he recognized sitting in the back of the vehicle. It was no surprise when the passenger door opened and their leader, AKA, emerged.

AKA walked over and knocked casually. Yasir, opened the door and greeted their visitor.

"Hello, Yasir. I need to talk with Zemar," AKA said, looking inside over the boy's shoulder.

"He can come in," Zemar instructed, knowing he didn't really have a choice.

AKA wandered in and looked around indifferently. The home was very modest with a few pillows and simple pieces of furniture on the floor. Several of Zemar's paintings decorated the walls of the dimly lit room.

"We need to speak alone," AKA said, looking at Yasir and the others sitting inside.

"It's okay. Go find something to do outside," Zemar directed to his friends. The young men filed out, all giving AKA dirty looks as they passed.

AKA ignored their expressions and waited for them to leave. He nudged a pillow toward Zemar and then sat down facing him.

"This is a nice little home you have, Zemar."

"What do you want?" Zemar asked, skipping any unnecessary small talk.

"Always the businessman..." AKA mused at Zemar's direct approach. "Then we'll talk business. Zemar, we have been very patient with the foreigners who have illegally occupied our country for many years. We hoped that they would feel they had done enough to placate the politicians in Washington, D.C. and would be on their way. Unfortunately, that hasn't happened. They're still here and this country has no direction because of it. We are going to change that. We have been waiting and building our strength and now we will be imposing our will. The tide is turning, Zemar, and you need to decide who you are going to support."

"That's a wonderful sales pitch, Abdul. However, if you are so strong why are you sitting in my meager home? Why do you need me?"

"Strength comes not just from the number of soldiers or weapons. It also involves knowing where to strategically hit your enemy. That's where you come in, Zemar."

"So what do you want?" Zemar asked, still trying to put on a brave face, despite his rising level of discomfort.

"Major John Lewis."

"You know where he is. Just go kill him," Zemar blurted, acting as though he didn't care about the fate of his friend.

"Calm down, Zemar," AKA said with the tone of an evil teacher. "You're not listening to me. There is a big difference between me killing him and you killing him. Again, you need to know your enemy. I have been abroad and know how their society works. The interpretation of an event means so much more than the event itself. We can kill one hundred of their soldiers in the hills and it will garner little attention. However, when a young Afghan assassinates one of their commanders, who trusted him, it will have a significant impact. Especially upon the politicians who control the strings of the military. Do you understand that, Zemar?"

Zemar cringed at the blatant statement of intent. "So you think I can just walk into MacKenzie and shoot Major Lewis?"

"Shoot him? No, no, Zemar you're still not listening. I want you to aspire to a higher goal: martyrdom."

Zemar had no reply. He sat there stunned at the thought of becoming a suicide bomber. It was even more unsettling as the possibility hadn't even occurred in Zemar's mind. They sat there together staring at each other in silence waiting for someone to make the next move.

AKA could sense Zemar's state of shock and continued on the offensive. "Being a businessman, I'm sure you're wondering - what is in it for me? I think you're smart enough to know the answer to that already, Zemar. You do very well peddling all of your haraam and *art*," AKA said holding his hands out toward the pictures on the wall. "You could afford a nicer place than this. But you send your money elsewhere, don't you? So much money in Afghanistan moves through the hawallahs. They are honorable money changers, but it is easy enough for us to determine where it goes. We know what you value the most, Zemar. I think it is a fair trade. Besides, you've lost so much already. Do you want to lose all that remains?"

Zemar still didn't know what to say. He'd always been fast on his feet and quick in thought. He was in a corner and couldn't find a way out. "How do I know you'll keep your side of the bargain?"

"If you do your part, Zemar, I will honor your memory and honor our agreement," AKA said smoothly.

Zemar wondered how he'd gotten himself into this position. He had thought his friendship with Major Lewis would be an asset; however, it had now become a massive liability. "You're saying I should trust you? You come here and blackmail me and I'm supposed to trust you. I'm not sure how I can do that."

"I'm not sure you have a choice," AKA added confidently.

"And you must have no conscience. To expect me to give everything for *your* ambitions. You're pathetic," Zemar said with his anger starting to grow. He wanted to jump on AKA and gouge his eyes out. Only the knowledge of a truck full of armed men outside stopped him.

"This conflict has forced all of us to make difficult choices, Zemar. Had they not come here none of this would be necessary."

Zemar just stared at AKA, even more angry about the man's arrogant rationalization.

"This is something that will happen one way or another. I came here today in order to give you the choice in how it occurs. Before I go, let me be very clear on the terms of my offer. You are a smart boy, Zemar, so don't do anything stupid. We now have eyes everywhere. Stay away from MacKenzie and from Major Lewis. If you try to warn him or retaliate against me we'll make it much worse for you and everyone else.

We will be back in a few days. That will give you time to prepare and get your affairs in order," AKA said, standing to leave. "Remember my terms, Zemar. Do not cross me, it will be a very big mistake."

AKA walked out, leaving Zemar sitting in his state of confusion. Outside there was a commotion as AKA rattled off orders as the vehicle sped off. Zemar ignored the sounds and considered what to do next.

Several quiet moments passed before his friend, Sayyid, return to the home.

"Zemar, why did they take Yasir?" the boy asked.

"What?" Zemar asked, truly not understanding the question.

"Abdul and his men grabbed Yasir and then left."

"Oh no..." Zemar moaned, realizing that AKA had taken his close friend as collateral and that his options were now even more limited.

"What should we do, Zemar?"

Zemar slumped over and put his face in his hands. "I don't know, Sayyid. I don't know."

***

The senior officers at FOB MacKenzie were gathered in the command center waiting for their secure teleconference link to be established. Major Lewis was seated in the middle in front of a large flat-screen monitor with a camera on top. All of the men were sitting particularly up right and still, as though the camera would be taking pictures rather than capturing video.

The television finally came to life and the face of Colonel Renfro appeared on the screen. He was sitting close to the camera on his end so his head appeared rather oversized. The resolution was exceptionally high so the men at MacKenzie could see every detail on his weathered, reddish face.

"Good morning, men," he proclaimed in a gruff, military-style voice.

"Good morning, sir," Major Lewis replied.

"Today we are going to review the details of the planned incursions in your region. Hopefully you had time to review the briefings we sent out."

"We have, sir," Major Lewis confirmed.

"Good-good. Beginning tonight we will be implementing Operation Tourniquet. The objective of the operation will be to disrupt increased insurgent activities in your area. Major Lewis we appreciate the intel that you have provided over the past several months and we are ready to act on certain high value targets."

Major Lewis just grinned, happy that his voice had finally been heard in Kabul.

Colonel Renfro continued, "Our primary objectives will be several suspected training camps located in the mountains north and east of FOB MacKenzie. These locations may also be serving as stopover points for enemy fighters moving through to other parts of the country. Additionally, we have located several remote farms that are being used for the cultivation of contraband. We have received numerous indications that the Taliban still situated in Afghanistan are getting back into the drug business, primarily for cash flow reasons."

"Many of the sites are outside of our direct operating range. What level of certainty do we have on the activities been carried out?" Major Lewis asked.

"Given their remote locations most of the reconnaissance has been accumulated from aerial and satellite tracking. There has been additional corroboration from land based assets operating in the region."

"I'm glad we've at least had some feet on the ground out there. Funny, though, the spooks never stop by to see us when they're in the neighborhood."

"I can understand your concerns, Major Lewis. If something goes wrong you are going to take the local heat even if you didn't carry out the attacks. We do not want you to conduct surveillance patrols in these locations prior to the exercises. Our concern being the possibility that the fighters get scared and depart, or decide to bring in human shields."

"We trust your sources, sir. It's just that we've found it increasingly difficult to differentiate hostile and non-hostile activities. Unfortunately they are often operating side by side."

"Noted, Major Lewis. The majority of the sorties will be carried out by the Special Ops Aviation Regiment. They have handled many such operations and are being drawn on increasingly as we step up our proactive efforts."

All of the men at MacKenzie nodded and smiled in acknowledgement of the group that would be handling the work. The Army's Special Operations Aviation Regiment, known as the Night Stalkers, was formed in the early 1980's in the wake of the failed attempt to rescue American hostages being held in Iran. The teams were specially trained and equipped for night missions and had played vital roles recently in the conflicts in Iraq and Afghanistan.

The unit operated with a variety of helicopters including: AH-6C Little Birds, MH-60K Black Hawks, and MH-47D Chinooks. Their machines were outfitted with the latest technology and weapons for night time maneuvers. There were also rumors that they had begun using a new generation of stealth helicopter in Afghanistan for operations along the border and even into neighboring Pakistan.

Colonel Renfro spent time going through the details and timing of each activity. "Upon completion of the exercises we want you to provide on-site follow-up to the selected targets noted in your briefing report. We need photographic and video documentation of the damage to prevent any staging."

"We're already working on the arrangements and assignments, sir," Major Lewis replied.

"Excellent. Is there anything else we need to cover?"

"Did you review the local target group I had provided? They are led by Abdul Karim Abdullah also known as AKA."

"Yes, Major. We were unable to determine any direct connections to the primary networks we are monitoring such as the Haqqani and other factions operating out of Waristan at this time. There could very well be another link in between or they could be tied to a fringe group. They are obviously not on the target list for this operation, but if you can provide a reasonable case we will gladly evaluate them in the future."

"I appreciate the update, sir," Major Lewis said. "We will continue to monitor them. They seem to have been somewhat of a sleeper cell, but our sense is that is changing."

"Major, we need you and your men to focus on this operation currently. However, once this is complete you have the autonomy to deal with local insurgents as you see fit. If necessary you know that you may act unilaterally."

"Thank you, sir. You have our full support."

The teleconference terminated and the men continued with their planning.

***

The first strikes began two nights later. Major Lewis received status reports and on-site night vision and thermal graphic video of the attacks. No matter how many times he saw similar footage, he never ceased to be amazed by what the military could do with technology. The video appeared very sterile and scientific. He knew that when they visited the sites the reality would be much different.

Lieutenant Davitch was tapped to run the initial examinations. His team arrived at one of the selected locations at midday and began documenting the scene. It was situated in a small valley east of FOB MacKenzie. They did preliminary surveillance from the surrounding hillsides before moving in on foot. There appeared to be no movement and destruction was thorough. What limited structures that had been there were completely erased. So much so that nothing was burning and there was not even any smoke rising from the site. This had been a smaller camp and there were roughly twenty suspected combatants staying here.

The men came in from two directions and met in the middle. They had specific protocols to follow, however, there was very little to document. Once the site had been evaluated and no survivors found, Lieutenant Davitch radioed to Major Lewis.

"Lieutenant Davitch, what do you have out there?" Major Lewis asked.

"Looks like a clean hit. We have all male casualties. There appear to be a number of small arms scattered around. Nothing that indicates these men were doing anything other than planning to fight."

"That's good news. I don't know what anyone would be doing out there other than hiding."

"It appears to have been a temporary settlement, no permanent structures, just tents and lean-tos. We don't see evidence of any kind of stockpiles either. They were stopping here on their way to someplace else."

Everything sounded as it should be. It was very common for foreign fighters to move in small groups rather than large units. When traveling the already compact teams would often break up even further with members sometimes traveling alone to the next destination. It was a simple, but very effective strategy to avoid detection. When they came together in a camp like this they were immediately more exposed to detection.

"Is there anyone we might know?" Major Lewis asked, not expecting to get a positive confirmation.

"No, sir. Honestly, many of the bodies are tough to recognize. The Night Stalkers don't leave much of a mess to clean up. It looks like a team of surgeons did this. We'll do our best to get pictures for the facial scans, but I don't think any of these men will turn out to be locals."

"Alright, Lieutenant Davitch. Finish up and move on to the next site. Take care of what needs to be done and get back here."

"Will do, sir."

Major Lewis was relieved that the attacks had started off successfully. He knew that more fighters would be on their way despite such operations. At least this would reduce the ranks of those currently operating in the area. Major Lewis now had twenty less things to worry about in the coming months.

14

After the encounter with AKA, Zemar spent the following days mired in depression. He wanted to take some kind of action, but saw no way out. Even if there were a solution he could not muster the strength to act. His friends did their best to cheer him up and manage the home and business. Unfortunately, Zemar was their leader and they were in many ways reliant on him. They were also worried about Yasir and feared that they could be targets as well.

It was early in the morning when Zemar heard vehicles pull up in front. He was sleeping on his mat and didn't even know what day it was.

"Zemar! Wake up," one of his friends hissed while shaking him.

"I'm awake," Zemar groaned.

"Abdul is here."

When there was a knock on the door no one said a word, somehow hoping the visitor would go away. A few seconds passed before AKA showed himself in. He stood inside the doorway staring at the young men scattered about the room and then focused on Zemar.

"Right where I left you, Zemar," AKA observed. "Come along. It is time for us to go."

"Where is Yasir?"

"Are you ready to fulfill your duty?"

"I'll go. Where's Yasir?"

AKA poked his head outside and called to his subordinates. They brought Yasir in and shoved him forward.

"I'm sorry, Zemar. They grabbed me before I knew what was happening."

"Don't worry. This isn't your fault. Take care of things here, Yasir, my brother," Zemar said, giving his friend a hug.

"Where are you going, Zemar?" Yasir asked nervously.

"I have to take care of something."

"When will you be back?"

Zemar patted his friend on the shoulder and turned to AKA. "Let's go."

They walked out leaving the others in stunned silence.

The other men all watched Zemar anxiously when he came outside. AKA opened the door on one of the trucks and motioned for Zemar to get inside. They squeezed into the cab and rode out of town in silence.

Zemar stared blankly ahead, not even paying attention to where they were going. His eyes were fixed on the road directly ahead while his head bobbed around randomly with the turbulence from the rutted terrain.

"Zemar, I know this is difficult, but you are doing something very important for your country. We are preparing to make a number of high impact attacks across Afghanistan. This will be a pivotal point in our history."

"Too bad I won't be around to see the wonderful place it becomes," Zemar said sarcastically.

"You cannot be selfish, Zemar. This is bigger than you or me. We must cleanse our land and set the example for our brothers around the world."

"I see you can find your religion when it suits your needs."

"Our ability to practice our faith properly has been interrupted. That is why we are taking action. Once we are back in control it will again be a way of life for all of us."

"Despite all of our problems right now there are too many people that won't be willing to go back. The world around us continues to move forward, while you insist on moving backward."

"You have indeed been spending too much time with your friend, Major Lewis. You are starting to sound like him," AKA noted.

"Even if you do succeed in driving out the Americans, which is unlikely, you will be left with overwhelming dissent from within," Zemar argued.

"That has been subdued in the past and can be controlled when the time comes. People can be persuaded."

"Persuaded? Threats, torture, and coercion would be a more accurate description of your approach."

"Zemar, do not get yourself all worked up. Do not make me go back to Baza Faqir-e and use *persuasion* on your friends."

"Where are we going?"

"To meet someone. An expert who will help us prepare you for your assignment.

***

It was mid-morning at FOB MacKenzie when one of the two Privates manning the entry control point noticed a small plume of dust rising along the access road in the distance. He double checked to be sure no arrivals were expected this morning and it was rare for the base to receive any unannounced visitors. He motioned to the fellow soldier who was relaxed and reading a book. They both watched through binoculars for several moments as the dusty apparition moved closer. The source of the activity finally moved onto a flat area and they were able to see someone riding a small motor scooter.

The first soldier instinctively called into the command center and notified them of the situation. Both guards picked up their rifles and took up positions behind concrete barriers located on either side of the entrance road. The arrival of a single Afghan was a definite red flag, however, the fact that he was not in a car lessened the threat as there was far less storage space for explosives. The first soldier continued to watch via his binoculars while the other began sighting the rider through the high-powered scope on his weapon.

The tension grew as the vehicle gradually closed the distance to the check point. Just inside the perimeter several additional soldiers had situated themselves along the large, fortified wall. As he neared, the guards could hear the sputtering engine and see that it was a young man riding the scooter. He was not carrying anything and the soldiers could not see any packages attached to the bike frame.

The rider slowed his pace and then stopped approximately fifty yards short of the gate near the warning signs that were posted in several languages including Pashto.

The first soldier stood up and held his hand out indicating for the young man to stay right where he was. He then yelled several basic commands in Pashto. "Get off the motorcycle! On your knees! Hands above your head!"

The rider dismounted and did as he was told.

The private then cautiously moved toward the visitor, while the others trained their sights on him and held their fingers on the triggers. As the soldier approached he called out, "Why are you here?"

The young man, who was clearly petrified, finally revealed his purpose in trembling words, "Major Lewis. Major Lewis."

The private looked the rider over and then tapped his radio, "Command. This is entry control point. See if you can locate Major Lewis. He has a visitor."

***

Major Lewis walked briskly toward the base entrance. All of the soldiers there watched nervously as he approached. With the initiation of recent activities everyone was even more on edge.

"Sir," the guard said when Major Lewis arrived, "he drove up and all he kept saying was your name. We searched him and ran him with the explosives sensor. He appears clean. He may have ingested a device though."

"Always a possibility," Major Lewis acknowledged, knowing the lengths that bombers would now go to in order to conceal their explosives.

Major Lewis, followed by his translator, Private Webster, moved closer to the young man, but maintained a reasonable distance.

"Hello, Yasir," Major Lewis said, greeting him in Pashto. "Ask him what he is doing here," Major Lewis added to Private Webster.

Webster asked and then translated the response. "He said that AKA has taken Zemar and thinks they intend to target you. He said he didn't know what else to do so he came out here to warn you and ask for your help."

"Oh, man," Major Lewis said quietly as he processed the situation he was now facing. He immediately knew from the emotions he was feeling that he had crossed the line. His first thought was that he had to rescue Zemar. The reality was that that was the last thing he should be doing right now.

"Does he know where they are?"

Private Webster relayed the question and translated the response. "They are using homes in several towns right now and also have camps in the mountains. He was taken hostage for several days and knows some of the locations. However, AKA separated from his captors so Yasir isn't sure where he is operating out of."

"How far?" Major Lewis asked.

"About an hour away."

Major Lewis stood still, thinking for a moment while everyone watched and waited. He was in a position where he had to do something. He couldn't simply send Yasir on his way back to Baza Faqir-e and he didn't want to take the risk of bringing the young man inside of FOB MacKenzie.

"Tell him to wait here. Keep an eye on him. Get him a bottle of water or something," Major Lewis finally said, clearly frustrated. "I'll be back in a few minutes."

Major Lewis's mind was churning at full capacity as he jogged back to the command center. He wanted to go after AKA, but with everything else in full swing it was the worst possible time. Lieutenants Davitch and Warner were both out on patrols with many of their best soldiers. Moreover, he'd assured Colonel Renfro that Operation Tourniquet would be his sole focus.

Captain Roth, who was monitoring the patrols, was in the center with several other soldiers when Major Lewis returned.

"What are the current locations?" Major Lewis requested.

Captain Roth pulled up an active map on his laptop and pointed out where the MacKenzie teams were currently operating. "Davitch is out here and Warner is over here."

As expected they were a significant distance from MacKenzie. Both teams had left early and covered a lot of ground en route to today's monitoring locations.

Major Lewis sat down and stared at the map knowing that he could not call his men off to rescue and Afghan boy.

"What's the problem, Major? Who was out there? Zemar?"

"No. It's his friend, Yasir. AKA took Zemar this morning, apparently in order to somehow kill me."

"I see," Captain Roth said, realizing what a difficult predicament his senior officer was in. He also guessed at the strategy Major Lewis was contemplating. "What's your plan?"

"I'm working on it. Not getting very far," Major Lewis said, shaking his head in consternation.

"You can't go out there alone, Major."

"I know, but I can't just wait here either."

"I'll go with you, sir," Captain Roth volunteered.

"Thanks for the offer, but I need you here no matter what. I'm just trying to figure out the best way to locate and engage them."

"Maybe that's what they want. They're setting a trap and Zemar is the bait."

"It could be, but my best bet is to act quickly before they can get set. If I wait then I know for certain it will be a trap and Zemar might be dead already."

Sergeant Terrance was sitting nearby listening to the discussion. "Major, you need a team to provide support. I'll get some of my guys and we'll go with you."

"I can't ask your men to go either," Major Lewis acknowledged.

"You didn't. I offered and my soldiers will be more than willing to go after a deceitful local. Trust me," Sergeant Terrance said.

"Alright. I hate to do it, but I'll take you up on that offer. Thanks, Sergeant," Major Lewis said gratefully, not admitting that taking Sergeant Terrance's men had been high on the list of options he was considering. "I'm hopeful that we can retrieve Zemar and we now have a strong reason to eliminate AKA. We'll take several trucks and have Yasir lead us to the most likely place to intercept them. Do you think you can be ready within a half hour?"

"Absolutely, sir. I'm on it," he said, getting up to leave.

"Captain Roth. Stay on top of things here. I'll keep you posted on our progress. Depending on what we run into I may request our guys to divert before returning."

"Sir, you're sure you want to do this?" Captain Roth asked in a quiet voice so as not to be heard by the others.

"I know it seems rash, but if it didn't happen now it would be happening soon enough."

"Yes, but in another scenario we would have more data to formulate a plan and be staffed and equipped properly."

"We're so much better than AKA and his fighters," Major Lewis said, sounding overconfident. "I know we'd like to engage them in an optimal situation, but that's not always how it works. Again, if anything that's what they'll expect us to do."

"Alright. You know you have my support no matter what, sir."

"Thank you, Captain. I need to get ready."

Captain Roth returned to his computer as Major Lewis walked out. Captain Roth believed in his commanding officer, but once again found himself questioning a vital decision.

***

The small convoy assembled and departed MacKanzie before noon. The line of three vehicles headed out with Major Lewis in the lead truck accompanied by Private Webster and Yasir providing navigation. As they headed north across the scalding, baked landscape it was comical listening to the two bantering in Pashto. Yasir had a basic understanding of the Army's maps, but preferred to stick with basic commands like: "Go here." and "Go there."

As they moved into populated areas the directions became much more serious. There were random locals wandering the rugged thoroughfares and they looked on with questioning scowls when the military vehicles passed. After coming up empty at the first two possible locations, they continued to head north into a region that Major Lewis had not yet visited. Yasir was confident that this was the most likely place for Zemar to be held. He had also been able to get help from a relative who lived near one of the major crossroads. The man confirmed that he'd seen several militia trucks go by earlier. He recognized some of AKA's men, but had not seen Zemar or AKA himself.

Major Lewis's instinct told him they were on the right path. He hoped his gut feeling was right as goose chases in Afghanistan were very dangerous endeavors. They continued cautiously toward a small settlement that had been abandoned some time ago. Just outside the town the road forked in two. Yasir felt that this was a likely hiding spot for AKA, but was not sure which way to proceed. The maps showed the road segments spreading out through town and then coming back together at the other end. Major Lewis was concerned that if they only took one side AKA would be able to escape unseen if the Army vehicles were detected. He was also considering the possibility of an ambush and he preferred not to have all of the vehicles together. Therefore, he sent Sergeant Terrance with the other truck down the left fork while he proceeded down the right.

Sergeant Terrance had one soldier who was competent in Pashto and Major Lewis had shown them photos of Zemar from the golf outings. If either team came across their targets they would notify the other. Major Lewis's primary strategy was to try to negotiate Zemar's release. Removal by force was secondary as there were many more things that could go wrong.

Major Lewis drove along the gradually curving road. He had been so consumed with thoughts of how to retrieve Zemar that he had been far less concerned about the safety of the roads compared to his normal, IED-fearing travel. They passed through an area of dilapidated groves lining the modestly sloped hillsides. They emerged into an open area with the first structures of the settlement. They were crumbling, earthen dwellings scattered in an uncoordinated fashion. Many were built into the sides of natural mounds while some were grafted one onto another. It was extremely quiet and there was no sign of anyone. It looked like a perfect place to hide, but Major Lewis was becoming worried that they were once again not in the right location.

What seemed like the main road snaked between the homes and led to a clearing. As he entered the open space, Major Lewis stopped the truck suddenly. Directly across from him was a parked vehicle with three men standing next to it. Major Lewis immediately recognized one of them, it was Atash.

He grabbed the radio and called, "We have contact."

Everyone sat there motionless for a moment, the surprise being absorbed by both sides. It felt like two gunslingers staring each other down, waiting for someone to draw. Major Lewis then stunned Private Webster by making his move - he got out of the truck.

"Sir! What are you doing?" Private Webster blurted out.

Major Lewis was wearing his body armor, but he was still very exposed. He also left his rifle inside the cab. He held up a hand toward Private Webster, indicating for him to remain calm. "Go up top so you can translate," Major Lewis said, sounding quite composed.

Private Webster did as he was told and carefully climbed into the protected turret built into the roof of the vehicle.

Atash recognized Major Lewis once he emerged from the truck. He shook his head in disbelief and then muttered a comment in Pashto.

"He is giving thanks to Allah for bringing them the gift they had been seeking," Private Webster said uncomfortably from his perch.

Major Lewis continued to move gradually with his hands up and was now completely clear from the protection afforded by the truck. "Tell them that no one needs to die today. This can all be avoided."

Private Webster provided the message and then relayed the response. "They don't intend to die, sir. However, if that is Allah's bidding then they are prepared to die in his glorious name."

"Great," Major Lewis said under his breath, trying to figure out the best way to talk down men who made statements like that.

The tension was broken momentarily as there was a noise behind the home closest to Atash's men.

"Sir, it looks like we have a runner," Private Webster observed, seeing an individual fleeing from the home.

"Does it look like AKA?" Major Lewis asked.

"Not sure, but I don't think so. He was moving pretty fast," Private Webster replied.

At the sound of the commotion Atash yelled something in that direction.

"Whoever it was, Atash is scolding him for being a coward," Private Webster said.

"Alright, let's not worry about him," Major Lewis decided. "Ask them if AKA is here. I'd like to speak with him directly."

Atash laughed slightly at the question before providing a response.

"He said that AKA is not here, but that it does not matter because he is in charge of this operation."

Major Lewis assumed that the "operation" was the "kill Major Lewis operation". "Okay. Ask them if Zemar is here."

Atash once again acted amused by the question. Atash would have been content for his men to open fire on Major Lewis, but AKA had been insistent that Zemar be the one to accomplish the objective. Despite his bravado, Atash was still very much subordinate to his leader and knew that the men would also defer to AKA's orders.

Private Webster continued, "He said that Allah has indeed provided good fortune to them today and they give many thanks for his magnificent power."

Atash then motioned for one of his men to open the truck door and provided instructions.

"He said: come and greet your friend, Zemar..."

As Private Webster translated, Zemar emerged from the vehicle. He looked directly at the ground and appeared to be crying.

The men shoved him toward Major Lewis and then backed off.

"Go, Zemar. Fulfill your destiny..." Atash preached via Private Webster.

Zemar stumbled forward and fell to his knees facing Major Lewis.

"Ajani, I'm so sorry," Zemar cried through streaming tears. "I didn't know what to do. I had no choice. They threatened to kill my sister and my friends if I didn't kill you."

Major Lewis was caught off guard by the statement. "Your sister?" he asked.

"Yes. I've kept her hidden, but they said they know where to find her."

"Where is she, Zemar?"

Zemar looked over his shoulder at Atash before turning back to Major Lewis. "She is in the heart of Afghanistan."

"That's where we are, Zemar," Major Lewis replied.

Atash did not care for the conversation and shouted the repetitive instructions at Zemar.

Zemar stood up and took several more steps toward Major Lewis. He was now about twenty feet away.

"Stop, Zemar," Major Lewis said firmly. "You don't need to do this."

Zemar stopped again and held out his arms in front of him. "What should I do, Ajani?" Zemar pleaded.

From above, Private Webster could see a wire with a loop on the end protruding from Zemar's sleeve. "Sir, he's already wired."

"I can see that," Major Lewis said, debating what to do next.

Meanwhile, Atash's orders became more forceful. "Now, Zemar! Now!"

"I'm sorry, Ajani," Zemar said again, beginning to wail.

"Zemar, calm down. It's going to be alright. You're better than these men. You know right from wrong. Think back to the rules I taught you when we were golfing."

"What do you mean, Ajani?" Zemar asked, settling down slightly.

Major Lewis motioned toward the boy's arm. "Zemar, if you are on their team you can't pull the pin when it's my shot."

Major Lewis gave a slight smile and then slowly closed his raised, right hand into a fist.

In the distance there were several blasts that sounded like one.

Major Lewis felt a dark sense of satisfaction as he saw Atash's body convulse and his torso burst open with an eruption of viscera. Chunks of his internal organs immediately became external and stained the dirt in front of where he stood. His legs collapsed and he crumbled to the earth. The other two fighters, who were standing behind the truck also jerked violently, slammed against the vehicle, and then slid to the ground.

"How many more are there, Zemar?" Major Lewis asked coolly as he ducked back to his truck.

"Just them, Ajani. The bomb maker was inside, but ran away."

"You're sure?"

"Yes, Ajani. We separated from the others earlier and came here. They were going to get me ready and then meet back up somewhere else. Abdul was working on a plan to get you out of MacKenzie."

Major Lewis leaned inside and radioed to Sergeant Terrance. "You can come on down. That's all of them. Nice shots."

"Ajani, how did you find me?" Zemar asked.

Major Lewis opened the back door and retrieved Yasir, who was huddled on the floor. He emerged and ran to his friend.

"Yasir!" Zemar said, beaming with joy. He then instructed his friend not to get too close.

Sergeant Terrance and several of his men walked into the clearing and observed their work up close. "One shot, one kill," one of the snipers said to the others, exchanging high fives.

"Thanks, guys. I knew I could count on you," Major Lewis said.

"Our pleasure, sir," Sergeant Terrance said with pride. "My other two men are tracking the runner still."

Major Lewis looked to Zemar. "It's the bomb maker. I don't think there is any way we can trust him to disarm Zemar. He may be able to help us locate AKA, however. Have your men try to detain him. If he proves hostile they can go ahead and take him out."

Sergeant Terrance radioed the orders to his men.

"We got one of their top men," Major Lewis said, pointing to the bodies bleeding out across the way. "However, AKA is still out here somewhere. We need to get him before he gets us...or at least me."

"What are we going to do now, sir?"

"I'm working on that. I'm amazed we got this far today," Major Lewis admitted.

15

After documenting the scene in the settlement Major Lewis and his team began the journey back to MacKenzie. They notified the nearest ANP unit to provide clean up and disposal services. One thing that Major Lewis didn't mind about opposition casualties in Afghanistan was that it was normally someone else's job to coordinate a proper burial service.

According to Sergeant Terrance's men the bomb maker had indeed proven hostile. When they caught up to him he appeared ready to detonate a device that he was carrying so they shot him on the spot. Major Lewis would have liked to have captured him, but at this point he wasn't going to worry about it.

Private Webster had gladly taken Major Lewis up on his offer to ride back with Sergeant Terrance. With Zemar still wired and live Major Lewis was responsible for transporting him. Major Lewis also gave Yasir the option of riding with the others, but he chose to ride with his potentially explosive friend instead.

There would be no need for a translator with Zemar, however, it was a moot point since there was no conversation in the vehicle whatsoever. Major Lewis had told Zemar to sit still and do the best he could to relax. Major Lewis didn't want apologies; he just wanted to be sure that Zemar didn't go off accidentally.

He had Zemar and Yasir in the back seat to avoid attention as they drove through the populated areas. Yasir looked intently at Zemar who stared vacantly out the small window. Major Lewis was portraying an air of control; however, inside he was fraying. The way that Zemar had been drawn into the conflict was very unsettling and Major Lewis was racked with guilt. Sitting by himself at the wheel, his mind cycled continuously between what had just occurred and what he should do next. The first priority was disarming the explosive device. Beyond that there were no good solutions. Zemar would still be in great danger and there was no way for Major Lewis to protect him. He started to think of ways to get Zemar out of Uruzgan or even out of Afghanistan.

The mental disarray was accentuated by his heightened level of paranoia. He was now hyper-aware of everyone and everything around him. While slowing down at a crossroads Major Lewis's focus bounced from face to face of the Afghans standing along the road. He scrutinized their beards, their eyes and noses, every wrinkle and pock mark, searching for some clue of their intentions. Most of the men looked quickly at the truck and then turned away, acting as though it wasn't even there.

Major Lewis didn't recognize anyone, but he knew that a random, anonymous killer might be looking for him or Zemar. Despite having Sergeant Terrance and the other men driving right behind him, Major Lewis felt completely alone.

The convoy was rolling steadily through a seemingly endless stretch of pale brown hills when Major Lewis was startled by a call from Captain Roth back at FOB MacKenzie. Major Lewis had already called in after they retrieved Zemar so he was not expecting another contact.

"Captian Roth, what's going on?"

"Sir, it sounds like we may have a problem," Captain Roth said hesitantly.

"A problem? I thought I'd already solved my problem for the day."

"I know, sir. I didn't want to call you, but Lieutenant Davitch reported in and indicated that they have a number of potential civilian casualties at one of their sites."

"How many?"

"Around a dozen women and children."

"What was on the site?" Major Lewis asked.

"It looks like a transient location, not a lot of permanent structures so they could be refugees or shields. They were all close together."

"What about fighters?"

187

"Davitch said there are weapons, but mainly small arms. Hard to tell if they were insurgents or just a group protecting themselves."

"Alright, go ahead and have him follow procedure and notify the ANP to get a unit out there to verify everything. With all of these attacks I figured there'd be some collateral damage."

"Yes, sir, Davitch is already doing that. The reason I'm calling is that a number of locals showed up on scene and were getting very vocal. Word has spread about the campaign so people know we are carrying out nighttime sorties. Davitch's men settled most of them down and dispersed the crowd, but several of the elders were not content. One of them said he was close with Dehqan and was going to get him so that he could see the atrocities that the Americans had perpetrated."

"Great. Just what we needed."

"Davitch told them not to, but they didn't listen to him and left saying they'd be back shortly. They also said that we should send out more senior officers to handle the situation. We're assuming that means you, Major. Davitch didn't want to leave the site unguarded so he is still there."

Major Lewis stopped his truck and radioed the others. He grabbed his laptop and opened his mapping application. "Where is Davitch?"

"He's actually not too far away since this was on his return leg. Look up Mount Kijra. He's just north of there. I plotted a course where you can head south and then west and be there in under an hour."

"Yes, but I don't think I should show up there packing an explosive strapped Afghan kid. That's probably not going to help our cause."

"I was considering that already, Major. Lieutenant Warner has completed his work and is in transit. If we redirect him he could meet you near the town of Shibah and you could hand off Zemar. As you know, he's got Specialist Fergamo with him and the EOD suit."

"That's a good idea. I'd much rather handle the removal away from MacKenzie...just in case," Major Lewis said, his voice tapering off as he finished the sentence.

"Do you want me to call Lieutenant Warner to confirm?"

Major Lewis hesitated for a moment considering this change and the ramifications. There was a big difference between thinking quickly and making rash decisions. There were too many lives on the line today and Major Lewis knew that the wrong move could prove costly. He also didn't like the fact that his decisions were all reactive. It felt as though someone else was pulling the strings and all he could do was respond.

"Let's do it," Major Lewis replied, hoping he was making the right choice.

"I'm on it, sir. I will tell them to be ready for the disarm and I'll send you both the exact coordinates."

"Thanks, Captain. Keep me posted if anything changes," Major Lewis said before hanging up. He turned to the two occupants in the back. "Wait here. I'll be back in a minute."

Major Lewis climbed out and walked back to speak with Sergeant Terrance.

"What's happening, sir?" Sergeant Terrance asked, stepping out of his truck.

"We have a slight change of plans. We're going to meet Lieutenant Warner and then I have to go out to where Lieutenant Davitch is operating. There appears to be some civilian casualties and some unhappy locals."

"Why do you need to be there?"

"They are barking up to one of the local power brokers that I work with. You know how the Afghans are about seniority so if their top representative is there they expect to have the same from us. Also, we still have several sites to target so we need to prevent any unrest from spreading. What I'll probably do is switch teams so you can head back to MacKenzie. In which case I'll need for you to take these two with you."

"Oh, I see," Sergeant Terrance answered somewhat surprised.

"But we are going to remove the device from Zemar at the rendezvous location," Major Lewis added.

"No, I just figured we'd continue on with you since Lieutenant Warner went out so early today."

Major Lewis had already thought about the scenario that had brought Sergeant Terrance's men to MacKenzie. He was concerned about a similar situation unfolding this afternoon. Major Lewis felt that he could trust Dehqan, but was still uneasy about the possibility that this could be a trap. Sergeant Terrance's men were already jaded about trusting local authorities and this could be a bad position for them to be in so soon. They had performed well so far, but he didn't want to push his luck.

"Do you think your troops are up for it?"

"Absolutely, sir. You have to understand that my men and I are more than willing to kill any traitorous Afghans. If anything the incident in Nuristan has made our judgment clearer. But you can't confuse that with just being trigger happy. We are willing to shoot when necessary and with cause."

"Alright. We'll still probably pick up some of Warner's team, but I'll send him back to MacKenzie with Zemar and Yasir."

"Thank you, sir. I think my men were glad to be back in action today and this will help them to re-engage."

"I appreciate the support, Sergeant. Let's go."

***

Captain Roth had selected an unpopulated area outside of Shibah as the meeting point. Warner's unit arrived first and was waiting when Major Lewis pulled into the field. The men were scattered around and were relaxing after a tense morning. The laughing stopped and the smiles disappeared when their commanding officer showed up with yet another challenge.

Major Lewis pulled off to one side and left the two Afghans in his truck while he tracked down Lieutenant Warner.

"Lieutenant, how did your runs go this morning?"

"Pretty well, sir. Everything went according to plan and it looked like some clean work again. I understand Davitch wasn't so lucky."

"Yes. I would have been surprised if we made it through these attacks without any problems. Hopefully this will be it. Thanks for coming over to meet us. I've created a bit of a problem myself," Major Lewis said, gesturing toward his truck.

"That's what we're here for, sir, to fix problems. We're ready to go. There's a sheltered area over behind that rise. We checked it out and it should be a good place to defuse the kid."

"And Specialist Fergamo?"

"He's ready. We just need to get him in the EOD suit. We were waiting until you got here. Even with the cooling systems that thing gets a little warm this time of year. It's like wearing a character costume at Disney."

"That's fine. I'll be taking Sergeant Terrance and his men with me. Just in case, I'm going to take most of your team with me to support Davitch. I'm concerned that along with Dehqan there might be other local militia men coming up there to hassle us. I want to be in full control of the situation. I'll need you to transport Zemar and Yasir back to MacKenzie. Assuming all goes well here of course."

"Excellent, sir. Whatever you need. Are they going to stay with us?"

"For today, yes. Longer-term, no. That will never fly. I'll get grief from every direction if someone finds out we're putting up locals on the base, regardless of the reason. I could classify them as prisoners short-term, but then I'd have to turn them over to the ANP. I'll have to see what Zemar wants to do and then determine if I can help him. He's pretty messed up right now. Go ahead and get Specialist Fergamo dressed and let's get this over with."

The men organized their equipment and Major Lewis escorted Zemar to the designated area.

"Don't worry about anything, Zemar. Just relax and we'll get that thing off of you."

Zemar just stared into the distance and kept mumbling, "I'm sorry. I'm sorry."

"Zemar, I have to go somewhere else after this. Lieutenant Warner is going to take you and Yasir back to MacKenzie for now. Once I get back to base we'll figure out what to do next and what to do about this sister of yours," Major Lewis said in a warm, fatherly voice.

The mention of his sister seemed to scare Zemar even more. Major Lewis saw the reaction and put his hand on Zemar's shoulder as they walked. Looking down at the boy's arm he still had an undertow of fear that Zemar might be overwhelmed by remorse and become suicidal. All it would take was a tug on the wire. Major Lewis hoped the fear was unfounded.

Zemar had already been thinking about his sister on the ride here. He was worried that even if he did get out of the bomb vest and back to Baza Faqir-e it might already be too late. Being in the hands of the Americans and with Atash now dead, he knew that AKA would be furious. Having Yasir with him didn't help either. He realized that his sister was AKA's primary point of leverage, but Zemar also knew that each of his friends could be in trouble at any time now.

Major Lewis was standing with Zemar as Specialist Fergamo approached over the small hill. Wearing the full explosive ordnance disposal suit he looked like a green alien crossing a Martian landscape. Zemar had apparently never seen a soldier in the suit before and he grew even more nervous at the sight of it.

"Don't worry, Zemar. Specialist Fergamo is an expert in explosives and he'll take good care of you."

"Okay, Ajani."

"Thanks for helping us out, Specialist Fergamo. Is there anything else you need for me to do?"

"No, sir. I'm going to take a look and evaluate what type of device we are dealing with and then go from there. You can go ahead back over to get clear."

"Zemar, remember, just stand still and do as he says. No worries."

Zemar nodded.

Major Lewis returned to the others and joined Lieutenant Warner at the rear of his truck. Warner had a laptop open and the screen displayed the live feed coming from a suit mounted camera and microphone. Everything was being recorded and the footage would be shared with other explosive teams across Afghanistan.

"Zemar, did they attach anything to your clothing directly that you are aware of?" Specialist Fergamo asked.

"No, sir," Zemar answered respectfully.

"Go ahead and carefully take off your over shirt."

Zemar did as he was told and slowly unveiled the ominous vest that was strapped around his torso.

Everyone stared intently as Specialist Fergamo walked an inspection loop around the boy. The bomb consisted of explosive strips running vertically attached to a dense mesh fabric. On top of those were packets filled with shrapnel. There were a series of straps holding it in place and the detonation wire taped down the length of Zemar's arm.

Specialist Fergamo was wearing thick gloves so his natural tactile abilities were limited. He did, however, have small grabbing devices that he used to carefully probe Zemar.

"I think I know what to do, but I'm going to come back for a minute to confirm," Specialist Fergamo said to the listening soldiers. "Zemar, just wait here for a few minutes. I want to be sure of something first."

Specialist Fergamo slowly loped back to the trucks. He removed his helmet and gloves and started scanning through files on the laptop.

"What are you searching for, Specialist?" Major Lewis asked.

"One of our training sessions had information on devices like this one. They had video of vests that were strapped on otherwise unwilling Afghans. Typically they add a second trigger mechanism, unknown to the person wearing it. I think I located it on Zemar. I just want to be sure of the right way to bypass it. I've never done this and I don't want to overlook something simple. There's wiring hidden on the back of one of the straps. If Zemar had second thoughts and tried to undo it he'd blow himself up. It should be a pull only connection, however, I want to be certain it's not electrical and that cutting it won't cause detonation," Specialist Fergamo said.

He quickly found the document and scanned through it. They all watched as an American soldier gave a sterile description while a similar looking vest was being removed from a crying Afghan woman. She seemed equally upset about the bomb and being exposed in front of the foreign soldiers who were potentially risking their lives to save hers. She kept trying to cover her bare arms and shoulders while the soldier patiently asked her to sit still. He used a caliper device to test the wires before cutting the straps in two different spots.

"You see what he's doing? Another simple trick is to have it attached to the strap and then also fasten it at a second location. You get the binding undone and think you're in the clear, then boom, they still get you. The one on Zemar doesn't look any more sophisticated than this. Let's hope they haven't come up with any other tricks recently."

Specialist Fergamo headed back to Zemar who was now dripping with sweat. He did one more visual inspection before beginning the removal. A set of calipers appeared in sight of the cameras and Specialist Fergamo began testing different spots.

"I'm not picking up any current and I don't see a battery anywhere. They often use wire because they have it handy and it's easy to work with." Specialist Fergamo's voice remained calm; however, it was clear to the soldiers that his breathing was getting heavier and more rapid. "I'm going to go ahead and start cutting," he continued.

A pair of heavy-duty silver scissors entered the frame and moved toward Zemar. Specialist Fergamo carefully made cut after cut working his way up Zemar's left rib cage and then across his chest. He left the shoulder loops in place while he focused on the main detonation wire on Zemar's arm. The scissors slid underneath near the shoulder, but seemed to have a problem when Specialist Fergamo clamped down. They could hear him pushing harder and then the scissors popped sideways. Everyone flinched as though the physical explosion might travel through the camera.

"This one must be a heavier gauge wire," Specialist Fergamo said, shifting position to get more leverage.

The improved angle helped and he cut the line into several segments. He took one last look before cutting the final bindings and slowly peeling the entire device away from Zemar's skin. Specialist Fergamo set it to the side and instructed Zemar to rejoin the others. He gathered all of the loose pieces and placed them in a collection bag. He wanted to get as much evidence as possible to send to Kabul for examination. There was a small pit in the ground nearby and he put the rest of the vest at the bottom. On top of that he gently placed his own explosive charge with a remote detonator before walking over the hill.

Back at the truck he made sure everyone was out of range and then called out, "Fire in the hole. Fire in the hole. Fire in the hole."

He pushed the red button on a small hand-held box and immediately triggered an explosion over the nearby horizon. The reaction of the men was a combination of shock and awe. Shock about the size of the explosion and the thought that Zemar had been wearing the bomb just moments before. The awe was that natural reaction that men always had when things blew up. It was something engrained in them, not just fond remembrances of Fourth of July fireworks.

Specialist Fergamo returned to the blast site one last time to collect additional fragments and confirm a complete detonation. The small pit was now a black-streaked crater.

"We're all clear, sir," Specialist Fergamo reported.

Major Lewis thanked everyone again and reorganized the men. He went back to his truck and spoke with Zemar and Yasir. "You're going back with Lieutenant Warner. Listen to his orders and stay out of trouble. I should be back tonight and we'll talk then."

"I'm sorry, Ajani," Zemar mumbled once again.

Lieutenant Warner left with one additional escort vehicle while all of the other men departed with Major Lewis and began the journey to Lieutenant Davitch's location.

***

On the drive to Kijra, Major Lewis was a passenger rather than the driver so he had even more time to obsess about Zemar's situation. He was considering every option he could come up with and none of them were good. As they neared the site Major Lewis was glad to have something else to think about for a while.

The convoy pulled into the small valley and found the soldiers there standing around waiting for direction. The American troops were situated on one side of the wreckage while an ANP unit was loitering on the other side. There appeared to be no interaction going on between the two.

"Welcome to the waiting room, Major," Lieutenant Davitch griped as he greeted the arriving troops.

"What's going on, Lieutenant Davitch?" Major Lewis asked, looking beyond the men on the ground and up toward the hills.

"Absolutely nothing," Lieutenant Davitch answered, motioning toward the scene behind him. "Nobody wants to do anything until the Afghan elders come out and perform their Kabuki theater."

"I take it Dehqan hasn't arrived yet?"

"No. Word is that he is on his way and should be here any time now."

"What's the mood here?" Major Lewis asked, noting the ANP unit that was looking across the area curiously.

"Boredom. No animosity. They've just been hanging out. I think they're staying on their own so as not to appear too friendly with us. There have been some random locals flowing through and these ANP guys give them an update."

"Any visitors we need to worry about?"

"I don't think so. Mostly passerby's with nothing else to do. We told the ANP guys to make sure no one was armed otherwise we would be dealing with them accordingly. Also, we've been flying the UFO cam around the area and haven't seen anything suspicious," Lieutenant Davitch said, trying to reassure Major Lewis in terms of the threat of an ambush.

"And what about the guy that went to fetch Dehqan? Was he here already when you arrived?"

"We ID'd him as Mohamed Bindur. He's another fence-sitter. He has ties with the Taliban, but has never shown to be openly hostile towards our troops. He was pretty mad, although it was tough to know how much was real and how much was show. There were a number of locals here when we arrived and it almost seemed like he was waiting for us to get here so he could make his proclamations. He clearly knew that we weren't the ones who'd conducted the attack."

"Let's say hello to the ANP guys and then I'll survey things."

Major Lewis was greeted warmly by the Afghan forces. He had found that they typically showed respect toward ranking U.S. officers. He asked that their senior officer, who spoke almost no English, join him as they surveyed the site.

Lieutenant Davitch led the two men through the destruction and pointed out what his team had documented earlier. From a military target standpoint it was a gray area. Lieutenant Davitch identified the location of weapons and men who were likely fighters. He then showed them to the collapsed, mud-walled structure where the bullet-ridden bodies of several women and children lay strewn across the floor. The stench of decomposition was building quickly in the Afghan heat. The bodies were rigid and they all had the frozen stares of death on their faces. The only sound was the steady buzz of flies zipping from carcass to carcass. It was a scene that Major Lewis had witnessed countless times over the past several years.

What these people were doing before last night's attack was difficult to determine. The Night Stalkers moved so quickly and decisively that most of their targets didn't even have time to react. That of course was a cornerstone of their strategy.

Major Lewis considered how much effort he'd put into saving Zemar today and how quickly and anonymously these Afghans had been killed. The difference between winners and losers in a war zone was dramatic.

Lieutenant Davitch's team had already documented the site so there was little else to do. Major Lewis was wondering whether or not

Dehqan was even going to show up. He let everyone know that they would give him an hour otherwise they'd be leaving.

Fifteen minutes later Dehqan finally arrived. With Mohamed Bindur and Major Lewis in a procession, the bodies received another viewing. Afterward the men sat down together on a group of rocks away from the others.

"Major Lewis, it is unfortunate that we are meeting again under such circumstances. I understand that the military has been carrying out many attacks such as this recently. I know who you are targeting, but as is often the case the innocent now pay the price."

Major Lewis knew the proper protocol for these discussions. He wanted to question Dehqan about his knowledge of the people killed at the site, but starting with that topic would be disrespectful. Instead he was treated to a lengthy dissertation about all of the wrongs that had been brought upon Afghanistan by the Americans for the past decade. He listened intently and nodded graciously throughout.

When Major Lewis finally had the chance to speak freely he went over the procedure for providing reparations to the survivors of those killed in the attack. He was careful to express the Army's great sorrow for the losses without explicitly apologizing on his own behalf. He didn't sense any true anger on the Afghans' part, it seemed like they were still just going through the paces. This was something they were supposed to be doing, but not something that had any real emotion behind it. Unfortunately there was a similar lack of feeling for Major Lewis. He had conducted too many of these discussions during his career.

When the meeting finally came to an end, the Afghans signaled their acceptance of Major Lewis's response. They jointly directed the ANP to move forward with the grisly task of cleaning up the mess the U.S. Army had made.

Major Lewis intentionally let Mohamed Bindur wander out of earshot before grabbing Dehqan to prod a little further. "Dehqan, why do you think local Mohamed called you out here today?"

Dehqan looked a bit puzzled by the question. "Didn't we just fully cover the reason?"

"I mean, did he really need to have you here? He couldn't have met with me on his own?"

"Major Lewis, he is not my subordinate, but he does acknowledge my seniority and it was a show of respect to request my presence. Why is it that you are questioning his motive?"

Major Lewis had been debating just how much of the situation with AKA that he should share with Dehqan. He definitely didn't want to talk about Zemar or Atash yet. "This was a terrible tragedy, but often things aren't what they seem in battle. Does Mohamed Bindur have any affiliation with Abdul Karim Abdullah?"

"Major Lewis, I know it is difficult for the U.S. Army to admit when it makes a mistake. There has been some deception by the Taliban, however, you shouldn't always assume that they are to blame for your errors," Dehqan said, getting a bit aggravated by Major Lewis's inferences. "As for Abdul, I'm sure they have crossed paths, but you would need to ask Mohamed himself if you want further details."

"I'm not in any way trying to dodge responsibility, Dehqan. I am trying to clarify why things happened the way they did today."

"Well, you need to consult with your superiors who directed this," Dehqan said decisively, pointing to the carnage.

Major Lewis wasn't going to get anything further from Dehqan and he didn't want to alienate a potential ally so he backed off. Dehqan was smart enough that when he found out about Atash being killed he would be able to tie it back to Major Lewis's suspicion. "Fair enough, Dehqan. I hope we can avoid this situation in the future."

"As do I, Major," Dehqan said, turning to leave.

After preparing to depart Major Lewis reconvened with Lieutenant Davitch. "What did Dehqan have to say about Mohamed Bindur?" Davitch asked.

"He didn't reveal anything. I think he was telling the truth, but who knows. He might just be playing along. He must know that AKA is stepping up his offensive and doesn't want to become a target."

"What about these people here? Did he know who they were?"

"They were very vague. Said they were 'travelers' likely

passing through. We'll obviously need to revisit it with headquarters to see if surveillance was tracking them. It could be that they just made some poor travel plans that followed insurgent routes. Let's call it a day and get back to Mac. We need to be very careful. Keep your eyes sharp," Major Lewis said, scanning the hills one last time.

16

After separating from Major Lewis, Zemar suddenly became more talkative. He knew he was still in a lot of trouble and had to find a way out. What he'd done was very dishonorable and he certainly didn't expect any favors from Major Lewis. As soon as Lieutenant Warner drove away Zemar began peppering him with questions.

"Lieutenant Warner, am I going to be arrested for attempting to kill Major Lewis?"

"You are not under arrest right now. I don't know exactly what happened, but Major Lewis didn't sound like he had any intention of punishing you. Quite the opposite, he's going to find a way to help you. He knows full well that this wasn't your idea, Zemar."

"But he can't keep me at MacKenzie. He will get in trouble for that."

"Kid, don't worry about it. Major Lewis is a good man and a smart man. He got you out of that vest safely today. Trust me, he'll figure something out."

"Do you think I'll be able to go back to Baza Faqir-e? Everything, I have is there and I need to speak with my friends."

"That depends if it is safe or not. They tried to take out Major Lewis and we took out one of their top guys. My guess is that things are going to get a lot worse in the near term. I'm sure we'll have patrols going into Baza Faqir-e so we'll be able to sneak you in or at least pick up some of your stuff."

Zemar looked to his side and saw Yasir sitting there silently. "What about Yasir? Is he going to be able to stay with me for now?"

"He's in the truck with us, isn't he?" Lieutenant Warner replied, starting to get a bit irritated. "We'll find a spot for him."

Zemar gave it a rest for a few minutes before asking another question. "Are you going to hunt down Abdul now?"

"It will be high on our list. We've got some other things happening right now, but after this stunt today we will be taking decisive action against him when we find him. Are you going to help us do that?"

"I will tell Ajani everything I know and show him where I think Abdul may be. Unfortunately once he finds out that I am alive and Atash is dead he will stay on the move and use new locations."

"If he values his life he should be running away as fast as he can right now. If he stays in the area we will find him. We have technology that makes it difficult for him to hide for too long."

Zemar felt somewhat reassured; however, he was also aware of one of the Americans' weaknesses: they were honorable fighters. Even with better technology and weapons they could potentially be at a disadvantage against someone as deceitful as AKA.

The hulking presence of Lieutenant Warner also made the two youths feel safer. It was like having their own private bodyguard. They had always been in awe of the physical size of many of the American soldiers and Lieutenant Warner was probably the biggest one they'd ever seen.

"So where are you from, Lieutenant Warner?" Zemar asked.

"Iowa. Do you know where that is?"

"Yes. I am familiar with most of the states. That is in the farming region."

"That's right. I grew up on a farm."

"What is it like there?"

"Pretty much like this," Lieutenant Warner said, motioning toward the empty plain to the right side of the truck. "Flat. But depending on what time of year it is the land may be covered with crops."

"What do you grow?"

"All kinds of things. A lot of corn, wheat, some soybeans. We have a lot of animals as well - cows, pigs, horses."

"Do you like it there?"

"I do since I'm a country boy. It can get a little boring though. That's part of why I joined the Army - see some different places, have a little adventure. A lot of my friends have left and said they'll never go back. I plan to end up back there and do what my family has done for generations. It's good, wholesome work."

"Hopefully Afghanistan is providing you with plenty of adventure, Lieutenant Warner."

"That's an understatement my friend," Lieutenant Warner acknowledged. "So where would you go if you could choose any place?"

"I would like to see New York City. I have seen many pictures and it looks amazing. Major Lewis has told me about Chicago, so I would go there as well."

"I've been to Chicago. It's cool, but I'm not a big city guy. It's not too far from Iowa, so if you ever do make it be sure to look me up and come visit me on the farm."

"I will do that," Zemar assured him, thinking about all of the places in the world he'd rather be than Uruzgan right now.

They rode in silence for a while and soon entered a tight, winding road that led through a range of foothills. The varying terrain made it more difficult to keep a set distance from the lead vehicle. Lieutenant Warner was accelerating to close the gap when the truck in front of him disappeared in a towering explosion of black smoke and debris. The sound was deafening and inside the narrow pass it felt like a tidal wave had enveloped Lieutenant Warner's truck.

Zemar immediately fell back into a state of shock and stared at the lingering cloud in front of them wondering what might emerge next.

Lieutenant Warner was stunned temporarily and then quickly gathered his senses. He looked over his shoulder, "Are you guys alright?"

Zemar nodded slowly.

Lieutenant Warner grabbed his radio and began calling, "What's your status? Is anybody there?" No response. More urgently, "What's your status?"

The smoke began to clear and Lieutenant Warner could see the reason no one was replying. The lead vehicle, despite its heavy armor, had been shredded by a powerful IED. He looked around to evaluate his options and scanned the hills to see if he could identify any fighters. The wreckage had blocked his path forward and the road was not wide enough for him to turn around. Driving the truck in reverse was also not a solid choice. He felt trapped with no good alternatives.

No matter what he was going to need backup and support, so Lieutenant Warner reached down for the case containing the satellite phone. As he did, Zemar called out, "Here they come!"

Lieutenant Warner bounced up and instinctively grabbed his gun. A number of armed men swarmed the vehicle from both sides and began yelling and banging their guns on the windows. Lieutenant Warner had no viable way to shoot at them and Zemar and Yasir were unarmed. Then, one of the fighters appeared directly in front of the truck pointing a shoulder-mounted RPG at the windshield. Lieutenant Warner's limited options had just dwindled even further.

"They want us to get out," Zemar said, as the cacophony outside grew.

"I kind of figured that," Lieutenant Warner replied, unable to come up with any other ideas. He knew that reaching for the satellite phone now was a bad idea. He put his hands up for the fighters to see and gradually turned toward the door. As he did, he grazed his fingers along the ceiling in the cab. He snagged his index finger on a small cable and severed a junction switch that activated a tracking beacon. Even if he wasn't found, at least the truck would be.

Lieutenant Warner cautiously opened the door. Before he could fully exit the men grabbed him and pulled him out. Still on his feet, he towered over them. He had a brief thought of fighting, but realized there were just too many of them. They shoved him away from the truck and kicked at the back of his legs to bring him down to his knees. Even in this position he was nearly looking eye-to-eye with most of his captors. They acted like maniacal puppet masters, delighting in the fact that they were in control of an American soldier.

Several men stood watch over Lieutenant Warner with guns drawn while others retrieved Zemar and Yasir. After extracting the passengers two of the fighters climbed in and reveled inside the truck. One climbed into the turret and feigned firing the roof-mounted gun.

The other sat in the driver's seat and pretended to steer. The leader of the group tolerated the antics and began questioning Zemar.

"They want to know where Major Lewis is," Zemar shouted to Lieutenant Warner over the fighters' noise. The leader was clearly agitated that Major Lewis wasn't in the truck with Zemar.

"I don't know. I really don't," Lieutenant Warner said honestly.

The fighters continued to talk amongst themselves and with Zemar. The leader's voice rose steadily as he didn't get the answers he wanted. His fury flowed into his men who also became more excited. He paced back and forth making proclamations before stopping behind Lieutenant Warner. The leader made a final call of, "Allahu akbar," and the men mirrored him with their response. In a single motion he drew a handgun from his belt, pointed it at the back of Lieutenant Warner's head, and pulled the trigger.

Zemar watched in horror as a spray of blood burst from Lieutenant Warner's head before the soldier fell forward and crashed to the ground. The fighters paraded in circles and pistoned their rifles up and down in a ritualistic frenzy. The felled giant lay motionless on the ground and the only thing Zemar could think about were the fields of crops in Iowa. The insurgents had just brutally reaped their harvest.

The fighters spent several minutes scavenging the site for anything of value or interest. They also took turns yelling taunts and insults at Lieutenant Warner's body and the remains of the soldiers in the destroyed vehicle. The men bound Zemar and Yasir's hands and led them off into the hills.

From above Zemar looked back at the carnage and worried that Major Lewis would soon meet the same fate.

***

Before leaving the bombing site Major Lewis checked in with Captain Roth at MacKenzie. He provided an update on their status and let Roth know they'd be returning to base on a western and southern route. Captain Roth indicated that he had not heard from Warner, but expected them to arrive any time.

Approximately a half hour into their trip Major Lewis received another call from MacKenzie.

"Sir, I'm afraid something has happened to Lieutenant Warner's team," Captain Roth relayed to Major Lewis uncomfortably.

"Now what?" Major Lewis asked exasperatedly. He had hoped the day would end without any further conflict.

"He hasn't returned so I tried to reach him. I couldn't make contact with them and when I checked on their location it was stationary. The only signal registering was from Warner's truck. They were in some hills so I thought it might just be bad reception. I gave it a few minutes, checked again, and received the same data. I then switched over to the beacon application," Captain Roth said before pausing.

"And?"

"The truck Lieutenant Warner was driving is transmitting a distress signal. Nothing from the other vehicle."

Major Lewis quickly radioed to the other vehicles to stop.

"Okay, Captain Roth. Where are they?"

"The location is northwest of MacKenzie and due east of you. I'm sending you coordinates now."

Major Lewis reviewed the map and plotted a course. Unfortunately there was not a direct route via road. They would have to go back or south and then cut across, which would take extra time. He looked around their current location and then looked at the map again.

"Captain, it appears that if we go cross country here there is a small road we can catch and it will save us a lot of travel."

"I see that, sir. Let me check the terrain on the high resolution satellite imagery," Captain Roth said. After loading the photos and quickly scanning he added, "It looks good and flat most of the way, sir. Minimal elevation change and no major waterways."

Major Lewis thought about it for a moment. Crossing uncharted land in a hurry was never a good idea, however, compared to the danger of Afghanistan's roads it was still a viable option. Most of the mines in open land were intended for people so the armored trucks could handle them reasonably well. He hated the idea of putting the unit in additional danger, but there was no alternative. He consulted briefly with Lieutenant Davitch who agreed with taking the fastest route.

"We're going off-roading, Captain. I'll keep you posted and contact me if you hear anything."

"Will do, sir. Keep your eyes sharp. They could be trying to draw you in again."

"I know."

***

The convoy made good time and arrived on the edge of the foothills ahead of expectations. The men disembarked and surveyed the land in front of them.

"What's the plan, sir?" Lieutenant Davitch asked Major Lewis.

"Three prongs. You take a team on foot up to the right and Sergeant Terrance will do the same on the left. Try to remain in visual contact with the road and each other. I'll take two vehicles and we'll drive in. Let's roll."

"Yes, sir," the men replied.

Proceeding down the road, Major Lewis could see the heavy tracks of the Army vehicles that had passed this stretch earlier in the afternoon. He held out hope that the vehicles had broken down and lost communication, but he knew that was unlikely and prepared for the worst case scenario.

He drove slowly and periodically scanned the hillsides catching glimpses of the support teams moving in tandem. The sun was dipping behind the higher hills causing Major Lewis's eyes to constantly adjust while the road switched from bright light to shade. His hands clutched the wheel tighter as he neared the destination spot on the map.

When Major Lewis finally cleared the final bend he saw exactly what he had expected and also dreaded. He saw the wreckage in front and the body of a large soldier lying on the ground next to the other truck. He knew immediately it was Lieutenant Warner.

"I have visual contact," Major Lewis reported to the others. "What does it look like up above?"

"We haven't seen anyone. There are some recent foot prints leading away from our location," Lieutenant Davitch responded.

"Nothing over here," echoed Sergeant Terrance.

"I'm going to go out on foot. Stay up there for now and keep watch."

Major Lewis and his men left their vehicles and moved up the short stretch of road. Their glances bounced from the ground beneath their feet, to the trucks up ahead, to the surrounding hills. Danger could be anywhere.

When they reached Lieutenant Warner's body the men responded with profanity-laced growls containing a mix of sorrow and rage. Based on the entry wound they knew it had been a quick, but certain death. The anger grew steadily as they investigated the shell of the lead vehicle and found the remains of their fellow soldiers.

Major Lewis was the only one who seemed to notice what wasn't there: Zemar and Yasir. He looked inside and underneath the truck and found no sign of them. He could only wonder what their captors had in mind for the two boys. Right now, however, he had to deal with the grim task at hand.

"Lieutenant Davitch. Sergeant Terrance. Keep a few men on lookout and send the rest down here," Major Lewis requested.

"What happened down there, sir?" Lieutenant Davitch asked.

"They were ambushed. Everyone's dead. No trace of Zemar or Yasir."

"Warner?" Lieutenant Davitch pressed.

"Everyone's dead, Lieutenant," Major Lewis repeated.

Among their supplies, the unit carried an adequate quantity of body bags. The soldiers put on disposable surgical masks and latex gloves for the cleanup. They tended to their fallen comrades in complete reverent silence. Once finished they moved on to clearing the truck debris. The second truck was still functional so Major Lewis assigned himself the task of driving it back to MacKenzie.

The area now appeared clear of insurgents so they called up the other trucks and gathered the soldiers from the hillsides. Major Lewis led the somber procession alone. They snaked through the remaining stretch of hills and finally emerged on a plain that would lead back to MacKenzie. The sun had now dropped below the horizon. The high clouds reflected a fiery orange while the sky along the distant mountains bled into a deep red. The battle was now in full swing and blood had been spilled on both sides today. Major Lewis knew that more would be let soon.

***

The convoy crawled out of the darkness and pulled into MacKenzie. The men parked the vehicles and wanted to go right to their quarters, but their day was still not over.

Outside the men unloaded the depressing cargo. The remains of the soldiers were taken to the makeshift morgue, the existence of which the men tried to ignore. It was essentially a cellar that had been dug into the hard, sandy earth. Everyone was exhausted; however, they took their time in order to show respect for the men killed today.

Major Lewis then headed to the command center and met privately with Captain Roth.

"How are you doing, sir?"

"That was a long day, Captain. Unfortunately, we have an escalating conflict and now we have a score to settle as well."

Captain Roth considered the second part of the statement. It was not the kind of statement he expected to hear from Major Lewis. The tone in Lewis's voice and the look on his face were also different.

"I have already requested air resources for the casualties. The choppers will be here in the morning. What kind of response should we start planning?"

"I don't know," Major Lewis said, shaking his head in anger. "Now that Zemar is back in their hands who knows what they're considering. I can't believe that after all we did today to rescue him we ended up losing him again."

Captain Roth paused before asking his next question. "Sir, do you think there's any chance that Zemar wasn't captured?"

"What do you mean?"

"Just that...maybe...he and Yasir weren't killed along with Lieutenant Warner for a reason. Maybe they left with the insurgents."

That thought had not occurred to Major Lewis and it shocked him when he heard it. He started to respond and then stopped to think about it for a moment. *Could it have been possible that it was all part of the set up?* Perhaps Zemar was never meant to be a suicide bomber, just bait. *But if so why hadn't they killed Major Lewis in the morning?* He was obviously a higher target than Warner. Unless the expectation was that Major Lewis would be the one driving through the hills. There were too many what-ifs.

"I don't think so, Captain," Major Lewis answered, now with a twinge of doubt. "I can't see Zemar doing that. He's a good kid. Besides, there were too many chances where they could have killed me if they wanted to."

"I understand, Major. But given the circumstances it's hard to know what he might be capable of. Would you have seen him becoming a suicide bomber?"

"No," Major Lewis replied honestly.

"They might very well have been captured this afternoon. I'm just saying we need to consider all of the possibilities when crafting our response, sir."

"Yes. You're right. I need to think about this some more." He knew that Roth was just trying to think about every angle, but Roth had been here at MacKenzie all day and did not have the same perspective of the day's events.

"Why don't you get some sleep and we'll reconvene tomorrow."

"I think I'll do that."

Major Lewis drearily wandered back to his room and sat down on his bed. He rubbed his eyes and his temples and looked across to the pictures on his desk. The photos of his family and the men he had served with reminded him of everything that was on the line.

He then glanced over to Zemar's pictures hanging on the wall. Suddenly he felt angry. It wasn't anger toward Zemar, though. Major Lewis was mad at himself. He had put Zemar in this situation and he was responsible for the loss of Lieutenant Warner and the others today.

Major Lewis simply couldn't believe that the young man he'd come to know could be siding with the enemy. Tomorrow he would figure out a way to help Zemar and confirm that he was right.

Although his mind was still racing, his body was exhausted. He rolled back on the bed and stared at the ceiling until his eyes forced themselves shut.

***

First thing the next morning Major Lewis returned to the command center. He found Captain Roth right where he'd left him the night before.

"Did you ever leave?" Major Lewis asked only half joking.

"I just got back, sir. I got plenty of sleep. Now it's time to get back to work. I've been checking around already and haven't picked up any reports of significant activity. Pretty quiet out there. It was a perfect time for the Night Stalkers to take a break as well. Most of the upcoming attacks planned later this week will be further east and out of our coverage area."

"I won't miss being responsible for the follow up, but I wouldn't have minded if they kept going and happened to find the camp where AKA was staying. I guess I'm going to need to find him myself."

"Have you decided how to best do that without getting killed?"

"I'm going to request drone support to track him. I'm not sure HQ will approve it yet for someone at AKA's level, but it's worth a shot to keep trying. My other route is Dehqan. He's the only other link we have. I still don't know whether or not we can trust him, but I have to try. We have to stay on the offensive now. If we pull back and isolate here at Mac it will give them time to prepare and they'll be waiting for us when we do go back out."

Captain Roth moved to take an incoming call. "Sir, the chopper is almost here for pickup."

"Let's go."

The two officers walked out and joined the stream of soldiers headed toward the landing area. It was a solemn march and only glances were exchanged, no words. They found Lieutenant Davitch already at the cellar coordinating with several soldiers to transport the casualties. When they arrived at the helicopter pad most of the men stationed at MacKenzie were there to pay their respects to the fallen soldiers.

Everyone stood stoic and statue-like as the massive helicopter fell from above. They closed their eyes, but held their ground as the prop wash generated a large, inverted mushroom cloud of dust. The bodies were loaded quickly but carefully in the din of the idling engines. Once ready, the helicopter departed and the men of MacKenzie acknowledged their final goodbyes.

Before the assembled group could depart, Major Lewis grabbed their attention and gave an impromptu speech.

"Men, yesterday was another difficult day in Afghanistan. We lost good soldiers and good friends. You can't replace someone like Lieutenant Simon Warner. I had the honor of only knowing him for a short time, but he was truly a man among men. I take full responsibility for what happened yesterday. However, the enemy fighters that actually killed these fine men are still out there and need to be dealt with. Those men want to kill me, they want to kill you, and they want to kill any chance of this becoming a better place. My goal is to eliminate them before any of that can happen.

Losses are always difficult and we need to honor the men that just left us. We cannot afford to be afraid and we can't let this stop us. This is a dangerous place and we are the only ones that can change that. Yesterday was a setback. In the end, we will prevail in this struggle."

The men nodded in agreement and dispersed.

Major Lewis returned to the command center and contacted the senior officers in Kabul. The initial discussion centered on the bombing at Mount Kijra. Major Lewis provided his description to go with the report they'd filed and the photos they'd sent.

Colonel Renfro could tell that Major Lewis was disconcerted, but had misinterpreted the reason. "I know you had a tough day yesterday with multiple losses, Major. We're seeing increased activity throughout the country and dealing with a lot of casualties. We need you to maintain your resolve and keep your men focused."

"Sir, I just finished doing that. I've seen this before. However, the difference this time is that they've targeted me directly. It's hard to remain professional when they've made it personal. Additionally, their tactics have gone way beyond the pale."

"Major, they never play by the rules. That's always been the case, but we stick to our plan and prevail. Our offensive has stirred up the insurgency. We've been kicking the hornets' nest and now they're agitated. We're not going to run away, we're going to continue smashing them."

"I agree, sir. I do have a request, though. It's time to locate and track Abdul Karim Abdullah. He's now fully engaged and needs to be our top target. He also seems to always be on the move. I'd like to have more advanced drones involved so we can try to obtain facial recognition on him."

"I know you've been concerned about him for some time. We won't be able to do it immediately with all of the air traffic we already have planned. Let me see what we can do."

"Thank you, sir. He is the past of Uruzgan. We need to remove him and look toward the future."

After finishing the teleconference, Major Lewis typed a short e-mail to his wife. She already knew that he was constantly in jeopardy so there was no need for an update on the threat du jour. As usual, he sent his love to the family and assured them that everything was fine. At times like this he wanted to say more, especially to his kids. He always stopped himself, though. It was one of the lines he forced himself not to cross.

Major Lewis sat for a moment staring at the monitor. He highlighted and deleted the text and was left with a blank screen. He clicked the undo button and the message reappeared. He ran his fingers over the words and smiled. "They will not take me away from you," he said quietly and hit the send button.

He then scanned through a directory that had photos of their adversaries in Afghanistan. He quickly found the folder with shots of AKA. Scrolling over the thumbnails he found one that was very familiar. It was a picture that had been taken covertly during the meeting at Dehqan's country home. He double-clicked and the image filled his screen. For Major Lewis this was the face of evil. The look on AKA's face was how Uruzgan now felt: vacant, empty.

Major Lewis clicked the red X in the corner of the frame and AKA disappeared. Major Lewis creased a wry smile and thought: *I wish it was that easy*. He opened the picture again and scrutinized it closely, letting the image burn into his memory. "The next time I look at your picture it will be on an insurgents killed report," Major Lewis said to the screen and clicked the red X a final time.

The last item on his agenda was a call to Major Cierra down at Camp Ross. Both men had their hands full so there had been limited communication between them lately. Major Lewis called the video conference line and was glad to find Major Cierra available.

"Good morning, Ray."

"Johnny, how are you doing? When are we getting out to play?"

"Soon I hope. Been a little busy up here lately," Major Lewis replied.

"I hear ya'. Things have been heating up all over this country. How have the night attacks gone?"

"Not too bad until yesterday. It wasn't a total disaster, just had to calm down the locals. It was unfortunately exacerbated by another situation we had going on."

"What was that?"

"AKA turned my caddie into a bomb."

"What?"

"I won't go into all of the details, but AKA blackmailed Zemar and got a vest on him. We tracked him down and rescued him. Took out AKA's number two man in the process. I thought we were in good shape until I got sidetracked attending to an attack site. I had Lieutenant Warner transporting Zemar and Yasir back here when they were ambushed. We lost Warner and part of his team. They took the two boys, not sure what they are going to do with them."

"Jeez, Johnny. That's terrible."

"We just sent the bodies out a little while ago. Now I'm working on how to find Zemar and get rid of AKA."

"Johnny, there's only one of those two people you need to focus on. I'm sure Zemar's a good kid, but you know better than to get involved. I'm sorry about what happened, but I warned you. You need to go after AKA and if you find Zemar then great."

"I knew you'd say that, Ray. I have to take some responsibility for him, though. He got dragged into this because of me."

"He didn't get dragged into anything, Johnny. He was already knee-deep in it when you showed up. He just happened to meet you in the process. Zemar lived on his own and ran his own life. Zemar is responsible for Zemar. A sixteen year old kid here in Afghanistan is a lot different from one back in the States. Like I said, I hope you can find him, but he's secondary. I know I sound callous, but that's because I'm worried about *you*."

"I appreciate that, Ray. I'm going to do what I think is right."

"Alright, Johnny. Be careful and let me know if you need anything. Maybe things will settle down a bit and we can get together to play golf in the next few weeks. I need you around so I can take some of your money after you stole my trophy. Is that a deal?"

"Absolutely, Ray. I'll be looking forward to it. Take care."

"You do the same, Johnny."

17

The following day Major Lewis coordinated his team and prepared for the trip to Baza Faqir-e. Once again he had Sergeant Terrance and most of his men providing support. He had bonded with them in a short time and his confidence in them had grown immensely. After what had transpired he felt as though he was associating with them more closely, even morphing into their mentality about Afghanistan. Major Lewis had, however, once again excluded several of Sergeant Terrance's soldiers who had volunteered to go. Their tours were up and they were scheduled to leave Afghanistan in just a few days. There was no way he was going to put them in any further danger. Their orders were to stay put and stay safe at MacKenzie.

Lieutenant Davitch had also asked to participate. Major Lewis was concerned that Davitch was still very upset about the loss of Lieutenant Warner; however, he did want the extra support. He wanted to travel with a large show of force to intimidate any would-be attackers.

In Baza Faqir-e Major Lewis was hoping to find clues about Zemar and AKA's whereabouts from two potential sources: Zemar's friends and Dehqan. When they arrived the town felt surprisingly quiet. The morning heat had probably kept some of the residents inside, but that usually didn't stop the kids who would normally greet them. Major Lewis was not overly concerned as this was in no way a goodwill visit. He wasn't interested in giving things out to the populace, today he wanted something from them.

The convoy lined up outside Dehqan's compound and Major Lewis went to the gate along with Private Webster. The rest of the men remained close with weapons ready.

An agitated man answered the door and spoke quickly with Private Webster before ushering them inside.

"He said that Dehqan was expecting us and would meet with us immediately," Private Webster relayed as they crossed the courtyard.

This came as a surprise to Major Lewis who had intentionally planned for the visit to be unannounced. "Apparently he found out about Atash's demise," he said.

They were shown into the same room where they had gathered before. A moment later Dehqan appeared with his normal entourage.

"Good morning, Dehqan," Major Lewis said, standing to greet his host.

"Welcome, Major Lewis. Please let us sit down. Once again we have much to discuss. I'd hoped it wouldn't be so soon, however," Dehqan said brusquely.

"With violence on the rise we are all experiencing unfortunate outcomes," Major Lewis offered.

"Unfortunate indeed. We obviously need to address what measures we can take to make sure that the residents of Baza Faqir-e are no longer being slaughtered."

"Dehqan, you indicated that the people at Kijra were not from Baza Faqir-e," Major Lewis said, questioning if something had changed.

"I'm not referring to those individuals. I'm talking about your acquaintances: Zemar Durani and Yasir Hamidi."

"Slaughtered?" Major Lewis asked with astonishment.

"Yes, I assumed you knew this already. They, or should I say part of them, returned to Baza Faqir-e yesterday before dawn," he said before turning to one of his associates and dictating orders.

The other man fumbled through his robe and produced a smart phone. He tapped the screen several times and then handed it to Dehqan.

Dehqan shook his head and then passed the device to Major Lewis. "This is what our merchants were greeted with in the market that morning, Major. Very unpleasant."

Major Lewis looked down at the small screen and saw the gruesome image of Zemar and Yasir's severed heads sitting on the curb in front of Zemar's shop. He stared back at Dehqan, but could not come up with any words. His chest felt tight as though he couldn't breathe while his mind was enveloped with rage. *Who could possibly be so evil to do something like this?* He handed the phone over to Private Webster who examined it with morbid fascination.

"Did anyone see who put them there?" Private Webster asked, seeing Major Lewis's distress.

"No. No one was around at that time. Even if someone did it is unlikely that they would dare say who," Dehqan replied. "Do you know who is responsible?"

"Abdul Karim Abdullah," Major Lewis said quietly, still digesting the photo he'd just seen.

"That is who we thought as well. The question we had is: *why*? What was his motivation? I'm hoping you can provide us with some answers, Major Lewis."

"Abdul was using Zemar to get to me. They were forcing him to be a suicide bomber, but we got to him first and saved him. Zemar and Yasir were headed back to MacKenzie when they were ambushed. Four of my men were killed in the attack."

"That's regrettable. To what do you attribute this escalation?"

"You know him better than I do. Why don't you ask him yourself?" Major Lewis blurted, feeling that Dehqan was interrogating him.

"Major, there are a number of different parties operating in this region. I don't have a choice other than to deal with each accordingly. And frankly, I'd prefer to keep my head attached to my body."

"Well, you've just answered your question. He did this to scare you and your people. We've seen a number of groups suddenly spring into action around Afghanistan this summer. It's almost as though they were sleeper cells. Now that they are active they are seeking to send a message."

"Still, this is not the kind of action I would expect from Abdul. Is there anything else?"

"We killed Atash."

"When?"

"Two days ago. The morning of the day I met with you. Atash was the one with Zemar preparing him for the mission."

Dehqan considered this information. "Something you obviously didn't tell me at the time."

"You had enough on your plate already that day," Major Lewis said, not willing to reveal the real reason for the omission.

The two men scrutinized each other for a moment. Major Lewis wondered if Dehqan was revisiting their conversation from two days prior.

Finally Dehqan continued, "That could be part of the reason for the display. Atash was always more militant and extreme than Abdul. Many of Abdul's followers came via Atash. Abdul may have allowed this as a show of retaliation for your killing of Atash."

"I didn't have a choice. He was a militant fighter and we dealt with him accordingly. Zemar and Yasir were innocent civilians."

"We are both unhappy that your involvement here has dragged our citizens into the conflict unnecessarily."

Major Lewis was racked with guilt and felt responsible for what had happened to Zemar and his friend; however, he was flabbergasted at how Dehqan was trying to spin the cause and effect. "AKA is the responsible party and I intend to see that he is removed from Uruzgan. He is the one that initiated the fighting. If we forced his hand so be it."

"I had hoped that some form of détente could be reached between your unit and his group. Perhaps I can help broker a cease fire to prevent the situation from spiraling further out of control."

"Honestly, Dehqan, that's not really on my list of options right now. I came here today to make sure you still support us and to ask for your help in finding him. If you seriously care about your people dying you will help us. Abdul is the one who has killed your people, not us. The decision should be an easy one."

"There are no easy decisions here. You do realize that if you kill Abdul he will soon be replaced? Perhaps a known evil is better than an unknown one," Dehqan countered.

"I guess I'm not making myself clear," Major Lewis said with emphasis, remembering that he was dealing with a politician and not a soldier. "Negotiation is no longer on the table. That time has passed.

I understand what a difficult position you are in, however, you now need to move off the fence and choose a side. Are you going to be with us or against us?"

Dehqan sat pensively thinking about Major Lewis's ultimatum. He knew that Major Lewis had just stopped being a respectful collaborator and was now going to dictate terms from a position of power. "What is it you expect us to do?"

"I don't expect you to fight him or serve as bait for a trap. I came here today for information. He knows this area very well and seems to always be on the move. He made his aggressive push, but now he'll likely pull back knowing that we will be actively pursuing him. Where will he go? Does he have a favorite hiding spot? Does he have any patterns to his movements? Does he have any couriers? Someone we can follow to find him?"

"Up until recently I could have answered those types of questions. Lately, however, we have had minimal contact with him. In light of what has happened that is clearly by design on his part. Abdul is very smart and also very paranoid. The people he does work with know him well and will not readily turn on him, out of both respect and fear. I will make some inquiries and will provide you with whatever information I can find. I will also let you know if he contacts us directly."

Major Lewis stared intently at Dehqan attempting to read his body language. He was comfortable that Dehqan had not been involved in luring him to the Mount Kijra site, but was still not sure how much information he would voluntarily convey.

"So you have no idea where he is right now?" Major Lewis pressed.

"I do not," Dehqan replied in an even tone, staring directly back at Major Lewis to reinforce the fact that he was being honest. "I believe he is still in the area, however. This is his territory and the place where he is most comfortable fighting. It's unlikely that he brought the heads to Baza Faqir-e. That was probably left to subordinates."

"Alright, any assistance you can provide will be appreciated and I'll let you know if we find him," Major Lewis said, standing to leave.

"Take care, Major, and good luck," Dehqan said sincerely, knowing that he was now tying his fate and that of his people to the Americans.

***

Major Lewis and his men departed Dehqan's compound and headed for Zemar's house. Baza Faqir-e was still quiet and the residents they did encounter offered only somber scowls. Major Lewis did not feel that they were in any danger from the people here. He sensed in them only fear and disappointment.

A similar greeting awaited them when they entered Zemar's home. Three young men were there and Major Lewis recognized one of them as, Sayyid, who Zemar had brought as a caddie to the Ughust Valley. The boy spoke almost no English so Private Webster translated.

"They want to know what we are doing here now and how we could let this happen, sir."

"Let them know that I'm very sorry about what happened to Zemar and Yasir. We are here to find out more information about the people responsible for their deaths. They can honor their friends by helping us catch Abdul. It won't bring them back, but it will assure that it doesn't happen again."

The young men traded skeptical glances before Sayyid responded.

"After what happened they don't think they can trust us. Zemar and Yasir tried and now they're dead. They want us to leave now."

"One more question. Do they know anything about Zemar's sister? She is likely in serious danger and we need to find her quickly," Major Lewis said.

"Zemar was very secretive about her. Yasir was the only one that Zemar told of her location."

221

"Let them know that if they change their minds we are ready to act on any information they can give us," Major Lewis said before abruptly turning and walking out. He stomped off toward the market with the others following behind.

The normally active market was draped in a dark cloud today. Zemar was well known and well liked. The merchants seemed startled when the soldiers arrived. Many backed into their shops while shopping patrons headed away. A woman several stalls away began yelling at the men before she was quickly hushed and pulled back by others. Major Lewis didn't know what he'd find here, but somehow felt that he needed to visit the place he'd first met Zemar.

The area in front of Zemar's booth had been cleaned, but there were still two burgundy stains on the rugged concrete. There were flowers and green ribbons placed neatly nearby. It appeared that the merchandise remained as Zemar had left it. Major Lewis stepped in alone and looked around. He wondered what would become of the business now.

Major Lewis walked into the back hoping to find something of use. He doubted that Zemar would have any information on AKA here and it was unlikely that he'd leave a map to his sister lying around, but it was worth a shot. The only things there were a chair and several boxes of merchandise. He searched for any signs of a lock box or hidden compartment. The bare office yielded nothing.

Back out front he took one last scan around and lamented what a shame it was that the talented young man was dead. He gathered the men and left under the suspicious glares of the locals.

"Very frustrating," Major Lewis said to Private Webster.

"I agree, sir."

"I can appreciate all of their fears, but they have to change their mindset. AKA killed Zemar and Yasir. I need them to be angry at *him* the way I am. There's nothing else to gain here. Let's go."

Major Lewis was climbing back into his truck when he saw one of Dehqan's men approaching.

"Major Lewis," he called.

"Yes?" Major Lewis replied as several nearby soldiers put their fingers on the triggers of their weapons.

The man motioned for Private Webster to translate.

"He says he has something for you from Dehqan," Private Webster reported.

The man handed over several sheets of paper. They were crude, hand-drawn maps with writing scribbled on them. He continued, "Dehqan wanted you to have these. They are places you might want to look. Dehqan also said that AKA and many of his men are now traveling via motorcycle." The man quickly turned and hurried away.

"Looks like Dehqan is giving us some hints," Major Lewis said, handing the sheets to Webster who evaluated the directions.

"Basic, but we should be able to locate these spots. I guess he had a sudden recall after we left."

"Could be. My guess is that he didn't want to give us anything in front of all of his men just in case any of them were to change allegiances. He trusts that guy. We'll check these locations and compare them with our intelligence when we get back to base."

***

After returning to MacKenzie Major Lewis headed to the command center to review the information. He kept his expectations in check, but was glad to have at least come away from Baza Faqir-e with something in hand.

He spent time with Captain Roth evaluating the locations Dehqan had provided. Roth continued to play the role of skeptic and warned Major Lewis that these too could be traps. However, at this point Major Lewis had made the firm decision that Dehqan was throwing his lot in with the Americans. He would not intentionally send them into an ambush.

There were four primary locations. They spent a good part of the afternoon pouring over satellite data and looking for signs of activity captured recently on film. They then moved on to logistics and the best ways to monitor the sites.

Major Lewis wanted to act quickly, but he also knew that he needed to do it properly. The primary targets had several routes that allowed for attack and escape. He wanted to be sure that when they did make their move that AKA would not be able to slip away.

By nightfall Major Lewis was glad to have a game plan for the coming days. Sending numerous patrols out for surveillance and potential combat was going to drastically increase the danger level. Nonetheless, Major Lewis felt that his troops were ready and willing to take action.

Major Lewis ate a quick dinner and returned to his quarters exhausted. He had brought back several satellite map printouts and other documents to review. At this point, though, he set them down on his desk and just leaned back in his chair. He couldn't help but replay the events of the day through is mind.

Once again he looked at Zemar's artwork on the wall. The reddish splotch in the middle of the Afghanistan picture unfortunately reminded him of the bloodstains on the ground at the market. He then remembered his thought in the back office: *Zemar wouldn't just leave a map lying around.* Major Lewis stood up and pulled the picture from the wall. Suddenly he recalled Zemar's words from the site where they rescued him: *"She's in the heart of Afghanistan."* Major Lewis took the picture and ran to find Private Webster.

After locating his translator in the barracks the two men returned to the command center and pulled up several maps. Major Lewis now knew she was in the Day Kundi Province and he hoped that the writing and symbols on the picture would narrow down a more specific location.

"What are you seeing, Webster?" Major Lewis asked nervously.

"These are definitely directions. Here it says the town of Panja-Deh. Over here it indicates that approaching from the south edge of town you count six streets and go right. This note along the side mentions some kind of business or company, Azizi. Does that mean anything to you?"

"No, nothing. Maybe that's where she works?" Major Lewis postulated.

"This last part along the bottom says the two important names are: Kinah and Behnam. Did Zemar ever mention those people? The first one is a female name."

"Again, no idea. If he did I don't recall. My guess is that's his sister's name."

"Looking at our base locations, there's really nothing close to Panja-Deh. There doesn't appear to be much of anything out there, honestly."

"It doesn't matter. I can't send someone else out there for this. I have to go myself."

"And then what, sir?"

"I have no idea. I hadn't gotten that far," Major Lewis admitted, examining the maps and possible routes from Uruzgan. "My only focus has been AKA, but now this has arisen. I need to think about it some more and figure out what to do. Nothing else to do about it tonight so I guess I'll sleep on it. Thanks again for all of your help, Private."

"My pleasure, sir."

***

Despite everything that had happened in the past few days, Major Lewis found himself in a surprisingly good mood the next morning. Potentially gaining the upper hand against AKA and locating Zemar's sister had re-energized him. He now had goals that he intended to achieve.

He was greeted by Captain Roth who, as always, seemed to beat him to the command center.

"Good morning, Major. Are we ready to start moving forward with your plans?"

"We've had a change in plans, Captain," Major Lewis said,

producing his map and information on Day Kundi. "Private Webster helped me locate Zemar's sister last night."

"How did he do that?"

"Actually it was Zemar. This drawing he did for me discloses where she is hiding."

"That's incredible."

"My objective is to head out with a large patrol convoy tomorrow and then break off and head north to find her."

"Why do you need to go there? What if *they* don't know where she is and you end up leading them to her? Or if they are just waiting for you to arrive?"

"Captain Roth, despite being contrary to all of my plans recently I appreciate the fact that you continue to think very rationally about the possible risks and outcomes. It's probably not a good sign that I don't have strong arguments against you. The simple answer is that I *think* it is the right thing to do. I need to meet her and let her know about Zemar in case she hasn't already heard. I need to know what will happen to her without Zemar being able to support her any longer. I need to know if she is aware of the risk from AKA and if she needs to go elsewhere. Bottom line reason: I owe it to Zemar."

"Again, I understand, sir. I can appreciate your motivation. What can I do to help?"

"The usual. Stay here and hold down the fort. We'll head out early and should be able to make it there and back in a day. My plan is to have Lieutenant Davitch run the patrols while I take Sergeant Terrance and some of his men. I don't even know if she speaks English so I'm going to recruit Webster as well."

He spent part of the morning going over the routes to Panja-Deh with Captain Roth and then sought out the other members of his team.

Sergeant Terrance was lifting weights and sweating profusely when Major Lewis found him at the outdoor gym.

"Good morning, Major."

"Sergeant Terrance. Am I interrupting?"

"No, sir. I need to take a breather anyway."

"I'm planning another mission tomorrow. Looking to leave early for Day Kundi Province. I'm confident that we've located Zemar's sister and I need to make contact with her. I'll obviously need some support and I've become very reliant on you and your men in my recent quests. Are you up for another run?"

"Absolutely, sir. All of this activity has been good for those of us who are staying a while longer. We need to stay engaged."

"Even if it's to potentially rescue an Afghan girl that none of us has ever met and might not even still be alive?"

"Rescuing a damsel in distress? It doesn't get any better than that, sir. Seriously, I'm fine with it and my men will be as well. We certainly don't bear any grudges against someone like her. She's an innocent and the kind of person we should be helping. It would be nice to have a positive outcome for once."

"Thanks, Sergeant Terrance. Once we locate her I'll hopefully figure out what to do. I have a couple of ideas. Depending on how it goes I may have one more favor to ask of your men."

"Anything you need, sir."

"Don't commit yet. It would be a biggy," Major Lewis warned.

He then located Private Webster who was also more than willing to participate once again. He too was glad to be involved and putting his skills to use.

***

The line of trucks rolled out at dawn and headed north and west away from MacKenzie. After about an hour Major Lewis and his team peeled off and then headed due north. They followed a route that Captain Roth thought would get them there the fastest and also be the safest. There were limited areas of population and the topography made ambushes more difficult.

After an uneventful trip they approached the town near mid-day. The people they encountered on the outskirts seemed to be indifferent to the soldiers' presence. Typically the further north that troops went in the central part of Afghanistan the more tolerant the people were of them.

At a reasonable distance Major Lewis stopped and scouted the town. It seemed quiet and very much like every other village in the area. They pulled in slowly and drove around the edge before heading down what appeared to be the main thoroughfare. Major Lewis counted off the side streets and pulled down the one that they had located on the map. One of the trucks remained at the intersection to guard the route. Private Webster saw the small sign that read, Azizi, and notified Major Lewis that this was the building.

Major Lewis and the men slowly disembarked and surveyed the street. It was narrow and the buildings were two stories, which made it feel uncomfortably tight. Several men moved out in each direction, sliding down the street and hugging the wall as they went.

The small front door had detailed wood carving and a coat of purple paint that was faded and peeling. Private Webster ran the thermal scanner to make sure no one was directly behind it. Major Lewis took one last look around before stepping forward and knocking firmly. There was the sound of approaching footsteps followed by the clicking of latches. A small inset in the door popped open and the eyes of woman clad in a black head covering appeared from the darkness on the other side.

"Yes, what do you want?" she asked in Pashto. Although Dari was a more common language in Day Kundi, this part of the province still had a mixture of ethnicities.

"We are looking for someone," Private Webster answered. He turned to Major Lewis for confirmation before continuing. "A girl named, Kinah. Is she here?"

"Kinah? No. There is no one here with that name," the woman replied.

"Perhaps we have the wrong name. The person we are looking for is the sister of Zemar Durani. Does that help? Is she here?"

The woman studied them and looked at the street beyond them before answering. "Who are you and how do you know Zemar?"

Major Lewis immediately felt a surge of enthusiasm realizing they were in the right place.

"I am Private Webster and this is Major Lewis. We are with the U.S. Army stationed at Forward Operating Base MacKenzie. It is located in Uruzgan Province near the town of Baza Faqir-e. Zemar asked Major Lewis to come here to help his sister," Private Webster explained. They had agreed not to mention Zemar's death until they met with his sister in person.

"Wait here," she said, snapping the small hatch shut.

"I think we found her," Major Lewis said excitedly.

"It appears promising," Private Webster agreed.

"Keep the thermal running just in case. Make sure no more than two people return," Major Lewis instructed.

A few moments passed before the woman returned alone.

"Is there someone else you are looking for?" she asked.

"The man's name," Major Lewis said.

"Behnam," Private Webster relayed.

The woman peered beyond the soldiers again before closing the hatch and unlocking the main door. She motioned for them to follow and scurried down a dim hallway. The woman stopped at a door and knocked.

"Come in," came a voice from the other side.

The woman opened the door and escorted the two men inside. It was a small room with cold, dreary walls lit by a narrow window in the far wall. There were two beds and two tiny dressers. Mounted in perfectly even rows on one wall were a number of small, ornate paintings. They immediately reminded Major Lewis of Zemar's work, albeit with a feminine touch.

Sitting on one of the beds was a girl wearing a plain, taupe dress with a thick, veiled headscarf draped across her face. Major Lewis could tell little about her other than the fact that she was very slender and petite.

"Hello, are you Zemar's sister?" Private Webster asked in Pashto.

"I speak English," she said in a soft voice. "Yes, I am Uzuri. Is Zemar in trouble?"

"I'm Major John Lewis. I met your brother several months ago. He's not in trouble, but I have some difficult news to tell you."

"Yes?"

"Zemar was killed several days ago."

"Oh, no..." she said, her voice trailing off into choked tears. The woman at the door began to step forward to console Uzuri, but then stopped. It seemed as though she had experienced this situation before and felt it best to remain detached.

They sat for several moments without saying a word before Major Lewis continued, "I'm very sorry. He was a great young man."

"What happened?" Uzuri asked, sobbing quietly.

"He was killed by a man named Abdul Karim Abdullah."

"I know of him. What did Zemar do to him?"

Major Lewis knew that he needed to be completely honest with her. "Zemar didn't do anything to him. The only thing he did wrong was get to know me. Abdul has launched an offensive push against us and Zemar got caught in the middle. Losing Zemar was a terrible tragedy. I came here to hopefully prevent another one. I'm afraid that your life may also be in jeopardy. I know Zemar kept your location secret, but Abdul may have discovered it. I have no idea of his intentions; however, I felt that I had to contact you. I'm willing to help you in any way I can."

"Zemar obviously trusted you to reveal my location and tell you our parents' names. That was our code for anyone he might send to visit me."

"I see," Major Lewis said, realizing the significance of the two names.

"Mehri," she said, motioning to the woman at the door, "has been very good to me and protected me and others here. I could never put them at risk. I will have to leave here no matter what."

"Do you have any other relatives or somewhere else we can take you where you'd be safe?"

"Unfortunately no. Zemar was all I had left. My father had family in Iran, but we never knew them. My mother was an only child and her parents died long ago."

"Iran?" Major Lewis asked.

"Yes, that is where he was from. He was born and raised there. His work brought him to Afghanistan."

"The way things are going that might be our next stop," Major Lewis said facetiously. "Definitely not a good option right now. There are a number of organizations in Kabul that might be able to help you, but I haven't had any direct experience with them."

"There is one other thing," she said.

"What's that?"

"Zemar had given me a map. He told me to follow it to items he had hidden if anything ever happened to him."

"Zemar loved his maps," Major Lewis said, smiling fondly.

"Yes, he did. If I go with you could we go there? It is in an area outside Baza Faqir-e."

"I think so. Probably not today though. How long will it take you to get ready?"

"This is everything I have," she said, spreading her arms across the room.

"I'm assuming those are your paintings." Major Lewis said.

"Yes, something to keep my mind busy. Mehri also sells them in one of her shops."

"A very talented family indeed."

"Thank you, Major."

"I know this is very sudden, but we can take you with us back to MacKenzie. We'll have helicopters going to Kabul in two days. We'll be exposing you to more danger short-term to get you to a better place long-term."

"Sadly, I expected this day would come. Please let me say goodbye to everyone here and then I'll be ready."

"Excellent, we'll grab some gear bags to put your belongings in."

Driving out of Panja-Deh with Uzuri tucked away in the back of his truck Major Lewis wondered if he was making another mistake. That was logic talking. In his heart he knew he was doing the right thing. He also considered how strange it was for them to show up, introduce themselves to Uzuri, and have her agree to leave with them. To an American it seemed bizarre, but to millions of people in other parts of the world it was common place. Huge populations were regularly displaced and forced to leave their homes. They simply took whatever they could carry and departed. Throughout this part of the world waves of refugees surged from one unstable place to another. Uzuri was now another drifting soul searching for a new place to settle.

18

On the way back to MacKenzie Major Lewis was once again obsessing about the options running through his head. There were no good choices in Afghanistan. He thought about, Sindo, the friend he'd met at the Buzkashi match. Major Lewis assumed that the last thing he needed was an orphaned girl. Kabul was the most obvious route; however, it would be a short-term solution. Dropping Uzuri off in a safe place and saying goodbye would not clear his conscience. He needed to determine something more permanent and he only had a short time to do it. The one possibility that kept coming to the forefront was getting her to a country where she could seek asylum.

Pulling into the base Major Lewis was greeted outside the command center by Captain Roth.

"Were you worried?" Major Lewis asked.

"Just glad you made it back in one piece, sir."

"Captain Roth, I'd like you to meet Zemar's sister, Uzuri," Major Lewis said, helping the girl step out of the truck.

"Welcome to FOB MacKenzie."

"Thank you, sir. It's not where I thought I'd finish the day when I woke up this morning, but I'm glad to be here nonetheless."

"Let's head inside," Major Lewis directed. "What happened with Davitch today, Captain?"

They had a couple of hit and run attacks, minor skirmishes. The group wasn't very organized so it was likely some freelance Taliban trying to stay busy. Nothing else out of the ordinary."

Inside they sat down and introduced Uzuri to Private Karen Jensen, who was newly arrived and currently the only female soldier at MacKenzie.

"Uzuri, I certainly want to respect your desires, but I think it would be best if we had you change into some standard issue military clothes while you are on base. Otherwise you are going to stick out like a sore thumb to anyone who might be observing us. You can keep your headscarf and we have some outfits that will provide full coverage," Major Lewis said cautiously.

"That will be fine, Major Lewis. I am comfortable in any style of clothing. I maintained my traditional dress in Panja-Deh to blend in there and as a show of respect to Mehri," Uzuri said. She then reached up and pulled back the veil covering her face. It was a strange moment as all three of the soldiers stared intently, wondering what she looked like underneath. They were even more mesmerized when they saw that she was stunningly beautiful. She had caramel skin and perfect features framed by her black hair. She smiled at them and revealed her brilliant, glowing teeth. They seemed almost unnaturally white juxtaposed against her dark skin. All of that, however, seemed insignificant when she flashed her piercing, grey eyes. They instantly reminded Major Lewis of the famous National Geographic cover from the 1980's featuring a mysterious Afghan girl.

"Wow!" Captain Roth said without even realizing it.

"You are absolutely gorgeous," Private Jensen raved.

Major Lewis shot them both glances as though they might be saying something offensive; however, his reaction was the same.

"So how old are you?" Private Jensen asked.

Major Lewis was glad that Jensen had broached the subject as he had been too embarrassed to ask when they picked her up.

"Nineteen."

"Oh my. We're definitely going to need to keep you hidden," Private Jensen added with a girlish laugh.

Uzuri responded with a shy grin, obviously knowing the effect she had on members of the opposite sex.

Getting back to topic, Major Lewis continued, "Tomorrow we will have a patrol heading out toward the area shown on Zemar's map. If you prefer to be the one to locate the item I will allow you to go with them. However, I would much prefer that you stay here. Lieutenant Davitch will be in charge and he is a very trustworthy soldier. He will deliver whatever it is that he finds out there. Additionally, they will be able to sweep for mines in case someone else found it and decided to leave a trap."

"I trusted you enough to come here so I think I can trust your men as well. That will be fine, Major Lewis. I appreciate that you even considered the request."

"The following day we will have a transport helicopter departing for Kabul. From there we'll have to work on the next step. At worst we can work with the agencies I mentioned until we can figure something else out."

Captain Roth looked at Major Lewis with surprise. The transport was for Sergeant Terrance's men who were completing their tours and he wondered how Major Lewis intended to convince the pilot to take her.

"What are your thoughts about that?" Major Lewis asked Uzuri.

"I also think that is best. It is sudden, but I knew my time to leave was coming. I did not want to rely on Zemar indefinitely and my only other option was to marry. Mehri would have hopefully found me a good man, but I would have had very little say in the selection."

"That's too bad," Private Jensen opined, trying to reconcile the fact that someone as attractive as Uzuri would not be able to choose her own husband.

"That is the just the way things are here. Hopefully someday that will change. What I really hope to do is return to school. Our parents did a great job educating us when we were young. The last few years, however, I have had very few chances to study."

"That's part of why we are here. It's easy for us to build schools, but they do no good if young people aren't allowed to attend them," Major Lewis said.

"Zemar was the one who really would have benefitted. He was so smart," Uzuri said with a distant look in her eyes.

"He was very bright and extremely talented," Major Lewis concurred. "It is late so I'll let Private Jensen show you to your quarters. We'll talk again tomorrow."

"Goodnight, gentlemen," she said, following Private Jensen out the door.

As soon as they'd left Captain Roth returned to his parental form. "Sir, how are you going to get her on the helicopter?"

"No worries, Captain. I've got that figured out. What I need to decide now is how to get her out of Kabul."

"Sir, I know you want to help, but you're really starting to push the bounds. I understand that she is important, as well as exceptionally attractive, I just hope you are still considering all of the risks you are taking."

Major Lewis shook his head. "I hear you, Captain, but I'm not listening. I passed the point of no return quite some time ago. I have to do this. Then I can get back to our normal business, whatever that is. Don't worry, if anything goes wrong I'll take full responsibility. I'm off to find Sergeant Lazarus. I think he may be able to help me. I'll see you in the morning."

***

Before departing, Major Lewis briefed Lieutenant Davitch on the proposed side trip. They reviewed the map with Private Webster to make sure they weren't missing anything in the instructions.

The patrol was successful and by mid-afternoon Lieutenant Davitch had returned to base with the bounty. They had located the crate hidden in the wall of an obscured cave and there were no signs that anyone had been there since Zemar. He carried it into the command center where Major Lewis was waiting with Uzuri and placed it gently on the conference table. It was approximately three feet by three feet and several inches deep. It looked like the kind of container used to transport art work. Major Lewis wondered if Zemar had somehow gotten his hands on a missing masterpiece.

"So that's it?" Major Lewis asked.

"It's the only thing that was there, sir."

"Uzuri?" Major Lewis said, waiting for her approval.

"Let's open it," she replied.

Major Lewis unsheathed a large survival knife and used it to torque open the rusted metal bands binding the corners. He slowly lifted the lid and everyone peered inside.

"More maps," Lieutenant Davitch said, sounding disappointed.

Major Lewis reached in and lifted the large squares of heavily laminated paper. He looked at the first one and then handed it to Uzuri. "Is Zemar showing you somewhere else to go?"

"These are not Zemar's maps. They are my father's maps. These are geological survey and resource maps," she said, gracefully running her fingers across the surface. "This is the work he was doing for the government before the Taliban came to power. They wanted to establish mining operations to help grow the economy."

"What do they say?" Major Lewis asked.

"They show the locations of the mineral and metals deposits they discovered. Here is gold, over here copper, and cobalt across here," she said pointing at different icons.

There were large scale maps covering broad areas of the country and detailed maps showing specific territory.

"So this is what Zemar was talking about when he said Afghanistan had plenty of resources. Here's one showing Uruzgan," Major Lewis said.

Lieutenant Davitch looked it over and noted the symbol. "There's gold in them thar hills, Major. We can go do some prospecting in our down time."

"These are very interesting, but they don't belong to us," Major Lewis reminded. "If these are accurate I can't believe no one has gone after all of this wealth. Modern technology would probably have a dramatic impact on access and yield as well."

"Major, this is Afghanistan," Uzuri said. "There are so many different tribes and factions operating across these lands. They don't trust each other and can never seem to work together. And none of them trust a central government. Just another opportunity squandered."

Major Lewis reached the final map and set it on the table. In the bottom of the box was small canvas bag. He picked it up and was surprised by the weight. He undid the drawstring and emptied the contents out onto the table for everyone to see.

"What's that?" Davitch asked.

"Samples," Major Lewis answered, separating the small chunks of raw metal. "There's your gold, this is copper, and I think this is cobalt," he said lifting an odd looking piece.

They passed around the pieces and admired them before Major Lewis returned them to the bag and handed them to Uzuri.

Major Lewis looked at the maps and the crate and considered the problem. "The bag should be easy for you to transport, these not so much. Perhaps we can roll them up for you."

"That won't be necessary, Major. I will take these as a memento," she said, holding up the bag, "but I want you to keep the maps. Whatever reward you might get you deserve for risking your life for our people and our country. You are already giving me my reward tomorrow and I want to thank you."

"I appreciate that. Rest assured that I will see that these make it to the right people in Kabul to see if anything can be further developed. Our leaders would much rather have Afghans mining gold rather than harvesting poppies."

"I know you'll do the right thing, Major."

The group spent the rest of the afternoon talking and finding out more about Uzari. Despite the challenges she'd faced and the way she'd been living recently she was a delightful person. She had a calming presence and seemed very much at peace with the world. Major Lewis wished that they would have more time to spend with her, but he knew that leaving Uruzgan immediately was the best thing for her.

***

The arrival of a transport helicopter early the next morning marked the "turning of the tide" – new soldiers rolling in and departing ones rolling out. Recently an increasing portion of the incoming soldiers were specialists and support personnel serving not only

MacKenzie, but other bases to the south as well. This increased Major Lewis's numbers, but not necessarily his strength. He was glad that Sergeant Terrance and many of his men would be remaining here through the end of the year. They were the type of men he would need most in the coming months.

There was a frenzy of activity as soldiers and equipment moved back and forth. Major Lewis was in the midst of it all greeting the new arrivals and sending off soldiers whose tours were up. He quickly disappeared when he saw the last of Sergeant Terrance's men, Private Scanlon, loading his gear into the back of the helicopter.

Major Lewis returned a moment later rolling his golf travel bag on its wheels in front of him. He headed straight for the helicopter and quickly rolled it up the ramp, parking it carefully next to Private Scanlon.

"Travel safe and take good care of my clubs, Private," Major Lewis said, shaking hands.

"Will do, sir," Private Scanlon responded with a smile and a nod.

Major Lewis walked off and then watched as the hatch was secured and the helicopter powered up. He felt a sense of closure when it finally disappeared over the horizon.

***

The next two days were spent waiting and watching. Uruzgan was ominously quiet. The recent raids had certainly had an impact on the enemy and a brutal heat wave had brought even normal activity to a standstill. Additionally, it was not uncommon for fighters like AKA to go from brazen to bashful. It was difficult to say whether this was due to cleverly implemented strategy or because of a complete lack of one.

Major Lewis was in the command center after dinner when a group of surveillance reports arrived. The first one, highlighted to his attention, indicated that there had been activity detected near one of the sites provided by Dehqan. A number of individuals had converged on an otherwise uninhabited area near a rock formation known as the Pillars of Ghari. Many of the subjects had arrived on motorcycles.

The site was not far from MacKenzie and Major Lewis's first thought was to leave immediately and engage the group at night. Unfortunately the location was not easily accessed by vehicles the size of those used by the Army. Most of the nearby routes were single track, allowing only foot or cycle crossing. The troops would have to stop at a distance and cover the rest of the ground on foot. Without any preparation or planning there were too many things that could go wrong. He would have to wait at least another day. He and Captain Roth spent the evening analyzing the area and deciding on the best plan of attack.

The next day Major Lewis led a small reconnaissance team that headed out for the hills near the Pillars. They arrived at the designated drop off point and then toiled across the dusty hillside to reach their observation sites. They had located two outcroppings that would provide excellent vantage points for anything happening at the Pillars across the valley. They settled in shortly before dusk as the oppressive heat was finally releasing its grip on the heavily equipped soldiers.

Major Lewis had brought two skilled snipers in case an opportunity presented itself, however, the main objective was to confirm the presence of AKA or his men and plan for a full scale attack. Major Lewis made use of the remaining daylight to photograph the area from ground level and make note of anything that might provide an advantage or be a pitfall.

The biggest issue that Major Lewis saw was the lack of protected areas from which to approach the entrances. There were spans of hundreds of yards in each direction where they would be easy targets for anyone already inside. Trying to attack under the cover of an artillery barrage would risk the possibility of collapsing the formation. Major Lewis didn't want to risk that scenario unless he was one hundred percent sure that AKA would be entombed inside. He did not want to be in a situation where he ended up uncertain about whether or not AKA was still alive. He wanted definitive proof.

A nighttime assault seemed to be the best alternative. Assuming they could make it to the entrances unchallenged, the troops would gain an advantage by being able to operate with night vision gear.

As night fell anticipation dissolved into boredom. They had not seen or heard a single thing. Several hours passed before Major Lewis decided to move in for a closer look. He and two of his men made their way down the slope until they reached a path on level ground. They took the trail until they were within several hundred yards of the south entrance. At that point Major Lewis moved forward alone with an explosives detection device. He walked carefully, visually inspecting the path and waving the wand in front of him. He reached the wall without incident and then radioed for the others to follow.

Major Lewis stood still and listened for any sounds from inside. It was dead silent. He also ran the thermal scanner which showed no one inside the first stretch that it could penetrate. The passages inside were narrow and Major Lewis assumed that if AKA had arrived by motorcycle he would only be able to pull it a short distance inside.

He conferred with the soldiers who agreed that after coming this far they might as well probe a little deeper. They called back to the other troops to notify them of the plan. Major Lewis took the lead and moved cautiously ahead. He was soon maneuvering inside a tight passage that glowed luminescent green through his goggles. He also turned on a handheld device that would map his steps inside. It was designed to operate where GPS could not and Major Lewis did not want to waste the opportunity to build intelligence on the site.

They slid through the crevices checking various offshoot routes as they went. Periodically they would come to a halt and listen and scan. The only sound they heard was their own steady, controlled breathing.

By Major Lewis's estimation they were approximately halfway through when the tunnel opened into a large room. He scanned again before entering the empty chamber. This was clearly used as a meeting place as several large rocks were arranged for seating. They also found scraps of garbage and several bullets, but that was it. They crawled into side rooms and explored further in the other direction before heading back the way they had come.

It was 1:00 a.m. when they rejoined the others. The walk back had been peaceful and Major Lewis marveled at the number of stars visible from the dark valley.

With no traces of insurgents everyone agreed to spend the night camped out under the clear, serene sky. They contacted MacKenzie to notify the base that they would be returning in the morning. The mission had come up empty, but in a way Major Lewis was not disappointed. As he eased back on his bed roll and let his eyes wander across the heavens he was more relaxed than he had been for quite some time. He drifted off reminiscing about camping out as a child and slept like a rock.

***

Major Lewis spent a good part of the following afternoon on a regional briefing call that included Major Cierra. Major Lewis was not particularly interested in the discussions and had not participated at all. Immediately after it ended he received a call from his friend.

"Hey, Johnny. Just calling to make sure you were awake."

"I'm actually wide awake, Ray. I slept great last night."

"Any luck getting your man yet? I haven't seen his name pop up on the enemy killed reports yet."

"We were out stalking him last night. Thought we had a good lead, but it turned out to be cold. They probably use it as a meeting site and for storage rather than a camp. It was late so we camped out on a hillside. Who knew manhunting could be so much fun?"

"I'm glad you're enjoying yourself, Johnny. What about your girl? Did you locate her?"

"Sure did," Major Lewis replied, offering nothing else.

"And?"

"Things worked out pretty well."

"Did you get her somewhere safe? She's not at MacKenzie is she?"

"She was here briefly, but she's gone now. As for safe? It's a relative term obviously. I'm comfortable with where she is now."

"Are you going to keep it a secret from me too, Johnny? Why are you jerking me around?"

"You don't want to know, Ray. In fact it's probably better that you don't."

"Johnny...what did you do?"

"I wish you could have met her," Major Lewis said, still avoiding the question. "She's a great kid like Zemar. Very smart and talented, speaks perfect English. And extremely attractive on top of all that."

"Johnny. I'm still here and I'm still waiting. Where did you put her?"

"Ray," Major Lewis began, looking around to make sure no one was within earshot, "my approach to this job has changed. I know we are not supposed to play favorites. Unfortunately sometimes we have to. Zemar should have been a winner. Instead he lost everything. I had to make sure that didn't happen to Uzuri."

"Johnny, we've already covered this ground. I get it. I just want to make sure you've cleared your conscience and can move on."

"I'm fine, Ray. In the past I would have been very guilty about breaking the rules. Right now, though, I'm very much at peace with my decisions."

"Alright, you win. I hope you didn't do something that's going to get you booted. I need you here, buddy."

"I plan to stick around," Major Lewis said confidently.

"I'll ask one more time. Where is she? I'm dying to know now."

"Two days ago she arrived in Texas. She was met by my sister and Private Lazarus's brother, Daniel. Daniel is an attorney and has experience dealing with the government. They have already helped her connect with an Afghan aid organization that will be providing assistance. She'll be applying for asylum and it sounds like there's an excellent chance she'll have it granted. Sending a young, intelligent, attractive girl back to Afghanistan right now probably wouldn't be real popular. She also has Iranian lineage, which will only add to her case. I think things are going to work out well for her."

"And?"

"Oh, how did she get there?"

"Yeah, that's the part I'm still missing."

"The U.S. military was nice enough to take care of the transportation. She was safely tucked inside my travel golf bag and escorted by Sergeant Terrance's men who were heading home. The helicopter ride was rough, but once they got her onboard the transport plane they were able to hide her in an area where only they could see her and she could use the head. The worst part was probably having to eat the MREs we sent with her. Her story is that she stowed away on her own – a desperate move to avoid oppression. It will be hard to question her motive and getting there was likely the biggest hurdle."

"So you sent an Afghan girl, who you'd just met and didn't even know existed until a few days ago, half way around the planet in your golf bag?"

"Yep, that pretty well sums it up."

"That's definitely a first. I hope this doesn't blow up on you or Terrance's men."

"I put Private Scanlon in charge. He is leaving the service so he didn't have any qualms about helping out. Who would have the time to prosecute this anyway? Rest assured this was a one-time thing, unless I can borrow your bag...It's not like we're running a human trafficking ring."

"Are you forgetting about Winslow and Davenport already?"

"Yeah, but that was different."

"I suppose."

"Did I tell you about the email I received from Winslow?" Major Lewis asked.

"No."

"Thanked us again for helping them out. Let me know that he was sending a CARE package, including a lot of golf equipment."

"That's the least he could do!"

"Still bitter I see."

"Let's not re-open that wound. Take care, Johnny. I hope you get your man so you can get some closure."

"I will."

***

"Major Lewis, it looks like we are going to have some visitors today," Captain Roth said, pointing out a bulletin that had just arrived with the morning reports.

"What's that?"

"Not exactly sure, sir. It says to expect some helicopters for a stop-over. Doesn't appear that they will be staying overnight."

"And they're not dropping anyone off?"

"It doesn't list anyone."

"Maybe they are on a long transit and need a rest on the way to their eventual destination."

"Could be. No big deal I guess. It's just a notification. I don't see anything we need to do in preparation."

"We'll be hospitable and then send them on their way. Anything else of interest?" Major Lewis asked, hoping for a report of possible AKA sightings.

"Pretty quiet, Major."

***

Later that afternoon Major Lewis took a break and headed for the driving range. He had not had many opportunities to play recently and was glad just to loosen up and swing. His motions were smooth and easy and his shots were perfect. AKA was ever-present in the back of his mind, but positive thoughts of Uzuri overwhelmed those. He kept thinking of how bright her future would be in the U.S. He was truly content with what he'd done.

Major Lewis was between shots and chatting with another soldier when Captain Roth arrived.

"Sir, I think we've got him."

"AKA?"

"Yes. There were low-flight drones out today and they were able to get facial recognition with a high degree of certainty. The position was close to Talqani, which is on Dehqan's list."

"Let's go," Major Lewis said as the adrenaline immediately started to flow.

Inside the command center they once again ran through their maps and satellite imagery. It was a bit frustrating for Major Lewis as everything was static and the situation was dynamic. He wanted to have a tracking device on AKA so he could pin point the enemy's position at any moment. Find the moving dot and then erase it.

Major Lewis was studying close up shots of the hillsides around Talqani when Lieutenant Davitch interrupted.

"Sir, the helicopters are here."

"What? I didn't hear any choppers coming in," Major Lewis said, looking at Roth for confirmation.

Roth shrugged indicating he hadn't heard anything either.

"I know. There's a reason. You've got to see these things," Lieutenant Davitch said, clearly giddy with excitement.

"I can't wait," Major Lewis said, as he and Roth followed Davitch out.

Parked on the helicopter pad were two of the most unusual looking helicopters Major Lewis had ever seen. They were low and angular with varying geometric body panels. The skins were a pale, khaki color that blended perfectly with the surrounding land and there were no markings whatsoever. On top there was not one set of rotors, but rather several. They were in a stack and the blades themselves appeared to be missing pieces. Down below it looked as though they were standing on jointed insect legs, clearly a retractable form of landing gear. Only one word came to Major Lewis's mind as he evaluated the helicopters: stealth.

The officers walked over and joined the other men who were admiring the machines and talking with the pilots.

"Welcome to FOB MacKenzie," Major Lewis said, shaking hands.

"Thank you, sir. I'm Captain Swift. We appreciate you letting us stop by for a visit."

"We're glad you did. Tell us about your UFOs here."

"Obviously not top secret anymore," Captain Swift began. "We just received approval for in-theater testing. They are definitely ready for full deployment, but we need to make sure there isn't some Achilles heel that the designers missed.

As you probably noticed, or rather didn't, they are mystically quiet. I had heard all about the engine and rotor technology and was skeptical that it could do what they said. I'm a believer now. Beyond the sound issue, the skin borrows from and improves on a lot of existing stealth capabilities. What do you think about the color?"

"It's perfect for here," Major Lewis complimented.

"What about at night?"

"Probably not so good. It would be too light."

"No problem. It changes colors. It's a new chameleon skin. It changes on its own depending on the environment and we can also adjust the appearance. You can't really see it, but the belly matches the blue sky. When you change it coming in for landing it's like turning off a cloaking device. It's kind of creepy."

"How many men can it hold?"

"Two pilot seats and room for five men plus equipment."

"And weapons?" Major Lewis asked, not noticing any visible guns.

"The standard guns and missiles are all retractable and if need be we can mount others. They will be equipped with some new micro-bombs. Bigger bang from a smaller package. The term they use when describing the capabilities is vaporize."

"These are awesome. How long are you staying?"

"We will be making flights the rest of the day. We come down periodically to run diagnostics and check all of the landing capabilities."

As soon as he had seen the new birds Major Lewis had been formulating a plan. "So are you giving rides?" he joked.

"Actually we are. Do you and a few men want to go up?"

"Maybe. Do you have a minute so I can show you something?"

"Sure."

Back inside the command center he quickly briefed Captain Swift on AKA's location. Major Lewis knew he was overstepping his bounds, but was pleasantly surprised when Captain Swift showed interest in helping them.

"In terms of my rules, we are not supposed to engage with the enemy unless absolutely necessary. If attacked our orders are to: 'run like invisible chickens'. As for transport, I think I can get you and several men here," he said, pointing at the map, "with no problem. If you can complete your mission and return in under two hours we'll be able to pick you up. Otherwise you'll need to call your own ground support."

"That's no problem," Captain Roth assured.

"Can you be ready in thirty minutes?" Captain Swift asked.

"We'll be ready," Major Lewis confirmed.

***

On the silent ride out to Talqani Major Lewis was reminded of the morning flight he'd taken to Kabul several months ago. Major Lewis was no longer concerned with "changing hearts and minds". Today was about stomping out the roaches.

The team was mostly the same group from the other night. After their insertion they once again made their way to vantage points they'd identified earlier.

In the fading light of dusk Major Lewis surveyed the valley below them. Among a sparse group of trees he saw several men

248

gathered around a low fire. Parked nearby were several motorcycles. Major Lewis set up a high powered scope and looked closer. He went from man to man until he found who he was looking for: Abdul Karim Abdullah. He stayed steady and watched for a moment while AKA conversed with one of the men.

"That's him. The one sitting on the left," Major Lewis said. "I want two shots on him, then worry about the others. They're not going anywhere."

The snipers calculated their measurements and confirmed that they were ready. One of them asked, "Sir, I have him locked on. Would you like the honor?"

Major Lewis considered the question and gave a partial smile. "No need. We're playing by local rules here. Fire."

THE END

About the author

Tate Volino lives with his wonderful family in Osprey, Florida. This is his second novel. He enjoys playing golf, watching golf, and reading about golf.